Tell
Me Your
Dreams

BOOKS BY SIDNEY SHELDON

Tell
Me Your
Dreams

❖

Sidney Sheldon

William Morrow and Company, Inc.
New York

ISBN 0-688-16282-7

Printed in the United States of America

www.williammorrow.com

This is a work of fiction based on actual cases.

Book One

---❖

Chapter One

SOMEONE was following her. She had read about stalkers, but they belonged in a different, violent world. She had no idea who it could be, who would want to harm her. She was trying desperately hard not to panic, but lately her sleep had been filled with unbearable nightmares, and she had awakened each morning with a feeling of impending doom. *Perhaps it's all in my imagination,* Ashley Patterson thought. *I'm working too hard. I need a vacation.*

She turned to study herself in her bedroom mirror. She was looking at the image of a woman in her late twenties, neatly dressed, with patrician features, a slim figure and intelligent, anxious brown eyes. There was a quiet elegance about her, a subtle attractiveness. Her dark hair fell softly to her shoulders. *I hate my looks,* Ashley thought. *I'm too thin. I must start eating more.* She walked into the kitchen and began to fix breakfast, forcing her mind to forget about the frightening thing that was happening, and concentrating on preparing a fluffy omelette. She turned on the coffeemaker and put a slice of bread in the toaster. Ten minutes later, everything was ready. Ashley placed the dishes on the table and sat down. She picked up a fork, stared at the food for a moment, then shook her head in despair. Fear had taken away her appetite.

This can't go on, she thought angrily. *Whoever he is, I won't let him do this to me. I won't.*

Ashley glanced at her watch. It was time to leave for work. She looked around the familiar apartment, as though seeking some kind of reassurance from it. It was an attractively furnished third-floor apartment on Via Camino Court, with a living room, bedroom and den, bathroom, kitchen and guest powder room. She had lived here in Cupertino, California, for three years. Until two weeks ago, Ashley had thought of it as a comfortable nest, a haven. Now it had turned into a fortress, a place where no one could get in to harm her. Ashley walked to the front door and examined the lock. *I'll have a dead bolt put in,* she thought. *Tomorrow.* She turned off all the lights, checked to make sure the door was firmly locked behind her and took the elevator to the basement garage.

The garage was deserted. Her car was twenty feet from the elevator. She looked around carefully, then ran to the car, slid inside and locked the doors, her heart pounding. She headed downtown, under a sky the color of malice, dark and foreboding. The weather report had said rain. *But it's not going to rain,* Ashley thought. *The sun is going to come out. I'll make a deal with you, God. If it doesn't rain, it means that everything is all right, that I've been imagining things.*

Ten minutes later, Ashley Patterson was driving through downtown Cupertino. She was still awed by the miracle of what this once sleepy little corner of Santa Clara Valley had become. Located fifty miles south of San Francisco, it was where the computer revolution had started, and it had been appropriately nicknamed Silicon Valley.

Ashley was employed at Global Computer Graphics Corporation, a successful, fast-growing young company with two hundred employees.

As Ashley turned the car onto Silverado Street, she had the uneasy feeling that *he* was behind her, following her. *But who? And why?* She looked into her rearview mirror. Everything seemed normal.

Every instinct told her otherwise.

Ahead of Ashley was the sprawling, modern-looking building that housed Global Computer Graphics. She turned into the parking lot, showed the guard her identification and pulled into her parking space. She felt safe here.

As she got out of the car, it began to rain.

At nine o'clock in the morning, Global Computer Graphics was already humming with activity. There were eighty modular cubicles, occupied by computer whizzes, all young, busily building Web sites, creating logos for new companies, doing artwork for record and book publishing companies and composing illustrations for magazines. The work floor was divided into several divisions: administration, sales, marketing and technical support. The atmosphere was casual. The employees walked around in jeans, tank tops and sweaters.

As Ashley headed toward her desk, her supervisor, Shane Miller, approached her. "Morning, Ashley."

Shane Miller was in his early thirties, a burly, earnest man with a pleasant personality. In the beginning, he had tried to persuade Ashley to go to bed with him, but he had finally given up, and they had become good friends.

He handed Ashley a copy of the latest *Time* magazine. "Seen this?"

Ashley looked at the cover. It featured a picture of a distinguished-looking man in his fifties, with silver hair. The caption read "Dr. Steven Patterson, Father of Mini Heart Surgery."

"I've seen it."

"How does it feel to have a famous father?"

Ashley smiled. "Wonderful."

"He's a great man."

"I'll tell him you said so. We're having lunch."

"Good. By the way . . ." Shane Miller showed Ashley a photograph of a movie star who was going to be used in an ad for a client. "We have a little problem here. Desiree has gained about ten pounds, and it shows. Look at those dark circles under her eyes. And even with makeup, her skin is splotchy. Do you think you can help this?"

Ashley studied the picture. "I can fix her eyes by applying the blur filter. I could try to thin her face by using the distort tool, but—No. That would probably end up making her look odd." She studied the picture again. "I'll have to airbrush or use the clone tool in some areas."

"Thanks. Are we on for Saturday night?"

"Yes."

Shane Miller nodded toward the photograph. "There's no hurry on this. They want it last month."

Ashley smiled. "What else is new?"

She went to work. Ashley was an expert in advertising and graphic design, creating layouts with text and images.

Half an hour later, as Ashley was working on the photograph,

she sensed someone watching her. She looked up. It was Dennis
Tibble.

"Morning, honey."

His voice grated on her nerves. Tibble was the company's computer genius. He was known around the plant as "The Fixer."
Whenever a computer crashed, Tibble was sent for. He was in his
early thirties, thin and bald with an unpleasant, arrogant attitude.
He had an obsessive personality, and the word around the plant
was that he was fixated on Ashley.

"Need any help?"

"No, thank you."

"Hey, what about us having a little dinner Saturday night?"

"Thank you. I'm busy."

"Going out with the boss again?"

Ashley turned to look at him, angry. "Look, it's none of your—"

"I don't know what you see in him, anyway. He's a nerd,
cubed. I can give you a better time." He winked. "You know
what I mean?"

Ashley was trying to control her temper. "I have work to do,
Dennis."

Tibble leaned close to her and whispered, "There's something
you're going to learn about me, honey. I don't give up. Ever."

She watched him walk away, and wondered: *Could he be the
one?*

At 12:30, Ashley put her computer in suspend mode and headed
for Margherita di Roma, where she was joining her father for
lunch.

She sat at a corner table in the crowded restaurant, watching her
father come toward her. She had to admit that he was handsome.
People were turning to stare at him as he walked to Ashley's table.
"How does it feel to have a famous father?"

Years earlier, Dr. Steven Patterson had pioneered a breakthrough
in minimally invasive heart surgery. He was constantly invited to
lecture at major hospitals around the world. Ashley's mother had
died when Ashley was twelve, and she had no one but her father.

"Sorry I'm late, Ashley." He leaned over and kissed her on the
cheek.

"That's all right. I just got here."

He sat down. "Have you seen *Time* magazine?"

"Yes. Shane showed it to me."

He frowned. "Shane? Your boss?"

"He's not my boss. He's—he's one of the supervisors."

"It's never good to mix business with pleasure, Ashley. You're seeing him socially, aren't you? That's a mistake."

"Father, we're just good—"

A waiter came up to the table. "Would you like to see a menu?"

Dr. Patterson turned to him and snapped, "Can't you see we're in the middle of a conversation? Go away until you're sent for."

"I—I'm sorry." The waiter turned and hurried off.

Ashley cringed with embarrassment. She had forgotten how savage her father's temper was. He had once punched an intern during an operation for making an error in judgment. Ashley remembered the screaming arguments between her mother and father when she was a little girl. They had terrified her. Her parents had always fought about the same thing, but try as she might, Ashley could not remember what it was. She had blocked it from her mind.

Her father went on, as though there had been no interruption. "Where were we? Oh, yes. Going out with Shane Miller is a mistake. A big mistake."

And his words brought back another terrible memory.

She could hear her father's voice saying, "Going out with Jim Cleary is a mistake. A big mistake . . ."

Ashley had just turned eighteen and was living in Bedford, Pennsylvania, where she was born. Jim Cleary was the most popular boy in Bedford Area High School. He was on the football team, was handsome and amusing and had a killer smile. It seemed to Ashley that every girl in school wanted to sleep with him. *And most of them probably have,* she had thought, wryly. When Jim Cleary started asking Ashley out, she was determined not to go to bed with him. She was sure he was interested in her only for sex, but as time went on, she changed her mind. She liked being with him, and he seemed to genuinely enjoy her company.

That winter, the senior class went for a weekend skiing trip in the mountains. Jim Cleary loved to ski.

"We'll have a great time," he assured Ashley.

"I'm not going."

He looked at her in astonishment. "Why?"

"I hate cold weather. Even with gloves, my fingers get numb."

"But it will be fun to—"

"I'm not going."

And he had stayed in Bedford to be with her.

They shared the same interests and had the same ideals, and they always had a wonderful time together.

When Jim Cleary had said to Ashley, "Someone asked me this morning if you're my girlfriend. What shall I tell him?" Ashley had smiled and said, "Tell him yes."

Dr. Patterson was worried. "You're seeing too much of that Cleary boy."

"Father, he's very decent, and I love him."

"How can you love him? He's a goddamned *football* player. I'm not going to let you marry a football player. He's not good enough for you, Ashley."

He had said that about every boy she had gone out with.

Her father kept making disparaging remarks about Jim Cleary, but the explosion occurred on the night of the high school graduation. Jim Cleary was taking Ashley to an evening graduation party. When he came to pick her up, she was sobbing.

"What's the matter? What's happened?"

"My—my father told me he's taking me away to London. He's registered me in—in a college there."

Jim Cleary looked at her, stunned. "He's doing this because of us, isn't he?"

Ashley nodded, miserable.

"When do you leave?"

"Tomorrow."

"No! Ashley, for God's sake, don't let him do this to us. Listen to me. I want to marry you. My uncle offered me a really good job in Chicago with his advertising agency. We'll run away. Meet me tomorrow morning at the railroad station. There's a train leaving for Chicago at seven A.M. Will you come with me?"

She looked at him a long moment and said softly, "Yes."

Thinking about it later, Ashley could not remember what the graduation party was like. She and Jim had spent the entire evening excitedly discussing their plans.

"Why don't we fly to Chicago?" Ashley asked.

"Because we would have to give our names to the airline. If we go by train, nobody will know where we've gone."

As they were leaving the party, Jim Cleary asked softly, "Would you like to stop off at my place? My folks are out of town for the weekend."

Ashley hesitated, torn. "Jim . . . we've waited this long. A few more days won't matter."

"You're right." He grinned. "I may be the only man on this continent marrying a virgin."

When Jim Cleary brought Ashley home from the party, Dr. Patterson was waiting, in a rage. "Do you have any idea how late it is?"

"I'm sorry, sir. The party—"

"Don't give me any of your goddamn excuses, Cleary. Who the hell do you think you're fooling?"

"I'm not—"

"From now on, you keep your goddamned hands off my daughter, do you understand?"

"Father—"

"You keep out of this." He was screaming now. "Cleary, I want you to get the hell out of here and stay out."

"Sir, your daughter and I—"

"Jim—"

"Get up to your room."

"Sir—"

"If I ever see you around here again, I'll break every bone in your body."

Ashley had never seen him so furious. It had ended with everyone yelling. When it was over, Jim was gone and Ashley was in tears.

I'm not going to let my father do this to me, Ashley thought, determinedly. *He's trying to ruin my life.* She sat on her bed for a long time. *Jim is my future. I want to be with him. I don't belong here anymore.* She rose and began to pack an overnight bag. Thirty minutes later, Ashley slipped out the back door and started toward Jim Cleary's home, a dozen blocks away. *I'll stay with him tonight, and we'll take the morning train to Chicago.* But as she got nearer to his house, Ashley thought, *No. This is wrong. I don't want to spoil everything. I'll meet him at the station.*

And she turned and headed back home.

* * *

Ashley was up the rest of that night thinking about her life with Jim and how wonderful it was going to be. At 5:30, she picked up her suitcase and moved silently past the closed door of her father's bedroom. She crept out of the house and took a bus to the railroad station. When she reached the station, Jim had not arrived. She was early. The train was not due for another hour. Ashley sat on a bench eagerly waiting. She thought about her father awakening and finding her gone. He would be furious.

But I can't let him live my life. One day he'll really get to know Jim, and he'll see how lucky I am. 6:30 . . . 6:40 . . . 6:45 . . . 6:50 . . . There was still no sign of Jim. Ashley was beginning to panic. What could have happened? She decided to telephone him. There was no answer. *6:55 . . . He'll be coming at any moment.* She heard the train whistle in the distance, and she looked at her watch. *6:59.* The train was pulling into the station. She rose to her feet and looked around frantically. *Something terrible has happened to him. He's had an accident. He's in the hospital.* A few minutes later, Ashley stood there watching the train to Chicago pull out of the station, taking all her dreams with it. She waited another half hour and tried to telephone Jim again. When there was still no answer, she slowly headed home, desolate.

At noon, Ashley and her father were on a plane to London. . . .

She had attended a college in London for two years, and when Ashley decided she wanted to be involved in working with computers, she applied for the prestigious MEI Wang Scholarship for Women in Engineering at the University of California at Santa Cruz. She had been accepted, and three years later, she was recruited by the Global Computer Graphics Corporation.

In the beginning, Ashley had written half a dozen letters to Jim Cleary, but she had torn them all up. His actions and his silence had told her only too clearly how he felt about her.

Her father's voice jarred Ashley back to the present.

"You're a million miles away. What are you thinking about?"

Ashley studied her father across the table. "Nothing."

Dr. Patterson signaled the waiter, smiled at him genially and said, "We're ready to look at menus now."

It was only when Ashley was on her way back to the office that she remembered she had forgotten to congratulate her father on his cover of *Time* magazine.

When Ashley walked up to her desk, Dennis Tibble was waiting for her.

"I hear you had lunch with your father."

He's an eavesdropping little creep. He makes it his business to know everything that's going on here. "Yes, I did."

"That can't have been much fun." He lowered his voice. "Why don't you ever have lunch with me?"

"Dennis . . . I've told you before. I'm not interested."

He grinned. "You will be. Just wait."

There was something eerie about him, something scary. She wondered again whether he could be the one who . . . She shook her head. *No.* She had to forget about it, move on.

On her way home, Ashley stopped and parked her car in front of the Apple Tree Book House. Before she went in, she studied the reflection in the storefront mirror to see if there was anyone behind her whom she recognized. No one. She went inside the store.

A young male clerk walked up to her. "May I help you?"

"Yes. I— Do you have a book on stalkers?"

He was looking at her strangely. *"Stalkers?"*

Ashley felt like an idiot. She said quickly, "Yes. I also want a book on—er—gardening and—and animals of Africa."

"Stalkers and gardening and animals of Africa?"

"That's right," she said firmly.

Who knows? Maybe someday I'll have a garden and I'll take a trip to Africa.

When Ashley returned to the car, it began to rain again. As she drove, the rain beat against the windshield, fracturing space and turning the streets ahead into surreal pointillistic paintings. She turned on the windshield wipers. They began to sweep across the window, hissing, "He's gonna get you . . . gonna get you . . . gonna get you. . . ." Hastily, Ashley turned them off. *No,* she thought. *They're saying, "No one's there, no one's there, no one's there."*

She turned the windshield wipers on again. "He's gonna get you . . . gonna get you . . . gonna get you. . . ."

Ashley parked her car in the garage and pressed the button for the elevator. Two minutes later, she was heading for her apartment. She reached the front door, put the key in the lock, opened the door and froze.

Every light in the apartment had been turned on.

Chapter Two

"All around the mulberry bush,
The monkey chased the weasel.
The monkey thought 'twas all in fun,
Pop! goes the weasel."

Toni Prescott knew exactly why she liked to sing that silly song. Her mum had hated it. *"Stop singing that stupid song. Do you hear me? You have no voice, anyway."*

"Yes, Mother." And Toni would sing it again and again, under her breath. That had been long ago, but the memory of defying her mother still gave her a glow.

Toni Prescott hated working at Global Computer Graphics. She was twenty-two years old, impish, vivacious, and daring. She was half smoldering, half firecracker. Her face was puckishly heart shaped, her eyes were a mischievous brown, her figure alluring. She had been born in London and she spoke with a delightful British accent. She was athletic and loved sports, particularly winter sports: skiing and bobsledding and ice-skating.

Going to college in London, Toni had dressed conservatively during the day, but at night, she had donned miniskirts and disco gear and made the swinging rounds. She had spent her evenings and nights at the Electric Ballroom on Camden High Street, and at Subterania and the Leopard Lounge, mixing with the trendy West End crowd. She had a beautiful voice, sultry and sensuous, and at some of the clubs, she would go to the piano and play and sing, and the patrons would cheer her. That was when she felt most alive.

The routine inside the clubs would always follow the same pattern:

"Do you know you're a fantastic singer, Toni?"

"Ta."

"Can I buy you a drink?"

She smiled. "A Pimm's would be lovely."

"My pleasure."

And it would end the same way. Her date would lean close to her and whisper in her ear, "Why don't we go up to my flat and have a shag?"

"Buzz off." And Toni would be out of there. She would lie in her bed at night, thinking about how stupid men were and how bloody easy it was to control them. The poor sods did not know it, but they *wanted* to be controlled. They *needed* to be controlled.

And then came the move from London to Cupertino. In the beginning, it had been a disaster. Toni hated Cupertino and she loathed working at Global Computer Graphics. She was bored with hearing about plug-ins and dpi's and halftones and grids. She desperately missed the exciting nightlife of London. There were a few nightspots in the Cupertino area, and Toni frequented those: San Jose Live or P. J. Mulligan's or Hollywood Junction. She wore tight-fitting miniskirts and tube tops with open-toed shoes having five-inch heels or platform shoes with thick cork soles. She used a lot of makeup—thick, dark eyeliner, false eyelashes, colored eye shadow and bright lipstick. It was as though she were trying to hide her beauty.

Some weekends, Toni would drive up to San Francisco, where the real action was. She haunted the restaurants and clubs that had music bars. She would visit Harry Denton's and One Market restaurant and the California Café, and during the evening, while the musicians took their break, Toni would go to the piano and play and sing. The customers loved it. When Toni tried to pay her dinner bills, the owners would say, "No, this is on the house. You're wonderful. Please come back again."

Did you hear that, Mother? "You're wonderful. Please come back again."

*   *   *

On a Saturday night, Toni was having dinner in the French Room at the Cliff Hotel. The musicians had finished their set and left the bandstand. The maître d' looked at Toni and nodded invitingly.

Toni rose and walked across the room to the piano. She sat down and began to play and sing an early Cole Porter number. When she was finished, there was enthusiastic applause. She sang two more songs and returned to her table.

A bald, middle-aged man came up to her. "Excuse me. May I join you for a moment?"

Toni started to say no, when he added, "I'm Norman Zimmerman. I'm producing a road company of *The King and I.* I'd like to talk to you about it."

Toni had just read a glowing article about him. He was a theatrical genius.

He sat down. "You have a remarkable talent, young lady. You're wasting your time fooling around in places like this. You should be on Broadway."

Broadway. Did you hear that, Mother?

"I'd like to audition you for—"

"I'm sorry. I can't."

He looked at her in surprise. "This could open a lot of doors for you. I mean it. I don't think you know how talented you are."

"I have a job."

"Doing what, may I ask?"

"I work at a computer company."

"I'll tell you what. I'll start by paying you double whatever you're getting now and—"

Toni said, "I appreciate it, but I . . . I can't."

Zimmerman sat back in his chair. "You're not interested in show business?"

"I'm very interested."

"Then what's the problem?"

Toni hesitated, then said carefully, "I'd probably have to leave in the middle of the tour."

"Because of your husband or—?"

"I'm not married."

"I don't understand. You said you're interested in show business. This is the perfect showcase for you to—"

"I'm sorry. I can't explain."

If I did explain, he wouldn't understand, Toni thought miserably. *No one would. It's the unholy curse I have to live with. Forever.*

A few months after Toni started working at Global Computer Graphics, she learned about the Internet, the worldwide open door to meeting men.

She was having dinner at the Duke of Edinburgh with Kathy Healy, a friend who worked for a rival computer company. The restaurant was an authentic pub from England that had been torn down, packed in containers and shipped to California. Toni would go there for Cockney fish and chips, prime ribs with Yorkshire pudding, bangers and mash and English sherry trifle. *One foot on the ground,* she would say. *I have to remember my roots.*

Toni looked up at Kathy. "I want you to do me a favor."

"Name it."

"I want you to help me with the Internet, luv. Tell me how to use it."

"Toni, the only computer I have access to is at work, and it's against company policy to—"

"Sod company policy. You know how to use the Internet, don't you?"

"Yes."

Toni patted Kathy Healy's hand and smiled. "Great."

The following evening, Toni went to Kathy Healy's office, and Kathy introduced Toni to the world of the Internet. After clicking on the Internet icon, Kathy entered her password and waited a moment to connect, then double clicked another icon and entered a chat room. Toni sat in amazement, watching rapid, typed conversations taking place among people all over the globe.

"I've got to have that!" Toni said. "I'll get a computer for my flat. Would you be an angel and set me up on the Internet?"

"Sure. It's easy. All you do is click your mouse into the URL field, the uniform resource locator, and—"

"Like the song says, 'Don't tell me, show me.'"

The next night, Toni was on the Internet, and from that time on, her life changed. She was no longer bored. The Internet became a magic carpet that flew her all over the world. When Toni got home from work, she would immediately turn on her computer and go on-line to explore various chat rooms that were available.

It was so simple. She accessed the Internet, pressed a key and a window opened on the screen, split into an upper portion and a lower portion. Toni typed in "Hello. Is anyone there?"

The lower portion of the screen flashed the words "Bob. I'm here. I'm waiting for you."

She was ready to meet the world.

There was Hans in Holland:

"Tell me about yourself, Hans."

"I'm a DJ in Amsterdam at a great club. I'm into hip-hop, rave, world beat. You name it."

Toni typed in her reply. "Sounds great. I love to dance. I can go all night long. I live in a horrible little town that has nothing to offer except a few disco nights."

"Sounds sad."

"It bloody well is."

"Why don't you let me cheer you up? What are the chances of our meeting?"

"Ta ta." She exited the chat room.

There was Paul, in South Africa:

"I've been waiting for you to check back in, Toni."

"I'm here. I'm dying to know all about you, Paul."

"I'm thirty-two. I'm a doctor at a hospital in Johannesburg. I—"

Toni angrily signed off. *A doctor!* Terrible memories came flooding through her. She closed her eyes a moment, her heart pounding. She took several deep breaths. *No more tonight,* she thought, shakily. She went to bed.

The following evening, Toni was back on the Internet. On-line was Sean from Dublin:

"Toni . . . That's a pretty name."

"Thank you, Sean."

"Have you ever been to Ireland?"

"No."

"You'd love it. It's the land of leprechauns. Tell me what you look like, Toni. I'll bet you're beautiful."

"You're right. I'm beautiful, I'm exciting and I'm single. What do you do, Sean?"

"I'm a bartender. I—"

Toni ended the chat session.

* * *

Every night was different. There was a polo player in Argentina, an automobile salesman in Japan, a department store clerk in Chicago, a television technician in New York. The Internet was a fascinating game, and Toni enjoyed it to the fullest. She could go as far as she wanted and yet know that she was safe because she was anonymous.

And then one night, in an on-line chat room, she met Jean Claude Parent.

"*Bon soir.* I am happy to meet you, Toni."

"Nice to meet you, Jean Claude. Where are you?"

"In Quebec City."

"I've never been to Quebec. Would I like it?" Toni expected to see the word *yes* on the screen.

Instead, Jean Claude typed, "I do not know. It depends on what kind of person you are."

Toni found his answer intriguing. "Really? What kind of person would I have to be to enjoy Quebec?"

"Quebec is like the early North American frontier. It is very French. Quebecois are independent. We do not like to take orders from anyone."

Toni typed in, "Neither do I."

"Then you would enjoy it. It is a beautiful city, surrounded by mountains and lovely lakes, a paradise for hunting and fishing."

Looking at the typed words appearing on her screen, Toni could almost feel Jean Claude's enthusiasm. "It sounds great. Tell me about yourself."

"*Moi?* There is not much to tell. I am thirty-eight years old, unmarried. I just ended a relationship, and I would like to settle down with the right woman. *Et vous?* Are you married?"

Toni typed back, "No. I'm looking for someone, too. What do you do?"

"I own a little jewelry store. I hope you will come and visit it one day."

"Is that an invitation?"

"*Mais oui.* Yes."

Toni typed in, "It sounds interesting." And she meant it. *Maybe I'll find a way to go there,* Toni thought. *Maybe he's the person who can save me.*

Toni communicated with Jean Claude Parent almost every night. He had scanned in a picture of himself, and Toni found herself looking at a very attractive, intelligent-looking man.

When Jean Claude saw the photograph of Toni that she scanned in, he wrote, "You are beautiful, *ma chérie*. I knew you would be. Please come to visit me."

"I will."

"Soon."

"Ta ta." Toni signed off.

On the work floor the next morning, Toni heard Shane Miller talking to Ashley Patterson and thought, *What the hell does he see in her? She's a right git.* To Toni, Ashley was a frustrated, spinsterish Miss Goody Two-shoes. *She doesn't bloody know how to have any fun,* Toni thought. Toni disapproved of everything about her. Ashley was a stick-in-the-mud who liked to stay home at night and read a book or watch the History Channel or CNN. She had no interest in sports. *Boring!* She had never entered a chat room. Meeting strangers through a computer was something Ashley would never do, *the cold fish. She doesn't know what she's missing,* Toni thought. *Without the on-line chat room, I never would have met Jean Claude.*

Toni thought about how much her mother would have hated the Internet. But then her mother had hated everything. She had only two means of communicating: screaming or whining. Toni could never please her. *"Can't you ever do anything right, you stupid child?"* Well, her mother had yelled at her once too often. Toni thought about the terrible accident in which her mother had died. Toni could still hear her screams for help. The memory of it made Toni smile.

> *"A penny for a spool of thread,*
> *A penny for a needle.*
> *That's the way the money goes,*
> *Pop! goes the weasel."*

Chapter Three

I N another place, at another time, Alette Peters could have been a successful artist. As far back as she could remember, her senses were tuned to the nuances of color. She could see colors, smell colors and hear colors.

Her father's voice was blue and sometimes red.

Her mother's voice was dark brown.

Her teacher's voice was yellow.

The grocer's voice was purple.

The sound of the wind in the trees was green.

The sound of running water was gray.

Alette Peters was twenty years old. She could be plain-looking, attractive or stunningly beautiful, depending on her mood or how she was feeling about herself. But she was never simply pretty. Part of her charm was that she was completely unaware of her looks. She was shy and soft-spoken, with a gentleness that was almost an anachronism.

Alette had been born in Rome, and she had a musical Italian accent. She loved everything about Rome. She had stood at the top of the Spanish Steps and looked over the city and felt that it was hers. When she gazed at the ancient temples and the giant Colosseum, she knew she belonged to that era. She had strolled in the Piazza Navona, listened to the music of the waters in the Fountain of the Four Rivers and walked the Piazza Venezia, with its wedding cake monument to Victor Emanuel II. She had spent endless hours at St. Peter's Basilica, the Vatican Museum and the Borghese Gallery, enjoying the timeless works of Raphael and Fra

Bartolommeo and Andrea del Sarto and Pontormo. Their talent both transfixed her and frustrated her. She wished she had been born in the sixteenth century and had known them. They were more real to Alette than the passers-by on the streets. She wanted desperately to be an artist.

She could hear her mother's dark brown voice: *"You're wasting paper and paint. You have no talent."*

The move to California had been unsettling at first. Alette had been concerned as to how she would adjust, but Cupertino had turned out to be a pleasant surprise. She enjoyed the privacy that the small town afforded, and she liked working for Global Computer Graphics Corporation. There were no major art galleries in Cupertino, but on weekends, Alette would drive to San Francisco to visit the galleries there.

"Why are you interested in that stuff?" Toni Prescott would ask her. "Come on to P. J. Mulligans with me and have some fun."

"Don't you care about art?"

Toni laughed. "Sure. What's his last name?"

There was only one cloud hanging over Alette Peter's life. She was manic-depressive. She suffered from anomie, a feeling of alienation from others. Her mood swings always caught her unaware, and in an instant, she could go from a blissful euphoria to a desperate misery. She had no control over her emotions.

Toni was the only one with whom Alette would discuss her problems. Toni had a solution for everything, and it was usually: "Let's go and have some fun!"

Toni's favorite subject was Ashley Patterson. She was watching Shane Miller talking to Ashley.

"Look at that tight-assed bitch," Toni said contemptuously. "She's the ice queen."

Alette nodded. "She's very serious. Someone should teach her how to laugh."

Toni snorted. "Someone should teach her how to fuck."

One night a week, Alette would go to the mission for the homeless in San Francisco and help serve dinner. There was one little old woman in particular who looked forward to Alette's visits. She was in a wheelchair, and Alette would help her to a table and bring her hot food.

The woman said gratefully, "Dear, if I had a daughter, I'd want her to be exactly like you."

Alette squeezed her hand. "That's such a great compliment. Thank you." And her inner voice said, *If you had a daughter, she'd look like a pig like you.* And Alette was horrified by her thoughts. It was as though someone else inside her was saying those words. It happened constantly.

She was out shopping with Betty Hardy, a woman who was a member of Alette's church. They stopped in front of a department store. Betty was admiring a dress in the window. "Isn't that beautiful?"

"Lovely," Alette said. *That's the ugliest dress I've ever seen. Perfect for you.*

One evening, Alette had dinner with Ronald, a sexton at the church. "I really enjoy being with you, Alette. Let's do this more often."

She smiled shyly. "I'd like that." And she thought, *Non faccia, lo stupido. Maybe in another lifetime, creep.* And again she was horrified. *What's wrong with me?* And she had no answer.

The smallest slights, whether intended or not, drove Alette into a rage. Driving to work one morning, a car cut in front of her. She gritted her teeth and thought, *I'll kill you, you bastard.* The man waved apologetically, and Alette smiled sweetly. But the rage was still there.

When the black cloud descended, Alette would imagine people on the street having heart attacks or being struck by automobiles or being mugged and killed. She would play the scenes out in her mind, and they were vividly real. Moments later, she would be filled with shame.

On her good days, Alette was a completely different person. She was genuinely kind and sympathetic and enjoyed helping people. The only thing that spoiled her happiness was the knowledge that the darkness would come down on her again, and she would be lost in it.

Every Sunday morning, Alette went to church. The church had volunteer programs to feed the homeless, to teach after-school art lessons and to tutor students. Alette would lead children's Sunday school classes and help in the nursery. She volunteered for all of the charitable activities and devoted as much time as she could to them. She particularly enjoyed giving painting classes for the young.

One Sunday, the church had a fair for a fund-raiser, and Alette brought in some of her own paintings for the church to sell. The pastor, Frank Selvaggio, looked at them in amaze-ment.

"These are—These are brilliant! You should be selling them at a gallery."

Alette blushed. "No, not really. I just do them for fun."

The fair was crowded. The churchgoers had brought their friends and families, and game booths as well as arts-and-crafts booths had been set up for their enjoyment. There were beautifully decorated cakes, incredible handmade quilts, homemade jams in beautiful jars, carved wooden toys. People were going from booth to booth, sampling the sweets, buying things they would have no use for the next day.

"But it's in the name of charity," Alette heard one woman explain to her husband.

Alette looked at the paintings that she had placed around the booth, most of them landscapes in bright, vivid colors that leaped from the canvas. She was filled with misgivings. *"You're wasting good money on paint, child."*

A man came up to the booth. "Hi, there. Did you paint these?" His voice was a deep blue.

No, stupid. Michelangelo dropped by and painted them.

"You're very talented."

"Thank you." *What do you know about talent?*

A young couple stopped at Alette's booth. "Look at those colors! I have to have that one. You're really good."

And all afternoon people came to her booth to buy her paintings and to tell her how much talent she had. And Alette wanted to believe them, but each time the black curtain came down and she thought, *They're all being cheated.*

An art dealer came by. "These are really lovely. You should merchandise your talent."

"I'm just an amateur," Alette insisted. And she refused to discuss it any further.

At the end of the day, Alette had sold every one of her paintings.

She gathered the money that people had paid her, put it in an envelope and handed it to Pastor Frank Selvaggio.

He took it and said, "Thank you, Alette. You have a great gift, bringing so much beauty into people's lives."

Did you hear that, Mother?

When Alette was in San Francisco, she spent hours visiting the Museum of Modern Art, and she haunted the De Young Museum to study their collection of American art.

Several young artists were copying some of the paintings on the museum's walls. One young man in particular caught Alette's eye. He was in his late twenties, slim and blond, with a strong, intelligent face. He was copying Georgia O'Keeffe's *Petunias,* and his work was remarkably good. The artist noticed Alette watching him. "Hi."

His voice was a warm yellow.

"Hello," Alette said shyly.

The artist nodded toward the painting he was working on. "What do you think?"

"*Bellissimo.* I think it's wonderful." And she waited for her inner voice to say, *For a stupid amateur.* But it didn't happen. She was surprised. "It's really wonderful."

He smiled. "Thank you. My name is Richard, Richard Melton."

"Alette Peters."

"Do you come here often?" Richard asked.

"*Sì.* As often as I can. I don't live in San Francisco."

"Where do you live?"

"In Cupertino." *Not—"It's none of your damn business" or "Wouldn't you like to know?" but—"In Cupertino." What is happening to me?*

"That's a nice little town."

"I like it." *Not—"What the hell makes you think it's a nice little town?" or "What do you know about nice little towns?" but—"I like it."*

He was finished with the painting. "I'm hungry. Can I buy you lunch? Café De Young has pretty good food."

Alette hesitated only a moment. "*Va bene.* I'd like that." *Not—"You look stupid" or "I don't have lunch with strangers," but—"I'd like that."* It was a new, exhilarating experience for Alette.

*   *   *

The lunch was extremely enjoyable and not once did negative thoughts come into Alette's mind. They talked about some of the great artists, and Alette told Richard about growing up in Rome.

"I've never been to Rome," he said. "Maybe one day."

And Alette thought, *It would be fun to go to Rome with you.*

As they were finishing their lunch, Richard saw his roommate across the room and called him over to the table. "Gary, I didn't know you were going to be here. I'd like you to meet someone. This is Alette Peters. Gary King."

Gary was in his late twenties, with bright blue eyes and hair down to his shoulders.

"It's nice to meet you, Gary."

"Gary's been my best friend since high school, Alette."

"Yeah. I have ten years of dirt on Richard, so if you're looking for any good stories—"

"Gary, don't you have somewhere to go?"

"Right." He turned to Alette. "But don't forget my offer. I'll see you two around."

They watched Gary leave. Richard said, "Alette . . ."

"Yes?"

"May I see you again?"

"I would like that." *Very much.*

Monday morning, Alette told Toni about her experience. "Don't get involved with an artist," Toni warned. "You'll be living on the fruit he paints. Are you going to see him again?"

Alette smiled. "Yes. I think he likes me. And I like him. I really like him."

It started as a small disagreement and ended up as a ferocious argument. Pastor Frank was retiring after forty years of service. He had been a very good and caring pastor, and the congregation was sorry to see him leave. There were secret meetings held to decide what to give him as a going-away present. A watch . . . money . . . a vacation . . . a painting . . . He loved art.

"Why don't we have someone do a portrait of him, with the church in the background?" They turned to Alette. "Will you do it?"

"Of course," she said happily.

Walter Manning was one of the senior members of the church and one of its biggest contributors. He was a very successful businessman, but he seemed to resent everyone else's success. He said, "My daughter is a fine painter. Perhaps she should do it."

Someone suggested, "Why not have them both do it, and we'll vote on which one to give Pastor Frank?"

Alette went to work. The painting took her five days, and it was a masterpiece, glowing with the compassion and goodness of her subject. The following Sunday, the group met to look at the paintings. There were exclamations of appreciation over Alette's painting.

"It's so real, he could almost walk off the canvas. . . ."

"Oh, he's going to love that. . . ."

"That should be in a museum, Alette. . . ."

Walter Manning unwrapped the canvas painted by his daughter. It was a competent painting, but it lacked the fire of Alette's portrait.

"That's very nice," one of the members of the congregation said tactfully, "but I think Alette's is—"

"I agree. . . ."

"Alette's portrait is the one. . . ."

Walter Manning spoke up. "This has to be a unanimous decision. My daughter's a professional artist"—he looked at Alette—"not a dilettante. She did this as a favor. We can't turn her down."

"But, Walter—"

"No, sir. This has to be unanimous. We're either giving him my daughter's painting or we don't give him anything at all."

Alette said, "I like her painting very much. Let's give it to the pastor."

Walter Manning smiled smugly and said, "He's going to be very pleased with this."

On his way home that evening, Walter Manning was killed by a hit-and-run driver.

When Alette heard the news, she was stunned.

Chapter Four

ASHLEY Patterson was taking a hurried shower, late for work, when she heard the sound. A door opening? Closing? She turned off the shower, listening, her heart pounding. *Silence.* She stood there a moment, her body glistening with drops of water, then hurriedly dried herself and cautiously stepped into the bedroom. Everything appeared to be normal. *It's my stupid imagination again. I've got to get dressed.* She walked over to her lingerie drawer, opened it and stared down at it, unbelievingly. Someone had gone through her undergarments. Her bras and pantyhose were all piled together. She always kept them neatly separated.

Ashley suddenly felt sick to her stomach. Had he unzipped his pants, picked up her pantyhose and rubbed them against himself? Had he fantasized about raping her? Raping her and murdering her? She was finding it difficult to breathe. *I should go to the police, but they would laugh at me.*

You want us to investigate this because you think someone got into your lingerie drawer?

Someone has been following me.

Have you seen who it is?

No.

Has anyone threatened you?

No.

Do you know why anyone would want to harm you?

No.

It's no use, Ashley thought despairingly. *I can't go to the police. Those are the questions they would ask me, and I would look like a fool.*

She dressed as quickly as she could, suddenly eager to escape from the apartment. *I'll have to move. I'll go somewhere where he can't find me.*

But even as she thought it, she had the feeling that it was going to be impossible. *He knows where I live, he knows where I work. And what do I know about him? Nothing.*

She refused to keep a gun in the apartment because she hated violence. *But I need some protection now,* Ashley thought. She went into the kitchen, picked up a steak knife, carried it to her bedroom and put it in the dresser drawer next to her bed.

It's possible that I mixed my lingerie up myself. That's probably what happened. Or is it wishful thinking?

There was an envelope in her mailbox in the downstairs entrance hall. The return address read "Bedford Area High School, Bedford, Pennsylvania."

Ashley read the invitation twice.

Ten-Year Class Reunion!
Rich man, poor man, beggar man, thief. Have you often wondered how your classmates have fared during the last ten years? Here's your chance to find out. The weekend of June 15th we're going to have a spectacular get-together. Food, drinks, a great orchestra and dancing. Join the fun.
    Just mail the enclosed acceptance card so we'll know you're coming. Everyone looks forward to seeing you.

Driving to work, Ashley thought about the invitation. *"Everyone looks forward to seeing you." Everyone except Jim Cleary,* she thought bitterly.

"I want to marry you. My uncle offered me a really good job in Chicago with his advertising agency. . . . There's a train leaving for Chicago at seven A.M. Will you come with me?"

And she remembered the pain of desperately waiting at the station for Jim, believing in him, trusting him. He had changed his mind, and he had not been man enough to come and tell her. Instead, he had left her sitting in a train station, alone. *Forget the invitation. I'm not going.*

Ashley had lunch with Shane Miller at TGI Friday's. They sat in a booth, eating in silence.

"You seem preoccupied," Shane said.

"Sorry." Ashley hesitated a moment. She was tempted to tell him about the lingerie, but it would sound stupid. *Someone got into your drawers?* Instead, she said, "I got an invitation to my ten-year high school reunion."

"Are you going?"

"Certainly not." It came out stronger than Ashley had intended.

Shane Miller looked at her curiously. "Why not? Those things can be fun."

Would Jim Cleary be there? Would he have a wife and children? What would he say to her? "Sorry I wasn't able to meet you at the train station. Sorry I lied to you about marrying you?"

"I'm not going."

But Ashley was unable to get the invitation out of her mind. *It would be nice to see some of my old classmates,* she thought. There were a few she had been close to. One in particular was Florence Schiffer. *I wonder what's become of her?* And she wondered whether the town of Bedford had changed.

Ashley Patterson had grown up in Bedford, Pennsylvania, a small town two hours east of Pittsburgh, deep in the Allegheny Mountains. Her father had been head of the Memorial Hospital of Bedford County, one of the top one hundred hospitals in the country.

Bedford had been a wonderful town to grow up in. There were parks for picnics, rivers to fish in and social events that went on all year. Ashley enjoyed visiting Big Valley, where there was an Amish colony. It was a common sight to see horses pulling Amish buggies with different colored tops, colors that depended on the degree of orthodoxy of the owners.

There were Mystery Village evenings and live theater and the Great Pumpkin Festival. Ashley smiled at the thought of the good times she had had there. *Maybe I will go back,* she thought. *Jim Cleary won't have the nerve to show up.*

Ashley told Shane Miller of her decision. "It's a week from Friday," she said. "I'll be back Sunday night."

"Great. Let me know what time you're getting back. I'll pick you up at the airport."

"Thank you, Shane."

*   *   *

When Ashley returned from lunch, she walked into her work cubicle and turned her computer on. To her surprise, a sudden hail of pixels began rolling down the screen, creating an image. She stared at it, bewildered. The dots were forming a picture of her. As Ashley watched, horrified, a hand holding a butcher knife appeared at the top of the screen. The hand was racing toward her image, ready to plunge the knife into her chest.

Ashley screamed, "No!"

She snapped off the monitor and jumped to her feet.

Shane Miller had hurried to her side. "Ashley! What is it?"

She was trembling. "On the . . . the screen—"

Shane turned on the computer. A picture of a kitten chasing a ball of yarn across a green lawn appeared.

Shane turned to look at Ashley, bewildered. "What—?"

"It's—it's gone," she whispered.

"What's gone?"

She shook her head. "Nothing. I—I've been under a lot of stress lately, Shane. I'm sorry."

"Why don't you go have a talk with Dr. Speakman?"

Ashley had seen Dr. Speakman before. He was the company psychologist hired to counsel stressed-out computer whizzes. He was not a medical doctor, but he was intelligent and understanding, and it was helpful to be able to talk to someone.

"I'll go," Ashley said.

Dr. Ben Speakman was in his fifties, a patriarch at the fountain of youth. His office was a quiet oasis at the far end of the building, relaxed and comfortable.

"I had a terrible dream last night," Ashley said. She closed her eyes, reliving it. "I was running. I was in a huge garden filled with flowers. . . . They had weird, ugly faces. . . . They were screaming at me. . . . I couldn't hear what they were saying. I just kept running toward something. . . . I don't know what. . . ." She stopped and opened her eyes.

"Could you have been running *away* from something? Was something chasing you?"

"I don't know. I—I think I'm being followed, Dr. Speakman. It sounds crazy, but— I think someone wants to kill me."

He studied her a moment. "Who would want to kill you?"

"I—I have no idea."

"Have you *seen* anyone following you?"

"No."

"You live alone, don't you?"

"Yes."

"Are you seeing anyone? I mean romantically?"

"No. Not right now."

"So it's been a while since you—I mean sometimes when a woman doesn't have a man in her life—well, a kind of physical tension can build up. . . ."

What he's trying to tell me is that I need a good— She could not bring herself to say the word. She could hear her father yelling at her, *"Don't ever say that word again. People will think you're a little slut. Nice people don't say fuck. Where do you pick up that kind of language?"*

"I think you've just been working too hard, Ashley. I don't believe you have anything to worry about. It's probably just tension. Take it a little easier for a while. Get more rest."

"I'll try."

Shane Miller was waiting for her. "What did Dr. Speakman say?"

Ashley managed a smile. "He says I'm fine. I've just been working too hard."

"Well, we'll have to do something about that," Shane said. "For openers, why don't you take the rest of the day off?" His voice was filled with concern.

"Thanks." She looked at him and smiled. He was a dear man. A good friend.

He can't be the one, Ashley thought. *He can't.*

During the following week, Ashley could think of nothing but the reunion. *I wonder if my going is a mistake? What if Jim Cleary does show up? Does he have any idea how much he hurt me? Does he care? Will he even remember me?*

The night before Ashley was to leave for Bedford, she was unable to sleep. She was tempted to cancel her flight. *I'm being silly,* she thought. *The past is the past.*

When Ashley picked up her ticket at the airport, she examined it and said, "I'm afraid there's been some mistake. I'm flying tourist. This is a first-class ticket."

"Yes. You changed it."

She stared at the clerk. "I what?"

"You telephoned and said to change it to a first-class ticket."
He showed Ashley a slip of paper. "Is this your credit card number?"

She looked at it and said slowly, "Yes . . ."

She had not made that phone call.

Ashley arrived in Bedford early and checked in at the Bedford
Springs Resort. The reunion festivities did not start until six
o'clock that evening, so she decided to explore the town. She
hailed a taxi in front of the hotel.

"Where to, miss?"

"Let's just drive around."

Hometowns were supposed to look smaller when a native returned years later, but to Ashley, Bedford looked larger than she
had remembered. The taxi drove up and down familiar streets,
passing the offices of the *Bedford Gazette* and television station
WKYE and a dozen familiar restaurants and art galleries. The
Baker's Loaf of Bedford was still there and Clara's Place, the Fort
Bedford Museum and Old Bedford Village. They passed the Memorial Hospital, a graceful three-story brick building with a por-
tico. It was there that her father had become famous.

She recalled again the terrible, screaming fights between her
mother and father. They had always been about the same thing.
About what? She could not remember.

At five o'clock, Ashley returned to her hotel room. She changed
clothes three times before finally deciding on what she was going
to wear. She settled on a simple, flattering black dress.

When Ashley entered the festively decorated gymnasium of
Bedford Area High School, she found herself surrounded by 120
vaguely familiar-looking strangers. Some of her former classmates
were completely unrecognizable, others had changed little. Ashley
was looking for one person: Jim Cleary. *Would he have changed
much? Would he have his wife with him?* People were approaching
Ashley.

"Ashley, it's Trent Waterson. You look great!"

"Thanks. So do you, Trent."

"I want you to meet my wife. . . ."

"Ashley, it *is* you, isn't it?"

"Yes. Er—"

"Art. Art Davies. Remember me?"

"Of course." He was badly dressed and looked ill at ease.

"How is everything going, Art?"

"Well, you know I wanted to become an engineer, but it didn't work out."

"I'm sorry."

"Yeah. Anyway, I became a mechanic."

"Ashley! It's Lenny Holland. For God's sake, you look beautiful!"

"Thank you, Lenny." He had gained weight and was wearing a large diamond ring on his little finger.

"I'm in real estate now, doing great. Did you ever get married?"

Ashley hesitated. "No."

"Remember Nicki Brandt? We got married. We have twins."

"Congratulations."

It was amazing how much people could change in ten years. They were fatter and thinner . . . prosperous and downtrodden. They were married and divorced . . . parents and parentless. . . .

As the evening wore on, there was dining and music and dancing. Ashley made conversation with her former classmates and caught up on their lives, but her mind was on Jim Cleary. There was still no sign of him. *He won't come,* she decided. *He knows I might be here and he's afraid to face me.*

An attractive-looking woman was approaching. "Ashley! I was *hoping* I'd see you." It was Florence Schiffer. Ashley was genuinely glad to see her. Florence had been one of her closest friends. The two of them found a table in the corner, where they could talk.

"You look great, Florence," Ashley said.

"So do you. Sorry I'm so late. The baby wasn't feeling well. Since I last saw you, I've gotten married and divorced. I'm going out with Mr. Wonderful now. What about you? After the graduation party, you disappeared. I tried to find you, but you'd left town."

"I went to London," Ashley said. "My father enrolled me in a college over there. We left here the morning after our graduation."

"I tried every way I could think of to reach you. The detectives thought I might know where you were. They were looking for you because you and Jim Cleary were going together.''

Ashley said slowly, "The *detectives*?''

"Yes. The ones investigating the murder.''

Ashley felt the blood drain from her face. "What . . . murder?''

Florence was staring at her. "My God! You don't know?''

"*Know what?*'' Ashley demanded fiercely. "What are you talking about?''

"The day after the graduation party, Jim's parents came back and found his body. He had been stabbed to death and . . . castrated.''

The room started to spin. Ashley held on to the edge of the table. Florence grabbed her arm.

"I'm—I'm sorry, Ashley. I thought you would have read about it, but of course . . . you had left for London.''

Ashley squeezed her eyes tightly shut. She saw herself sneaking out of the house that night, heading toward Jim Cleary's house. But she had turned and gone back home to wait for him in the morning. *If only I had gone to him,* Ashley thought miserably, *he would still be alive. And all these years I've hated him. Oh, my God. Who could have killed him? Who—?*

She could hear her father's voice, "*You keep your goddamned hands off my daughter, do you understand? . . . If I ever see you around here again, I'll break every bone in your body.*''

She got to her feet. "You'll have to excuse me, Florence. I— I'm not feeling very well.''

And Ashley fled.

The detectives. They must have gotten in touch with her father. *Why didn't he tell me?*

She took the first plane back to California. It was early in the morning before she could fall asleep. She had a nightmare. A figure standing in the dark was stabbing Jim and screaming at him. The figure stepped into the light.

It was her father.

Chapter Five

THE next few months were misery for Ashley. The image of Jim Cleary's bloody, mutilated body kept going through her mind. She thought of seeing Dr. Speakman again, but she knew she dare not discuss this with anyone. She felt guilty even *thinking* that her father might have done such a terrible thing. She pushed the thought away and tried to concentrate on her work. It was impossible. She looked down in dismay at a logo she had just botched.

Shane Miller was watching her, concerned. "Are you all right, Ashley?"

She forced a smile. "I'm fine."

"I really am sorry about your friend." She had told him about Jim.

"I'll—I'll get over it."

"What about dinner tonight?"

"Thanks, Shane. I—I'm not up to it just yet. Next week."

"Right. If there's anything I can do—"

"I appreciate it. There's nothing anyone can do."

Toni said to Alette, "Miss Tight Ass has a problem. Well, she can get stuffed."

"I feel *dispiace*—sorry for her. She is troubled."

"Sod her. We all have our problems, don't we, luv?"

As Ashley was leaving on a Friday afternoon before a holiday weekend, Dennis Tibble stopped her. "Hey, babe. I need a favor."

"I'm sorry, Dennis, I—"

"Come on. Lighten up!" He took Ashley's arm. "I need some advice from a woman's point of view."

"Dennis, I'm not in the—"

"I've fallen in love with somebody, and I want to marry her, but there are problems. Will you help me?"

Ashley hesitated. She did not like Dennis Tibble, but she could see no harm in trying to help him. "Can this wait until tomorrow?"

"I need to talk to you now. It's really urgent."

Ashley took a deep breath. "All right."

"Can we go to your apartment?"

She shook her head. "No." She would never be able to make him leave.

"Will you stop by my place?"

Ashley hesitated. "Very well." *That way I can leave when I want to. If I can help him get the woman he's in love with, maybe he'll leave me alone.*

Toni said to Alette, "God! Goody Two-shoes is going to the twerp's apartment. Can you believe she could be that stupid? Where's her sodding brains?"

"She's just trying to help him. There's nothing wrong with—"

"Oh, come on, Alette. When are you going to grow up? The man wants to bonk her."

"*Non va. Non si fa così.*"

"I couldn't have said it better myself."

Dennis Tibble's apartment was furnished in neo-nightmare. Posters of old horror movies hung from the walls, next to pinups of naked models and wild animals feeding. Tiny erotic wood carvings were spread out on tables.

It's the apartment of a madman, Ashley thought. She could not wait to get out of there.

"Hey, I'm glad you could come, baby. I really appreciate this. If—"

"I can't stay long, Dennis." Ashley warned him. "Tell me about this woman you're in love with."

"She's really something." He held out a cigarette. "Cigarette?"

"I don't smoke." She watched him light up.

"How about a drink?"

"I don't drink."

He grinned. "You don't smoke, you don't drink. That leaves an interesting activity, doesn't it?"

She said to him sharply, "Dennis, if you don't—"

"Only kidding." He walked over to the bar and poured some wine. "Have a little wine. That can't hurt you." He handed her the glass.

She took a sip of wine. "Tell me about Miss Right."

Dennis Tibble sat down on the couch next to Ashley. "I've never met anybody like her. She's sexy like you and—"

"Stop it or I'll leave."

"Hey, that was meant as a compliment. Anyway, she's crazy about me, but her mother and father are very social, and they hate me."

Ashley made no comment.

"So the thing is, if I push it, she'll marry me, but she'll alienate her family. She's really close to them, and if I marry her, they'll sure as hell disown her. Then one day, she'll probably blame me. Do you see the problem?"

Ashley took another sip of wine. "Yes. I . . ."

After that, time seemed to vanish in a mist.

She awakened slowly, knowing that something was terribly wrong. She felt as though she had been drugged. It was an enormous effort merely to open her eyes. Ashley looked around the room and began to panic. She was lying in a bed, naked, in a cheap hotel room. She managed to sit up, and her head started to pound. She had no idea where she was or how she had gotten there. There was a room service menu on the nightstand, and she reached over and picked it up. *The Chicago Loop Hotel.* She read it again, stunned. *What am I doing in Chicago? How long have I been here? The visit to Dennis Tibble's apartment had been on Friday. What day is this?* With growing alarm, she picked up the telephone.

"May I help you?"

It was difficult for Ashley to speak. "What—what day is this?"

"Today is the seventeenth of—"

"No. I mean what *day* of the week is this?"

"Oh. Today is Monday. Can I—"

Ashley replaced the receiver in a daze. *Monday.* She had lost two days and two nights. She sat up at the edge of the bed, trying to remember. She had gone to Dennis Tibble's apartment. . . . She had had a glass of wine. . . . After that, everything was a blank.

He had put something in her glass of wine that had made her temporarily lose her memory. She had read about incidents where a drug like that had been used. It was called the "date rape drug." That was what he had given her. The talk about wanting her advice had been a ruse. *And like a fool, I fell for it.* She had no recollection of going to the airport, flying to Chicago or checking into this seedy hotel room with Tibble. And worse—no recollection of what had happened in this room.

I've got to get out of here, Ashley thought desperately. She felt unclean, as though every inch of her body had been violated. What had he done to her? Trying not to think about it, she got out of bed, walked into the tiny bathroom and stepped into the shower. She let the stream of hot water pound against her body, trying to wash away whatever terrible, dirty things had happened to her. What if he had gotten her pregnant? The thought of having his child was sickening. Ashley got out of the shower, dried herself and walked over to the closet. Her clothes were missing. The only things inside the closet were a black leather miniskirt, a cheap-looking tube top and a pair of spiked high-heeled shoes. She was repelled by the thought of putting on the clothes, but she had no choice. She dressed quickly and glanced in the mirror. She looked like a prostitute.

Ashley examined her purse. Only forty dollars. Her checkbook and credit card were still there. *Thank God!*

She went out into the corridor. It was empty. She took the elevator down to the seedy-looking lobby and walked over to the checkout desk, where she handed the elderly cashier her credit card.

"Leavin' us already?" He leered. "Well, you had a good time, huh?"

Ashley stared at him, wondering what he meant and afraid to find out. She was tempted to ask him when Dennis Tibble had checked out, but she decided it was better not to bring it up.

The cashier was putting her credit card through a machine. He frowned and put it through again. Finally, he said, "I'm sorry. This card won't go through. You've exceeded your limit."

Ashley's mouth dropped open. "That's impossible! There's some mistake!"

The clerk shrugged. "Do you have another credit card?"

"No. I—I don't. Will you take a personal check?"

He was eyeing her outfit disapprovingly. "I guess so, if you have some ID."

"I need to make a telephone call. . . ."

"Telephone booth in the corner."

"San Francisco Memorial Hospital . . ."

"Dr. Steven Patterson."

"One moment, please . . ."

"Dr. Patterson's office."

"Sarah? This is Ashley. I need to speak to my father."

"I'm sorry, Miss Patterson. He's in the operating room and—"

Ashley's grip tightened on the telephone. "Do you know how long he'll be there?"

"It's hard to say. I know he has another surgery scheduled after—"

Ashley found herself fighting hysteria. "I need to talk to him. It's urgent. Can you get word to him, please? As soon as he gets a chance, have him call me." She looked at the telephone number in the booth and gave it to her father's receptionist. "I'll wait here until he calls."

"I'll be sure to tell him."

She sat in the lobby for almost an hour, willing the telephone to ring. People passing by stared at her or ogled her, and she felt naked in the tawdry outfit she was wearing. When the phone finally rang, it startled her.

She hurried back into the phone booth. "Hello . . ."

"Ashley?" It was her father's voice.

"Oh, Father, I—"

"What's wrong?"

"I'm in Chicago and—"

"What are you doing in Chicago?"

"I can't go into it now. I need an airline ticket to San Jose. I don't have any money with me. Can you help me?"

"Of course. Hold on." Three minutes later, her father came back on the line. "There's an American Airlines plane leaving O'Hare at ten-forty A.M., Flight 407. There will be a ticket waiting for you at the check-in counter. I'll pick you up at the airport in San Jose and—"

"No!" She could not let him see her like this. "I'll—I'll go to
my apartment to change."
"All right. I'll come down and meet you for dinner. You can
tell me all about it then."
"Thank you, Father. Thank you."

On the plane going home, Ashley thought about the unforgivable
thing Dennis Tibble had done to her. *I'm going to have to go to
the police,* she decided. *I can't let him get away with this. How
many other women has he done this to?*

When Ashley got back to her apartment, she felt as though she had
returned to a sanctuary. She could not wait to get out of the tacky
outfit she was wearing. She stripped it off as quickly as she could.
She felt as though she needed another shower before she met her
father. She started to walk over to her closet and stopped. In front
of her, on the dressing table, was a burned cigarette butt.

They were seated at a corner table in a restaurant at The Oaks.
Ashley's father was studying her, concerned. "What were you
doing in Chicago?"
"I—I don't know."
He looked at her, puzzled. "You don't know?"
Ashley hesitated, trying to make up her mind whether to tell
him what had happened. Perhaps he could give her some advice.
She said carefully, "Dennis Tibble asked me up to his apartment
to help him with a problem. . . ."
"Dennis Tibble? That *snake*?" Long ago, Ashley had intro-
duced her father to the people she worked with. "How could you
have anything to do with him?"
Ashley knew instantly that she had made a mistake. Her father
had always overreacted to any problems she had. Especially when
it involved a man.
*"If I ever see you around here again, Cleary. I'll break every
bone in your body."*
"It's not important," Ashley said.
"I want to hear it."
Ashley sat still for a moment, filled with a sense of foreboding.
"Well, I had a drink at Dennis's apartment and . . ."
As she talked, she watched her father's face grow grim. There

was a look in his eyes that frightened her. She tried to cut the story short.

"No," her father insisted. "I want to hear it all. . . ."

Ashley lay in bed that night, too drained to sleep, her thoughts chaotic. *If what Dennis did to me becomes public, it will be humiliating. Everyone at work will know what happened. But I can't let him do this to anyone else. I have to tell the police.*

People had tried to warn her that Dennis was obsessed with her, but she had ignored them. Now, looking back on it, she could see all the signs: Dennis had hated to see anyone else talking to her; he was constantly begging her for dates; he was always eavesdropping. . . .

At least I know who the stalker is, Ashley thought.

At 8:30 in the morning, as Ashley was getting ready to leave for work, the telephone rang. She picked it up. "Hello."

"Ashley, it's Shane. Have you heard the news?"

"What news?"

"It's on television. They just found Dennis Tibble's body."

For an instant the earth seemed to shift. "Oh, my God! What happened?"

"According to the sheriff's office, somebody stabbed him to death and then castrated him."

Chapter Six

DEPUTY Sam Blake had earned his position in the Cupertino Sheriff's Office the hard way: He had married the sheriff's sister, Serena Dowling, a virago with a tongue sharp enough to fell the forests of Oregon. Sam Blake was the only man Serena had ever met who was able to handle her. He was a short, gentle, mild-mannered person with the patience of a saint. No matter how outrageous Serena's behavior, he would wait until she had calmed down and then have a quiet talk with her.

Blake had joined the sheriff's department because Sheriff Matt Dowling was his best friend. They had gone to school together and grown up together. Blake enjoyed police work and was exceedingly good at it. He had a keen, inquiring intelligence and a stubborn tenacity. The combination made him the best detective on the force.

Earlier that morning, Sam Blake and Sheriff Dowling were having coffee together.

Sheriff Dowling said, "I hear my sister gave you a bad time last night. We got half a dozen calls from the neighbors complaining about the noise. Serena's a champion screamer, all right."

Sam shrugged. "I finally got her calmed down, Matt."

"Thank God she's not living with me anymore, Sam. I don't know what gets into her. Her temper tantrums—"

Their conversation was interrupted. "Sheriff, we just got a 911. There's been a murder over on Sunnyvale Avenue."

Sheriff Dowling looked at Sam Blake.

Blake nodded. "I'll catch it."

*   *   *

Fifteen minutes later, Deputy Blake was walking into Dennis Tibble's apartment. A patrolman in the living room was talking to the building superintendent.

"Where's the body?" Blake asked.

The patrolman nodded toward the bedroom. "In there, sir." He looked pale.

Blake walked to the bedroom and stopped, in shock. A man's naked body was sprawled across the bed, and Blake's first impression was that the room was soaked in blood. As he stepped closer to the bed, he saw where the blood had come from. The ragged edge of a broken bottle had punctured the victim's back, over and over again, and there were shards of glass in his body. The victim's testicles had been slashed off.

Looking at it, Blake felt a pain in his groin. "How the hell could a human being do a thing like this?" he said aloud. There was no sign of the weapon, but they would make a thorough search.

Deputy Blake went back into the living room to talk to the building superintendent. "Did you know the deceased?"

"Yes, sir. This is his apartment."

"What's his name?"

"Tibble. Dennis Tibble."

Deputy Blake made a note. "How long had he lived here?"

"Almost three years."

"What can you tell me about him?"

"Not too much, sir. Tibble kept pretty much to himself, always paid his rent on time. Once in a while he'd have a woman in here. I think they were mostly pros."

"Do you know where he worked?"

"Oh, yes. Global Computer Graphics Corporation. He was one of them computer nerds."

Deputy Blake made another note. "Who found the body?"

"One of the maids. Maria. Yesterday was a holiday, so she didn't come in until this morning—"

"I want to talk to her."

"Yes, sir. I'll get her."

Maria was a dark-looking Brazilian woman in her forties, nervous and frightened.

"You discovered the body, Maria?"

"I didn't do it. I swear to you." She was on the verge of hysteria. "Do I need a lawyer?"

"No. You don't need a lawyer. Just tell me what happened."

"Nothing happened. I mean— I walked in here this morning to clean, the way I always do. I—I thought he was gone. He's always out of here by seven in the morning. I tidied up the living room and—"

Damn! "Maria, do you remember what the room looked like before you tidied up?"

"What do you mean?"

"Did you move anything? Take anything out of here?"

"Well, yes. There was a broken wine bottle on the floor. It was all sticky. I—"

"What did you do with it?" he asked excitedly.

"I put it in the garbage compactor and ground it up."

"What else did you do?"

"Well, I cleaned out the ashtray and—"

"Were there any cigarette butts in it?"

She stopped to remember. "One. I put it in the trash basket in the kitchen."

"Let's take a look at it." He followed her to the kitchen, and she pointed to a wastebasket. Inside was a cigarette butt with lipstick on it. Carefully, Deputy Blake scooped it up in a coin envelope.

He led her back to the living room. "Maria, do you know if anything is missing from the apartment? Does it look as if any valuables are gone?"

She looked around. "I don't think so. Mr. Tibble, he liked to collect those little statues. He spent a lot of money on them. It looks like they're all here."

So the motive was not robbery. Drugs? Revenge? A love affair gone wrong?

"What did you do after you tidied up here, Maria?"

"I vacuumed in here, the way I always do. And then—" Her voice faltered. "I walked into the bedroom and . . . I saw him." She looked at Deputy Blake. "I swear I didn't do it."

The coroner and his assistants arrived in a coroner's wagon, with a body bag.

Three hours later, Deputy Sam Blake was back in the sheriff's office.

"What have you got, Sam?"

"Not much." Deputy Blake sat down across from Sheriff Dowling. "Dennis Tibble worked over at Global. He was apparently some kind of genius."

"But not genius enough to keep himself from getting killed."

"He wasn't just killed, Matt. He was slaughtered. You should have seen what someone did to his body. It has to be some kind of maniac."

"Nothing to go on?"

"We aren't sure what the murder weapon is, we're waiting for results from the lab, but it may be a broken wine bottle. The maid threw it in the compactor. It looks like there's a fingerprint on one of the pieces of glass in his back. I talked to the neighbors. No help there. No one saw anyone coming in or out of his apartment. No unusual noises. Apparently, Tibble stuck pretty much to himself. He wasn't the neighborly type. One thing. Tibble had sex before he died. We have vaginal traces, pubic hairs, other trace evidence and a cigarette stub with lipstick. We'll test for DNA."

"The newspapers are going to have a good time with this one, Sam. I can see the headlines now—MANIAC STRIKES SILICON VALLEY." Sheriff Dowling sighed. "Let's knock this off as fast as we can."

"I'm on my way over to Global Computer Graphics now."

It had taken Ashley an hour to decide whether she should go into the office. She was torn. *One look at me, and everyone will know that something is wrong. But if I don't show up, they'll want to know why. The police will probably be there asking questions. If they question me, I'll have to tell them the truth. They won't believe me. They'll blame me for killing Dennis Tibble. And if they do believe me, and if I tell them my father knew what he did to me, they'll blame him.*

She thought of Jim Cleary's murder. She could hear Florence's voice: *"Jim's parents came back and found his body. He had been stabbed to death and castrated."*

Ashley squeezed her eyes shut tightly. *My God, what's happening? What's happening?*

Deputy Sam Blake walked onto the work floor where groups of somber employees stood around, talking quietly. Blake could imagine what the subject of conversation was. Ashley watched him apprehensively as he headed toward Shane Miller's office.

Shane rose to greet him. "Deputy Blake?"

"Yes." The two men shook hands.

"Sit down, Deputy."

Sam Blake took a seat. "I understand Dennis Tibble was an employee here?"

"That's right. One of the best. It's a terrible tragedy."

"He worked here about three years?"

"Yes. He was our genius. There wasn't anything he couldn't do with a computer."

"What can you tell me about his social life?"

Shane Miller shook his head. "Not much, I'm afraid. Tibble was kind of a loner."

"Do you have any idea if he was into drugs?"

"Dennis? Hell, no. He was a health nut."

"Did he gamble? Could he have owed someone a lot of money?"

"No. He made a damned good salary, but I think he was pretty tight with a buck."

"What about women? Did he have a girlfriend?"

"Women weren't very attracted to Tibble." He thought for a moment. "Lately, though, he was going around telling people there was someone he was thinking of marrying."

"Did he happen to mention her name?"

Miller shook his head. "No. Not to me, anyway."

"Would you mind if I talked to some of your employees?"

"Not at all. Go ahead. I have to tell you, they're all pretty shaken up."

They would be more shaken up if they could have seen his body, Blake thought.

The two men walked out onto the work floor.

Shane Miller raised his voice. "May I have your attention, please? This is Deputy Blake. He'd like to ask a few questions."

The employees had stopped what they were doing and were listening.

Deputy Blake said, "I'm sure that all of you have heard what happened to Mr. Tibble. We need your help in finding out who killed him. Do any of you know of any enemies he had? Anyone who hated him enough to want to murder him?" There was a silence. Blake went on. "There was a woman he was interested in marrying. Did he discuss her with any of you?"

Ashley was finding it difficult to breathe. Now was the time to speak up. Now was the time to tell the deputy what Tibble had done to her. But Ashley remembered the look on her father's face when she had told him about it. They would blame him for the murder.

Her father could never kill anyone.

He was a doctor.

He was a surgeon.

Dennis Tibble had been castrated.

Deputy Blake was saying, ". . . and none of you saw him after he left here on Friday?"

Toni Prescott thought, *Go ahead. Tell him, Miss Goody Two-shoes. Tell him you went to his apartment. Why don't you speak up?*

Deputy Blake stood there a moment, trying to hide his disappointment. "Well, if any of you remembers anything that might be helpful, I'd appreciate it if you'd give me a call. Mr. Miller has my number. Thank you."

They watched as he moved toward the exit with Shane.

Ashley felt faint with relief.

Deputy Blake turned to Shane. "Was there anyone here he was particularly close to?"

"No, not really," Shane said. "I don't think Dennis was close to anybody. He was very attracted to one of our computer operators, but he never got anywhere with her."

Deputy Blake stopped. "Is she here now?"

"Yes, but—"

"I'd like to talk to her."

"All right. You can use my office." They walked back into the room, and Ashley saw them coming. They were headed straight for her cubicle. She could feel her face redden.

"Ashley, Deputy Blake would like to talk to you."

So he knew! He was going to ask her about her visit to Tibble's apartment. *I've got to be careful,* Ashley thought.

The deputy was looking at her. "Do you mind, Miss Patterson?"

She found her voice. "No, not at all." She followed him into Shane Miller's office.

"Sit down." They both took chairs. "I understand that Dennis Tibble was fond of you?"

"I—I suppose . . ." *Careful.* "Yes."

"Did you go out with him?"

Going to his apartment would not be the same as going out with him. "No."

"Did he talk to you about this woman he wanted to marry?"

She was getting in deeper and deeper. Could he be taping this? Maybe he already knew she had been in Tibble's apartment. They could have found her fingerprints. Now was the time to tell the deputy what Tibble had done to her. *But if I do,* Ashley thought in despair, *it will lead to my father, and they'll connect that to Jim Cleary's murder.* Did they know about that, too? But the police department in Bedford would have no reason to notify the police department in Cupertino. Or would they?

Deputy Blake was watching her, waiting for an answer. "Miss Patterson?"

"What? Oh, I'm sorry. This has got me so upset. . . ."

"I understand. Did Tibble ever mention this woman he wanted to marry?"

"Yes . . . but he never told me her name." That, at least, was true.

"Have you ever been to Tibble's apartment?"

Ashley took a deep breath. If she said no, the questioning would probably end. But if they had found her fingerprints . . . "Yes."

"You have been to his apartment?"

"Yes."

He was looking at her more closely now. "You said you'd never been out with him."

Ashley's mind was racing now. "That's right. Not on a date, no. I went to bring him some papers he had forgotten."

"When was this?"

She felt trapped. "It was . . . it was about a week ago."

"And that's the only time you've been to his place?"

"That's right."

Now if they had her fingerprints, she would be in the clear.

Deputy Blake sat there, studying her, and she felt guilty. She wanted to tell him the truth. Maybe some burglar had broken in and killed him—the same burglar who had killed Jim Cleary ten years earlier and three thousand miles away. If you believed in coincidences. If you believed in Santa Claus. If you believed in the tooth fairy.

Damn you, Father.

Deputy Blake said, "This is a terrible crime. There doesn't seem to be any motive. But you know, in all the years I've been on the force, I've never seen a crime without a motive." There was no response. "Do *you* know if Dennis Tibble was into drugs?"

"I'm sure he wasn't."

"So what do we have? It wasn't drugs. He wasn't robbed. He didn't owe anybody money. That kind of leaves a romantic situation, doesn't it? Someone who was jealous of him."

Or a father who wanted to protect his daughter.

"I'm as puzzled as you are, Deputy."

He stared at her for a moment and his eyes seemed to say, "I don't believe you, lady."

Deputy Blake got to his feet. He took out a card and handed it to Ashley. "If there's anything you can think of, I'd appreciate your giving me a call."

"I'll be happy to."

"Good day."

She watched him leave. *It's over. Father's in the clear.*

When Ashley returned to her apartment that evening, there was a message on the answering machine: "You got me real hot last night, baby. I'm talking blue balls. But you'll take care of me tonight, though, the way you promised. Same time, same place."

Ashley stood there, listening in disbelief. *I'm going crazy,* she thought. *This has nothing to do with Father. Someone else must be behind all this. But who? And why?*

Five days later, Ashley received a statement from the credit card company. Three items caught her attention:

A bill from the Mod Dress Shop for $450.

A bill from the Circus Club for $300.

A bill from Louie's Restaurant for $250.

She had never heard of the dress shop, the club or the restaurant.

Chapter Seven

ASHLEY Patterson followed the investigation of Dennis Tibble's murder in the newspapers and on television every day. The police appeared to have reached a dead end.

It's over, Ashley thought. *There's nothing more to worry about.*

That evening, Deputy Sam Blake appeared at her apartment. Ashley looked at him, her mouth suddenly dry.

"I hope I'm not bothering you," Deputy Blake said. "I was on my way home, and I just thought I'd drop in for a minute."

Ashley swallowed. "No. Come in."

Deputy Blake walked into the apartment. "Nice place you have here."

"Thank you."

"I'll bet Dennis Tibble didn't like this kind of furniture."

Ashley's heart began to pound. "I don't know. He's never been in this apartment."

"Oh. I thought he might have, you know."

"No, I don't know, Deputy. I told you, I never dated him."

"Right. May I sit down?"

"Please."

"You see, I'm having a big problem with this case, Miss Patterson. It doesn't fit into any pattern. Like I said, there's always a motive. I've talked to some of the people over at Global Computer Graphics, and no one seems to have known Tibble very well. He kept pretty much to himself."

Ashley listened, waiting for the blow to fall.

"In fact, from what they tell me, you're the only one he was really interested in."

Had he found out something, or was he on a fishing expedition? Ashley said carefully, "He was interested in me, Deputy, but I was not interested in him. I made that quite clear to him."

He nodded. "Well, I think it was nice of you to deliver those papers to his apartment."

Ashley almost said, "What papers?" and then suddenly remembered. "It—it was no trouble. It was on my way."

"Right. Someone must have hated Tibble a lot to do what they did."

Ashley sat there tense, saying nothing.

"Do you know what I hate?" Deputy Blake said. "Unsolved murders. They always leave me frustrated. Because when a murder goes unsolved, I don't think it means that the criminals were that smart. I think it means that the police weren't smart enough. Well, so far, I've been lucky. I've solved all the crimes that have come my way." He got to his feet. "I don't intend to give up on this one. If you can think of anything that will be helpful, you'll call me, won't you, Miss Patterson?"

"Yes, of course."

Ashley watched him leave, and she thought, *Did he come here as a warning? Does he know more than he's telling me?*

Toni was more absorbed than ever in the Internet. She enjoyed her chats with Jean Claude the most, but that did not stop her from having other chat-room correspondents. At every chance, she sat in front of her computer, and the typed messages flew back and forth, spilling onto the computer screen.

"Toni? Where have you been? I've been in the chat room waiting for you."

"I'm worth waiting for, luv. Tell me about yourself. What do you do?"

"I work at a pharmacy. I can be good to you. Do you do drugs?"

"Sod off."

"Is that you, Toni?"

"The answer to your dreams. Is it Mark?"

"Yes."

"You haven't been on the Internet lately."

"I've been busy. I'd like to meet you, Toni."

"Tell me, Mark, what do you do?"

"I'm a librarian."
"Isn't that exciting! All those books and everything. . . ."
"When can we meet?"
"Why don't you ask Nostradamus?"

"Hello, Toni. My name is Wendy."
"Hello, Wendy."
"You sound like fun."
"I enjoy life."
"Maybe I can help you enjoy it more."
"What did you have in mind?"
"Well, I hope you're not one of those narrow-minded people who are afraid to experiment and try exciting new things. I'd like to show you a good time."
"Thanks, Wendy. You don't have the equipment I need."

And then, Jean Claude Parent came back on.
"*Bonne nuit. Comment ça va?* How are you?"
"I'm great. How about you?"
"I have missed you. I wish very much to meet you in person."
"I want to meet you, too. Thanks for sending me your photograph. You're a good-looking bloke."
"And you are beautiful. I think it is very important for us to get to know each other. Is your company coming to Quebec for the computer convention?"
"What? Not that I know of. When is it?"
"In three weeks. Many big companies will be coming. I hope you will be here."
"I hope so, too."
"Can we meet in the chat room tomorrow at the same time?"
"Of course. Until tomorrow."
"*À demain.*"

The following morning, Shane Miller walked up to Ashley. "Ashley, have you heard about the big computer convention coming up in Quebec City?"
She nodded. "Yes. It sounds interesting."
"I was just debating whether we should send a contingent up there."
"All the companies are going," Ashley said. "Symantec, Mi-

crosoft, Apple. Quebec City is putting on a big show for them. A trip like that could be kind of a Christmas bonus."

Shane Miller smiled at her enthusiasm. "Let me check it out."

The following morning, Shane Miller called Ashley into his office. "How would you like to spend Christmas in Quebec City?"

"We're going? That's great," Ashley said, enthusiastically. In the past, she had spent the Christmas holidays with her father, but this year she had dreaded the prospect.

"You'd better take plenty of warm clothes."

"Don't worry. I will. I'm really looking forward to this, Shane."

Toni was in the Internet chat room. "Jean Claude, the company is sending a group of us to Quebec City!"

"*Formidable!* I am so pleased. When will you arrive?"

"In two weeks. There will be fifteen of us."

"*Merveilleux!* I feel as though something very important is going to happen."

"So do I." *Something very important.*

Ashley anxiously watched the news every night, but there were still no new developments in the Dennis Tibble murder. She began to relax. If the police could not connect her with the case, there was no way they could find a connection to her father. Half a dozen times she steeled herself to ask him about it, but each time she backed off. What if he were innocent? Could he ever forgive her for accusing him of being a murderer? *And if he is guilty, I don't want to know,* Ashley thought. *I couldn't bear it. And if he has done those terrible things, in his mind, he would have done them to protect me. At least I won't have to face him this Christmas.*

Ashley telephoned her father in San Francisco. She said, without preamble, "I'm not going to be able to spend Christmas with you this year, Father. My company is sending me to a convention in Canada."

There was a long silence. "That's bad timing, Ashley. You and I have always spent Christmas together."

"I can't help—"

"You're all I have, you know."

"Yes, Father, and . . . you're all I have."

"That's what's important."

Important enough to kill for?

"Where is this convention?"

"In Quebec City. It's—"

"Ah. Lovely place. I haven't been there in years. I'll tell you what I'll do. I haven't anything scheduled at the hospital around that time. I'll fly up, and we'll have a Christmas dinner together."

Ashley said quickly, "I don't think it's—"

"You just make a reservation for me at whatever hotel you're staying at. We don't want to break tradition, do we?"

She hesitated and said slowly, "No, Father."

How can I face him?

Alette was excited. She said to Toni, "I've never been to Quebec City. Do they have museums there?"

"Of course they have museums there," Toni told her. "They have everything. A lot of winter sports. Skiing, skating . . ."

Alette shuddered. "I hate cold weather. No sports for me. Even with gloves, my fingers get numb. I will stick to the museums. . . ."

On the twenty-first of December, the group from Global Computer Graphics arrived at the Jean-Lesage International Airport in Sainte-Foy and were driven to the storied Château Frontenac in Quebec City. It was below zero outside, and the streets were blanketed with snow.

Jean Claude had given Toni his home telephone number. She called as soon as she checked into her room. "I hope I'm not calling too late."

"*Mais non!* I cannot believe you are here. When may I see you?"

"Well, we're all going to the convention center tomorrow morning, but I could slip away and have lunch with you."

"*Bon!* There is a restaurant, Le Paris-Brest, on the Grande Allée Est. Can you meet me there at one o'clock?"

"I'll be there."

The Centre des Congrès de Quebec on René Lévesque Boulevard is a four-story, glass-and-steel, state-of-the-art building that can accommodate thousands of conventioneers. At nine o'clock in the morning, the vast halls were crowded with computer experts from all over the world, exchanging information on up-to-the-minute developments. They filled multimedia rooms, exhibit halls and video-conferencing centers. There were half a dozen seminars going on simultaneously. Toni was bored. *All talk and no action,* she thought. At 12:45, she slipped out of the convention hall and took a taxi to the restaurant.

Jean Claude was waiting for her. He took her hand and said warmly, "Toni, I am so pleased you could come."

"So am I."

"I will try to make certain that your time here is very agreeable," Jean Claude told her. "This is a beautiful city to explore."

Toni looked at him and smiled. "I know I'm going to enjoy it."

"I would like to spend as much time with you as I can."

"Can you take the time off? What about the jewelry store?"

Jean Claude smiled. "It will have to manage without me."

The maître d' brought menus.

Jean Claude said to Toni, "Would you like to try some of our French-Canadian dishes?"

"Fine."

"Then please let me order for you." He said to the maître d', "*Nous voudrions le Brome Lake Duckling.*" He explained to Toni, "It is a local dish, duckling cooked in calvados and stuffed with apples."

"Sounds delicious."

And it was.

During luncheon, they filled each other in on their pasts.

"So. You've never been married?" Toni asked.

"No. And you?"

"No."

"You have not found the right man."

Oh, God, wouldn't it be wonderful if it were that simple. "No."

They talked of Quebec City and what there was to do there.

"Do you ski?"

Toni nodded. "I love it."

"Ah, *bon, moi aussi.* And there is snowmobiling, ice-skating, wonderful shopping . . ."

There was something almost boyish about his enthusiasm. Toni had never felt more comfortable with anyone.

* * *

Shane Miller arranged it so his group attended the convention mornings and had their afternoons free.

"I don't know what to do here," Alette complained to Toni. "It's freezing. What are you going to do?"

"Everything." Toni grinned. "*A più tardi.*"

Toni and Jean Claude had lunch together every day, and every afternoon, Jean Claude took Toni on a tour. She had never seen any place like Quebec City. It was like finding a turn-of-the-century picturesque French village in North America. The ancient streets had colorful names like Break Neck Stairs and Below the Fort and Sailor's Leap. It was a Currier & Ives city, framed in snow.

They visited La Citadelle, with its walls protecting Old Quebec, and they watched the traditional changing of the guard inside the walls of the fort. They explored the shopping streets, Saint Jean, Cartier, Côte de la Fabrique, and wandered through the Quartier Petit Champlain.

"This is the oldest commercial district in North America," Jean Claude told her.

"It's super."

Everywhere they went, there were sparkling Christmas trees, nativity scenes and music for the enjoyment of the strollers.

Jean Claude took Toni snowmobiling in the countryside. As they raced down a narrow slope, he called out, "Are you having a good time?"

Toni sensed that it was not an idle question. She nodded and said softly, "I'm having a wonderful time."

* * *

Alette spent her time at museums. She visited the Basilica of Notre-Dame and the Good Shepherd Chapel and the Augustine Museum, but she had no interest in anything else that Quebec City offered. There were dozens of gourmet restaurants, but when she was not dining at the hotel, she ate at Le Commensal, a vegetarian cafeteria.

From time to time, Alette thought about her artist friend, Richard Melton, in San Francisco, and wondered what he was doing and if he would remember her.

* * *

Ashley was dreading Christmas. She was tempted to call her father and tell him not to come. *But what excuse can I give? You're a murderer. I don't want to see you?*

And each day Christmas was coming closer.

"I would like to show you my jewelry store," Jean Claude told Toni. "Would you care to see it?"

Toni nodded. "Love to."

Parent Jewelers was located in the heart of Quebec City, on rue Notre-Dame. When she walked in the door, Toni was stunned. On the Internet, Jean Claude had said, *"I have a little jewelry store."* It was a very large store, tastefully done. Half a dozen clerks were busy with customers.

Toni looked around and said, "It's—it's smashing."

He smiled. *"Merci.* I would like to give you a *cadeau*—a gift, for Christmas."

"No. That isn't necessary. I—"

"Please do not deprive me of the pleasure." Jean Claude led Toni to a showcase filled with rings. "Tell me what you like."

Toni shook her head. "Those are much too expensive. I couldn't—"

"Please."

Toni studied him a moment, then nodded. "All right." She examined the showcase again. In the center was a large emerald ring set with diamonds.

Jean Claude saw her looking at it. "Do you like the emerald ring?"

"It's lovely, but it's much too—"

"It is yours." Jean Claude took out a small key, unlocked the case and pulled out the ring.

"No, Jean Claude—"

"Pour moi." He slipped it on Toni's finger. It was a perfect fit. *"Voilà!* It is a sign."

Toni squeezed his hand. "I—I don't know what to say."

"I cannot tell you how much pleasure this gives me. There is a wonderful restaurant here called Pavillon. Would you like to have dinner there tonight?"

"Anywhere you say."

"I will call for you at eight o'clock."

*   *   *

At six o'clock that night, Ashley's father telephoned. "I'm afraid I'm going to have to disappoint you, Ashley. I won't be able to be there for Christmas. An important patient of mine in South America has had a stroke. I'm flying to Argentina tonight."

"I'm—I'm sorry, Father," Ashley said. She tried to sound convincing.

"We'll make up for it, won't we, darling?"

"Yes, Father. Have a good flight."

Toni was looking forward to dinner with Jean Claude. It was going to be a lovely evening. As she dressed, she sang softly to herself.

"Up and down the city road,
In and out of the Eagle,
That's the way the money goes,
Pop! goes the weasel."

I think Jean Claude is in love with me, Mother.

Pavillon is located in the cavernous Gare du Palais, Quebec City's old railroad station. It is a large restaurant with a long bar at the entrance and rows of tables spreading toward the back. At eleven o'clock each night, a dozen tables are moved to the side to create a dance floor, and a disc jockey takes over with a variety of tapes ranging from reggae to jazz to blues.

Toni and Jean Claude arrived at nine, and they were warmly greeted at the door by the owner.

"Monsieur Parent. How nice to see you."

"Thank you, André. This is Miss Toni Prescott. Mr. Nicholas."

"A pleasure, Miss Prescott. Your table is ready."

"The food is excellent here," Jean Claude assured Toni, when they were seated. "Let us start with champagne."

They ordered paillard de veau and torpille and salad and a bottle of Valpolicella.

Toni kept studying the emerald ring Jean Claude had given her. "It's so beautiful!" she exclaimed.

Jean Claude leaned across the table. *"Tu aussi.* I cannot tell you how happy I am that we have finally met."

"I am, too," Toni said softly.

The music began. Jean Claude looked at Toni. "Would you like to dance?"

"I'd love to."

Dancing was one of Toni's passions, and when she got out on the dance floor, she forgot everything else. *She was a little girl dancing with her father, and her mother said, "The child is clumsy."*

Jean Claude was holding her close. "You're a wonderful dancer."

"Thank you." *Do you hear that, Mother?*

Toni thought, *I wish this could go on forever.*

On the way back to the hotel, Jean Claude said, "*Chérie,* would you like to stop at my house and have a nightcap?"

Toni hesitated. "Not tonight, Jean Claude."

"Tomorrow, *peut-être?*"

She squeezed his hand. "Tomorrow."

At 3:00 A.M., Police Officer René Picard was in a squad car cruising down Grande Allée in the Quartier Montcalm when he noticed that the front door of a two-story redbrick house was wide open. He pulled over to the curb and stepped out to investigate. He walked to the front door and called, "*Bon soir. Y a-t-il, quelqu'un?*"

There was no answer. He stepped into the foyer and moved toward the large drawing room. "*C'est la police. Y a-t-il, quelqu'un?*"

There was no response. The house was unnaturally quiet. Unbuttoning his gun holster, Officer Picard began to go through the downstairs room, calling out as he moved from room to room. The only response was an eerie silence. He returned to the foyer. There was a graceful staircase leading to the floor above. "Allo!" Nothing.

Officer Picard started up the stairs. When he got to the top of the stairs, his gun was in his hand. He called out again, then started down the long hallway. Ahead, a bedroom door was ajar. He walked over to it, opened it wide and turned pale. "*Mon Dieu!*"

At five o'clock that morning, in the gray stone and yellow brick building on Story Boulevard, where Centrale de Police is located, Inspector Paul Cayer was asking, "What do we have?"

Officer Guy Fontaine replied, "The victim's name is Jean Claude Parent. He was stabbed at least a dozen times, and his body was castrated. The coroner says that the murder took place in the last three or four hours. We found a restaurant receipt from Pavillon in Parent's jacket pocket. He had dinner there earlier in the evening. We got the owner of the restaurant out of bed.''

''Yes?''

''Monsieur Parent was at Pavillon with a woman named Toni Prescott, a brunette, very attractive, with an English accent. The manager of Monsieur Parent's jewelry store said that earlier that day, Monsieur Parent had brought a woman answering that description into the store and introduced her as Toni Prescott. He gave her an expensive emerald ring. We also believe that Monsieur Parent had sex with someone before he died, and that the murder weapon was a steel-blade letter opener. There were fingerprints on it. We sent them on to our lab and to the FBI. We are waiting to hear.''

''Have you picked up Toni Prescott?''

''Non.''

''And why not?''

''We cannot find her. We have checked all the local hotels. We have checked our files and the files of the FBI. She has no birth certificate, no social security number, no driver's license.''

''Impossible! Could she have gotten out of the city?''

Officer Fontaine shook his head. ''I don't think so, Inspector. The airport closed at midnight. The last train out of Quebec City left at five-thirty-five last night. The first train this morning will be at six-thirty-nine. We have sent a description of her to the bus station, the two taxi companies and the limousine company.''

''For God's sake, we have her name, her description and her fingerprints. She can't just have disappeared.''

One hour later, a report came in from the FBI. They were unable to identify the fingerprints. There was no record of Toni Prescott.

Chapter Eight

FIVE days after Ashley returned from Quebec City, her father was on the telephone. "I just got back."

"Back?" It took Ashley a moment to remember. "Oh. Your patient in Argentina. How is he?"

"He'll live."

"I'm glad."

"Can you come up to San Francisco for dinner tomorrow?"

She dreaded the thought of facing him, but she could think of no excuse. "All right."

"I'll see you at Restaurant Lulu. Eight o'clock."

Ashley was waiting at the restaurant when her father walked in. Again, she saw the admiring glances of recognition on people's faces. Her father was a famous man. *Would he risk everything he had just to—?*

He was at the table.

"It's good to see you, sweetheart. Sorry about our Christmas dinner."

She forced herself to say, "So am I."

She was staring at the menu, not seeing it, trying to get her thoughts together.

"What would you like?"

"I—I'm not really hungry," she said.

"You have to eat something. You're getting too thin."

"I'll have the chicken."

She watched her father as he ordered, and she wondered if she dared to bring up the subject.

"How was Quebec City?"

"It was very interesting," Ashley said. "It's a beautiful place."

"We must go there together sometime."

She made a decision and tried to keep her voice as casual as possible. "Yes. By the way . . . last June I went to my ten-year high school reunion in Bedford."

He nodded. "Did you enjoy it?"

"No." She spoke slowly, choosing her words carefully. "I—I found out that the day after you and I left for London, Jim Cleary's body . . . was found . He had been stabbed . . . and castrated." She sat there, watching him, waiting for a reaction.

Dr. Patterson frowned. "Cleary? Oh, yes. That boy who was panting after you. I saved you from him, didn't I?"

What did that mean? Was it a confession? Had he saved her from Jim Cleary by killing him?

Ashley took a deep breath and went on. "Dennis Tibble was murdered the same way. He was stabbed and castrated." She watched her father pick up a roll and carefully butter it.

When he spoke, he said, "I'm not surprised, Ashley. Bad people usually come to a bad end."

And this was a doctor, a man dedicated to saving lives. *I'll never understand him,* Ashley thought. *I don't think I want to.*

By the time dinner was over, Ashley was no closer to the truth.

Toni said, "I really enjoyed Quebec City, Alette. I'd like to go back someday. Did you have a good time?"

Alette said shyly, "I enjoyed the museums."

"Have you called your boyfriend in San Francisco yet?"

"He's not my boyfriend."

"I'll bet you want him to be, don't you?"

"*Forse.* Perhaps."

"Why don't you call him?"

"I don't think it would be proper to—"

"Call him."

They arranged to meet at the De Young Museum.

"I really missed you," Richard Melton said. "How was Quebec?"

"*Va bene.*"

"I wish I had been there with you."

Maybe one day, Alette thought hopefully. "How is the painting coming along?"

"Not bad. I just sold one of my paintings to a really well-known collector."

"Fantastic!" She was delighted. And she could not help thinking, *It's so different when I'm with him. If it were anyone else, I would have thought, Who is tasteless enough to pay money for your paintings? or Don't give up your day job or a hundred other cruel remarks. But I don't do that with Richard.*

It gave Alette an incredible feeling of freedom, as though she had found a cure for some debilitating disease.

They had lunch at the museum.

"What would you like?" Richard asked. "They have great roast beef here."

"I'm a vegetarian. I'll just have a salad. Thank you."

"Okay."

A young, attractive waitress came over to the table. "Hello, Richard."

"Hi, Bernice."

Unexpectedly, Alette felt a pang of jealousy. Her reaction surprised her.

"Are you ready to order?"

"Yes. Miss Peters is going to have a salad, and I'm going to have a roast beef sandwich."

The waitress was studying Alette. *Is she jealous of me?* Alette wondered. When the waitress left, Alette said, "She's very pretty. Do you know her well?" Immediately she blushed. *I wish I hadn't asked that.*

Richard smiled. "I come here a lot. When I first came here, I didn't have much money. I'd order a sandwich, and Bernice would bring me a banquet. She's great."

"She seems very nice," Alette said. And she thought, *She has fat thighs.*

After they had ordered, they talked about artists.

"One day I want to go to Giverny," Alette said, "where Monet painted."

"Did you know Monet started out as a caricaturist?"

"No."

"It's true. Then he met Boudin, who became his teacher and persuaded him to start painting out of doors. There's a great story about that. Monet got so hooked on painting out of doors that when he decided to paint a picture of a woman in the garden, with a canvas over eight feet high, he had a trench dug in the garden so he could raise or lower the canvas by pulleys. The picture is hanging at the Musée d'Orsay in Paris.''

The time went by swiftly and happily.

After lunch, Alette and Richard walked around looking at the various exhibits. There were more than forty thousand objects in the collection, everything from ancient Egyptian artifacts to contemporary American paintings.

Alette was filled with the wonderment of being with Richard and her complete lack of negative thoughts. *Che cosa significa?*

A uniformed guard approached them. ''Good afternoon, Richard.''

''Afternoon, Brian. This is my friend, Alette Peters. Brian Hill.''

Brian said to Alette, ''Are you enjoying the museum?''

''Oh, yes. It's wonderful.''

''Richard's teaching me to paint,'' Brian said.

Alette looked at Richard. ''You are?''

Richard said modestly, ''Oh, I'm just guiding him a little bit.''

''He's doing more than that, miss. I've always wanted to be a painter. That's why I took this job at the museum, because I love art. Anyway, Richard comes here a lot and paints. When I saw his work, I thought, 'I want to be like him.' So I asked him if he'd teach me, and he's been great. Have you seen any of his paintings?''

''I have,'' Alette said. ''They're wonderful.''

When they left him, Alette said, ''It's lovely of you to do that, Richard.''

''I like to do things for people,'' and he was looking at Alette.

When they were walking out of the museum, Richard said, ''My roommate is at a party tonight. Why don't we stop up at my place?'' He smiled. ''I have some paintings I'd like to show you.''

Alette squeezed his hand. ''Not yet, Richard.''

''Whatever you say. I'll see you next weekend?''

''Yes.''

And he had no idea how much she was looking forward to it.

Richard walked Alette to the parking lot where she had parked her car. He waved good-bye as she drove off.

*   *   *

As Alette was going to sleep that night, she thought, *It's like a miracle. Richard has freed me.* She fell asleep, dreaming of him.

At two o'clock in the morning, Richard Melton's roommate, Gary, returned from a birthday party. The apartment was dark. He switched on the lights in the living room. "Richard?"

He started toward the bedroom. At the door he looked inside and was sick to his stomach.

"Calm down, son." Detective Whittier looked at the shivering figure in the chair. "Now, let's go over it again. Did he have any enemies, someone mad enough at him to do this?"

Gary swallowed. "No. Everyone . . . everyone liked Richard."

"Someone didn't. How long have you and Richard lived together?"

"Two years."

"Were you lovers?"

"For God's sake," Gary said indignantly. "No. We were friends. We lived together for financial reasons."

Detective Whittier looked around the small apartment. "Sure as hell wasn't a burglary," he said. "There's nothing here to steal. Was your roommate seeing anyone romantically?"

"No— Well, yes. There was a girl he was interested in. I think he was really starting to like her."

"Do you know her name?"

"Yes. Alette. Alette Peters. She works in Cupertino."

Detective Whittier and Detective Reynolds looked at each other. "Cupertino?"

"Jesus," Reynolds said.

Thirty minutes later, Detective Whittier was on the phone with Sheriff Dowling. "Sheriff, I thought you might be interested to know that we have a murder here that's the same M.O. as the case you had in Cupertino—multiple stab wounds and castration."

"My God!"

"I just had a talk with the FBI. Their computer shows that there have been three previous castration killings very similar to this one. The first one happened in Bedford, Pennsylvania, about ten years ago, the next one was a man named Dennis Tibble—that was your case—then there was the same M.O. in Quebec City, and now this one."

"It doesn't make sense. Pennsylvania . . . Cupertino . . . Quebec City . . . San Francisco . . . Is there any link?"

"We're trying to find one. Quebec requires passports. The FBI is doing a cross-check to see if anyone who was in Quebec City around Christmas was in any of the other cities at the times of the murders. . . ."

When the media got wind of what was happening, their stories were splashed across the front pages across the world:

SERIAL KILLER LOOSE . . .

QUATRES HOMMES BRUTALEMENT TUÉS ET CASTRÉS . . .

WIR SUCHEN FÜR EIN MANN DER CASTRIERT SEINE HOP-FER . . .

MANIAC DI HOMICIDAL SULLO SPREE CRESPO DI UCCISIÓNE.

On the networks, self-important psychologists analyzed the killings.

". . . and all the victims were men. Because of the way they were stabbed and castrated, it is undoubtedly the work of a homosexual who . . ."

". . . so if the police can find a connection between the victims, they will probably discover that it was the work of a lover the men had all scorned. . . ."

". . . but I would say they were random killings committed by someone who had a dominating mother. . . ."

Saturday morning, Detective Whittier called Deputy Blake from San Francisco.

"Deputy, I have an update for you."

"Go ahead."

"I just got a call from the FBI. Cupertino is listed as the residence of an American who was in Quebec on the date of the Parent murder."

"That's interesting. What's his name?"

"Her. Patterson. Ashley Patterson."

At six o'clock that evening, Deputy Sam Blake rang the bell at Ashley Patterson's apartment. Through the closed door he heard her call out cautiously, "Who is it?"

"Deputy Blake. I'd like to talk to you, Miss Patterson."

There was a long silence, then the door opened. Ashley was standing there, looking wary.

"May I come in?"

"Yes, of course." *Is this about Father? I must be careful.* Ashley led the deputy to a couch. "What can I do for you, Deputy?"

"Would you mind answering a few questions?"

Ashley shifted uncomfortably. "I—I don't know. Am I under suspicion for something?"

He smiled reassuringly. "Nothing like that, Miss Patterson. This is just routine. We're investigating some murders."

"I don't know anything about any murders," she said quickly. *Too quickly?*

"You were in Quebec City recently, weren't you?"

"Yes."

"Are you acquainted with Jean Claude Parent?"

"Jean Claude Parent?" She thought for a moment. "No. I've never heard of him. Who is he?"

"He owns a jewelry store in Quebec City."

Ashley shook her head. "I didn't do any jewelry shopping in Quebec."

"You worked with Dennis Tibble."

Ashley felt the fear beginning to rise again. This *was* about her father. She said cautiously, "I didn't work with him. He worked for the same company."

"Of course. You go into San Francisco occasionally, don't you, Miss Patterson?"

Ashley wondered where this was leading. *Careful.* "From time to time, yes."

"Did you ever meet an artist there named Richard Melton?"

"No. I don't know anyone by that name."

Deputy Blake sat there studying Ashley, frustrated. "Miss Patterson, would you mind coming down to headquarters and taking a polygraph test? If you want to, you can call your lawyer and—"

"I don't need a lawyer. I'll be glad to take a test."

The polygraph expert was a man named Keith Rosson, and he was one of the best. He had had to cancel a dinner date, but he was happy to oblige Sam Blake.

Ashley was seated in a chair, wired to the polygraph machine. Rosson had already spent forty-five minutes chatting with her, getting background information and evaluating her emotional state. Now he was ready to begin.

"Are you comfortable?"

"Yes."

"Good. Let's start." He pressed a button. "What's your name?"

"Ashley Patterson."

Rosson's eyes kept darting between Ashley and the polygraph printout.

"How old are you, Miss Patterson?"

"Twenty-eight."

"Where do you live?"

"10964 Via Camino Court in Cupertino."

"Are you employed?"

"Yes."

"Do you like classical music?"

"Yes."

"Do you know Richard Melton?"

"No."

There was no change on the graph.

"Where do you work?"

"At Global Computer Graphics Corporation."

"Do you enjoy your job?"

"Yes."

"Do you work five days a week?"

"Yes."

"Have you ever met Jean Claude Parent?"

"No."

Still no change on the graph.

"Did you have breakfast this morning?"

"Yes."

"Did you kill Dennis Tibble?"

"No."

The questions continued for another thirty minutes and were repeated three times, in a different order.

When the session was over, Keith Rosson walked into Sam Blake's office and handed him the polygraph test. "Clean as a whistle. There's a less than one percent chance that she's lying. You've got the wrong person."

Ashley left police headquarters, giddy with relief. *Thank God it's over.* She had been terrified that they might ask questions that would involve her father, but that had not happened. *No one can connect Father with any of this now.*

She parked her car in the garage and took the elevator up to her apartment floor. She unlocked the door, went inside and carefully locked the door behind her. She felt drained, and at the same time, elated. *A nice hot bath,* Ashley thought. She walked into the bathroom and turned dead white. On her bathroom mirror, someone had scrawled in bright red lipstick YOU WILL DIE.

Chapter Nine

SHE was fighting hysteria. Her fingers were trembling so hard that she dialed three times trying to reach the number. She took a deep breath and tried again. Two . . . nine . . . nine . . . two . . . one . . . zero . . . one . . . The phone began to ring.

"Sheriff's Office."

"Deputy Blake, please. Hurry!"

"Deputy Blake has gone home. Can someone else—?"

"No! I— Would you ask him to call me? This is Ashley Patterson. I need to talk to him right away."

"Let me put you on hold, miss, and I'll see if I can reach him."

Deputy Sam Blake was patiently listening to his wife, Serena, screaming at him. "My brother works you like a horse, day and night, and he doesn't give you enough money to support me decently. Why don't you demand a raise? *Why?*"

They were at the dinner table. "Would you pass the potatoes, dear?"

Serena reached over and slammed the dish of potatoes in front of her husband. "The trouble is that they don't appreciate you."

"You're right, dear. May I have some gravy?"

"Aren't you listening to what I'm saying?" she yelled.

"Every word, my love. This dinner is delicious. You're a great cook."

"How can I fight you, you bastard, if you won't fight back?"

He took a mouthful of veal. "It's because I love you, darling."

The telephone rang. "Excuse me." He got up and picked up

the receiver. "Hello . . . Yes . . . Put her through. . . . Miss Patterson?" He could hear her sobbing.

"Something—something terrible has happened. You've got to come over here right away."

"I'm on my way."

Serena got to her feet. "*What?* You're going out? We're in the middle of dinner!"

"It's an emergency, darling. I'll be back as soon as I can." She watched him strap on his gun. He leaned over and kissed her. "Wonderful dinner."

Ashley opened the door for him the instant he arrived. Her cheeks were tear stained. She was shivering.

Sam Blake stepped into the apartment, looking around warily. "Is anyone else here?"

"S-someone *was* here." She was fighting for self-control. "L-look. . . ." She led him to the bathroom.

Deputy Blake read the words on the mirror out loud: "You will die."

He turned to Ashley. "Do you have any idea who could have written that?"

"No," Ashley said. "This is my apartment. No one else has a key. . . . And someone has been coming in here. . . . Someone's been following me. Someone's planning to kill me." She burst into tears. "I can't s-stand this any longer."

She was sobbing uncontrollably. Deputy Blake put his arm around her and patted her shoulder. "Come on. It's going to be all right. We'll give you protection, and we'll find out who's behind this."

Ashley took a deep breath. "I'm sorry. I—I don't usually carry on like this. It's—it's just been horrible."

"Let's talk," Sam Blake said.

She managed to force a smile. "All right."

"How about a nice cup of tea?"

They sat talking over cups of hot tea. "When did all this start, Miss Patterson?"

"About—about six months ago. I felt I was being followed. At first it was just a vague feeling, but then it began to grow. I *knew* I was being followed, but I couldn't see anyone. Then at work, someone got into my computer and drew a picture of a hand with a knife in it trying to—to stab me.''

"And do you have any idea who it could have been?''

"No.''

"You said someone has gotten into this apartment before today?''

"Yes. Once, someone turned on all the lights when I was gone. Another time I found a cigarette butt on my dressing table. I don't smoke. And someone opened a drawer and went through my . . . my underwear.'' She took a deep breath. "And now . . . this.''

"Do you have any boyfriends who might feel rejected?''

Ashley shook her head. "No.''

"Have you had any business dealings where somebody's lost money because of you?''

"No.''

"No threats from anyone?''

"No.'' She thought of telling him about the lost weekend in Chicago, but that might involve mentioning her father. She decided to say nothing.

"I don't want to be alone here tonight,'' Ashley said.

"All right. I'll call the station and have them send someone here to—''

"No! Please! I'm afraid to trust anyone else. Could you stay here with me, just until morning?''

"I don't think I—''

"Oh, please.'' She was trembling.

He looked into her eyes and thought he had never seen anyone so terrified.

"Isn't there someplace you could stay tonight? Don't you have any friends who—?''

"What if it's one of my friends who's doing this?''

He nodded. "Right. I'll stay. In the morning, I'll arrange for twenty-four-hour protection for you.''

"Thank you.'' Her voice was filled with relief.

He patted Ashley's hand. "And don't worry. I promise you that we'll get to the bottom of this. Let me call Sheriff Dowling and tell him what's going on.''

He spoke on the phone for five minutes, and when he hung up, he said, "I'd better call my wife.''

"Of course.''

Deputy Blake picked up the telephone again and dialed. "Hello, darling. I won't be home tonight, so why don't you watch some tel—?"

"You won't *what*? Where are you, with one of your cheap whores?"

Ashley could hear her screaming over the phone.

"Serena—"

"You're not fooling me."

"Serena—"

"That's all you men think about—getting laid."

"Serena—"

"Well, I won't put up with it any longer."

"Serena—"

"That's the thanks I get for being such a good wife. . . ."

The one-sided conversation went on for another ten minutes. Finally, Deputy Blake replaced the receiver and turned to Ashley, embarrassed.

"I'm sorry about that. She's not like that."

Ashley looked at him and said, "I understand."

"No— I mean it. Serena acts that way because she's scared."

Ashley looked at him curiously. "Scared?"

He was silent for a moment. "Serena is dying. She has cancer. It was in remission for a while. It first started about seven years ago. We've been married for five years."

"So you knew . . . ?"

"Yes. It didn't matter. I love her." He stopped. "It's gotten worse lately. She's scared because she's afraid to die and she's afraid I'll leave her. All the yelling is a cover-up to hide that fear."

"I'm—I'm so sorry."

"She's a wonderful person. Inside, she's gentle and caring and loving. That's the Serena I know."

Ashley said, "I'm sorry if I caused any—"

"Not at all." He looked around.

Ashley said, "There's just the one bedroom. You can take it, and I'll sleep on the couch."

Deputy Blake shook his head. "The couch will be fine for me."

Ashley said, "I can't tell you how grateful I am."

"No problem, Miss Patterson." He watched her go into a linen closet and take out sheets and blankets.

She walked over to the couch and spread the linen out. "I hope that you'll—"

"Perfect. I don't plan on doing much sleeping, anyway." He

checked the windows to make sure they were locked and then walked over to the door and double-bolted it. "All right." He placed his gun on the table next to the couch. "You get a good night's sleep. In the morning, we'll get everything organized."

Ashley nodded. She walked over to him and kissed him on the cheek. "Thank you."

Deputy Blake watched her walk into the bedroom and close the door. He walked back to the windows and checked them again. It was going to be a long night.

At FBI headquarters in Washington, Special Agent Ramirez was talking to Roland Kingsley, the chief of his section.

"We have the fingerprints and DNA reports found at the murder scenes in Bedford, Cupertino, Quebec, and San Francisco. We just got in the final DNA report. The fingerprints from the scenes all match, and the DNA traces match."

Kingsley nodded. "So it's definitely a serial killer."

"No question."

"Let's find the bastard."

At six o'clock in the morning, Deputy Sam Blake's naked body was found by the wife of the building superintendent in the alley that ran behind Ashley Patterson's apartment building.

He had been stabbed to death and castrated.

Chapter Ten

THERE were five of them: Sheriff Dowling, two plainclothes detectives and two uniformed policemen. They stood in the living room watching Ashley, sitting in a chair, weeping hysterically.

Sheriff Dowling said, "You're the only one who can help us, Miss Patterson."

Ashley looked up at the men and nodded. She took several deep breaths. "I'll—I'll try."

"Let's start at the beginning. Deputy Blake spent the night here?"

"Y-yes. I asked him to. I—I was desperately afraid."

"This apartment has one bedroom."

"That's right."

"Where did Deputy Blake sleep?"

Ashley pointed to the couch, which had a blanket and a pillow on it. "He—he spent the night there."

"What time did you go to bed?"

Ashley thought for a moment. "It—it must have been around midnight. I was nervous. We had some tea and talked for a while, and I felt calmer. I brought out blankets and a pillow for him, then I went into my bedroom." She was fighting for self-control.

"Was that the last time you saw him?"

"Yes."

"And you went to sleep?"

"Not immediately. I finally took a sleeping pill. The next thing I remember, I was awakened by a woman's screams coming from the alley." She began to tremble.

"Do you think someone came into this apartment and killed Deputy Blake?"

"I—I don't know," Ashley said desperately. "Someone has been getting in here. They even wrote a threatening message on my mirror."

"He told me about that on the telephone."

"He might have heard something and—and gone outside to investigate," Ashley said.

Sheriff Dowling shook his head. "I don't think he would have gone out naked."

Ashley cried. "*I don't know! I don't know!* It's a nightmare." She covered her eyes with her hands.

Sheriff Dowling said, "I'd like to look around the apartment. Do I need a search warrant?"

"Of course not. G-go ahead."

Sheriff Dowling nodded to the detectives. One of them went into the bedroom. The other one went into the kitchen.

"What did you and Deputy Blake talk about?"

Ashley took a deep breath. "I—I told him about—about the things that have been happening to me. He was very—" She looked up at the sheriff. "Why would anyone kill him? *Why?*"

"I don't know, Miss Patterson. We're going to find out."

Lieutenant Elton, the detective who had gone into the kitchen, stood in the doorway. "Could I see you for a moment, Sheriff?"

"Excuse me."

Sheriff Dowling walked into the kitchen.

"What?"

Lieutenant Elton said, "I found this in the sink." He was holding up a bloodstained butcher knife by the edge of the blade. "It hasn't been washed. I think we're going to get some prints."

Kostoff, the second detective, came in from the bedroom and hurried into the kitchen. He was holding an emerald ring, mounted with diamonds. "I found this in the jewelry box in the bedroom. It fits the description we got from Quebec of the ring that Jean Claude Parent gave to Toni Prescott."

The three men were looking at one another.

"This doesn't make any sense," the sheriff said. Gingerly, he took the butcher knife and the ring and walked back into the living room. He held out the knife and said, "Miss Patterson, is this your knife?"

Ashley looked at it. "I— Yes. It could be. Why?"

Sheriff Dowling held out the ring. "Have you ever seen this ring before?"

Ashley looked at it and shook her head. "No."

"We found it in your jewelry box."

They watched her expression. She was completely bewildered. She whispered, "I— Someone must have put it there. . . ."

"Who would do a thing like that?"

Her face was pale. "I don't know."

A detective walked in the front door. "Sheriff?"

"Yes, Baker?" He motioned the detective over to a corner. "What have you got?"

"We found bloodstains on the corridor rug and in the elevator. It looks like the body was laid on a sheet, dragged into the elevator and dumped in the alley."

"Holy shit!" Sheriff Dowling turned to Ashley. "Miss Patterson, you're under arrest. I'm going to read you your rights. You have the right to remain silent. If you give up the right to remain silent, anything you say may be used against you in a court of law. You are entitled to an attorney. If you cannot afford an attorney, one will be appointed to you by the courts."

When they reached the sheriff's office, Sheriff Dowling said, "Fingerprint her and book her."

Ashley went through the procedure like an automaton. When it was finished, Sheriff Dowling said, "You have the right to make one phone call."

Ashley looked up at him and said dully, "I have no one to call." *I can't call my father.*

Sheriff Dowling watched Ashley being led into a cell.

"I'll be goddamned if I understand it. Did you see her polygraph test? I would swear she's innocent."

Detective Kostoff walked in. "Sam had sex before he died. We ran an ultraviolet light over his body and the sheet he was wrapped in. We got a positive result for semen and vaginal stains. We—"

Sheriff Dowling groaned. "Hold it!" He had been putting off the moment when he would have to give his sister the news. It had to be done now. He sighed and said, "I'll be back."

Twenty minutes later, he was at Sam's house.

"Well, this is an unexpected pleasure," Serena said. "Is Sam with you?"

"No, Serena. I have to ask you a question." This was going to be difficult.

She was looking at him curiously. "Yes?"

"Did—did you and Sam have sex within the last twenty-four hours?"

The expression on her face changed. "What? We . . . No. Why do you want to—? Sam's not coming back, is he?"

"I hate to tell you this, but he—"

"He left me for her, didn't he? I knew it would happen. I don't blame him. I was a terrible wife to him. I—"

"Serena, Sam's dead."

"I was always yelling at him. I really didn't mean it. I remember—"

He took her by the arms. "Serena, Sam's dead."

"One time we were going out to the beach and—"

He was shaking her. "Listen to me. Sam is dead."

"—and we were going to have a picnic."

As he looked at her, he realized that she had heard him.

"So we're at the beach and this man comes up and says, 'Give me your money.' And Sam says, 'Let me see your gun.' "

Sheriff Dowling stood there and let her talk. She was in a state of shock, in complete denial.

". . . that was Sam. Tell me about this woman he went away with. Is she pretty? Sam tells me I'm pretty all the time, but I know I'm not. He says it to make me feel good because he loves me. He'll never leave me. He'll be back. You'll see. He loves me." She went on talking.

Sheriff Dowling went to the phone and dialed a number. "Get a nurse over here." He went over and put his arms around his sister. "Everything's going to be all right."

"Did I tell you about the time that Sam and I—?"

Fifteen minutes later, a nurse arrived.

"Take good care of her," Sheriff Dowling said.

There was a conference in Sheriff Dowling's office. "There's a call for you on line one."

Sheriff Dowling picked up the phone. "Yeah?"

"Sheriff, this is Special Agent Ramirez at FBI headquarters in Washington. We have some information for you on the serial killer case. We didn't have any prints on file for Ashley Patterson because she had no criminal record, and before 1988, the DMV didn't require thumbprints in the state of California to get a driver's license.''

"Go ahead.''

"In the beginning, we thought it had to be a computer glitch, but we checked it out and . . .''

For the next five minutes, Sheriff Dowling sat there listening, an incredulous expression on his face. When he finally spoke, he said, "Are you sure there's no mistake? It doesn't seem . . . All of them . . . ? I see. . . . Thank you very much.''

He replaced the receiver and sat there for a long moment. Then he looked up. "That was the FBI lab in Washington. They've finished cross-checking the fingerprints on the bodies of the victims. Jean Claude Parent in Quebec was seeing an English woman named Toni Prescott when he was murdered.''

"Yes.''

"Richard Melton in San Francisco was seeing an Italian lady named Alette Peters when he was killed.''

They nodded.

"And last night Sam Blake was with Ashley Patterson.''

"Right.''

Sheriff Dowling took a deep breath. "Ashley Patterson . . .''

"Yes?''

"Toni Prescott . . .''

"Yes?''

"Alette Peters . . .''

"Yes?''

"They're all the same fucking person.''

Book Two

Book Two

Chapter Eleven

ROBERT Crowther, the real estate broker from Bryant & Crowther, opened the door with a flourish and announced, "Here's the terrace. You can look down on Coit Tower from here."

He watched the young husband and wife step outside and walk over to the balustrade. The view from there was magnificent, the city of San Francisco spread out far below them in a spectacular panorama. Robert Crowther saw the couple exchange a glance and a secret smile, and he was amused. They were trying to hide their excitement. The pattern was always the same: Prospective buyers believed that if they showed too much enthusiasm, the price would go up.

For this duplex penthouse, Crowther thought wryly, *the price is high enough already.* He was concerned about whether the couple could afford it. The man was a lawyer, and young lawyers did not make that much.

They were an attractive couple, obviously very much in love. David Singer was in his early thirties, blond and intelligent-looking, with an engaging boyishness about him. His wife, Sandra, was lovely looking and warm.

Robert Crowther had noticed the bulge around her stomach and had said, "The second guest room would be perfect for a nursery. There's a playground a block away and two schools in the neighborhood." He had watched them exchange that secret smile again.

The duplex penthouse consisted of an upstairs master bedroom with a bath and a guest room. On the first floor was a spacious living room, a dining room, a library, a kitchen, a second guest bedroom and two bathrooms. Almost every room had a view of the city.

Robert watched the two of them as they walked through the apartment again. They stood in a corner whispering.

"I love it," Sandra was saying to David. "And it would be great for the baby. But, darling, can we afford it? It's six hundred thousand dollars!"

"Plus maintenance," David added. "The bad news is that we can't afford it today. The good news is that we're going to be able to afford it on Thursday. The genie is coming out of the magic bottle, and our lives are going to change."

"I know," she said happily. "Isn't it wonderful!"

"Should we go ahead with it?"

Sandra took a deep breath. "Let's go for it."

David grinned, waved a hand and said, "Welcome home, Mrs. Singer."

Arm in arm, they walked over to where Robert Crowther was waiting. "We'll take it," David told him.

"Congratulations. It's one of the choicest residences in San Francisco. You're going to be very happy here."

"I'm sure we are."

"You're lucky. I have to tell you, we have a few other people who are very interested in it."

"How much of a down payment will you want?"

"A deposit of ten thousand dollars now will be fine. I'll have the papers drawn up. When you sign, we'll require another sixty thousand dollars. Your bank can work out a schedule of monthly payments on a twenty- or thirty-year mortgage."

David glanced at Sandra. "Okay."

"I'll have the papers prepared."

"Can we look around once more?" Sandra asked eagerly.

Crowther smiled benevolently. "Take all the time you want, Mrs. Singer. It's yours."

"It all seems like a wonderful dream, David. I can't believe it's really happening."

"It's happening." David took her in his arms. "I want to make all your dreams come true."

"You do, darling."

They had been living in a small, two-bedroom apartment in the Marina District, but with the baby coming, it was going to be crowded. Until now, they could never have afforded the duplex on Nob Hill, but Thursday was partnership day at the international law firm of Kincaid, Turner, Rose & Ripley, where David worked. Out of a possible twenty-five candidates, six would be chosen to enter the rarefied air of the firm's partnership, and everyone agreed that David was one of those who would be selected. Kincaid, Turner, Rose & Ripley, with offices in San Francisco, New York, London, Paris and Tokyo, was one of the most prestigious law firms in the world, and it was usually the number one target for graduates of all the top law schools.

The firm used the stick-and-carrot approach on their young associates. The senior partners took merciless advantage of them, disregarding their hours and illnesses and handing the younger lawyers the donkey's work that they themselves did not want to be bothered with. It was a heavy pressure, twenty-four-hour-a-day job. That was the stick. Those who stayed on did so because of the carrot. The carrot was the promise of a partnership in the firm. Becoming a partner meant a larger salary, a piece of the huge corporate-profit pie, a spacious office with a view, a private washroom, assignments overseas and myriad other perks.

David had practiced corporate law with Kincaid, Turner, Rose & Ripley for six years, and it had been a mixed blessing. The hours were horrific and the stress was enormous, but David, determined to hang in there for the partnership, had stayed and had done a brilliant job. Now the day was finally at hand.

When David and Sandra left the real estate agent, they went shopping. They bought a bassinet, high chair, stroller, playpen and clothes for the baby, whom they were already thinking of as Jeffrey.

"Let's get him some toys," David said.

"There's plenty of time for that." Sandra laughed.

After shopping, they wandered around the city, walking along the waterfront at Ghirardelli Square, past the Cannery to Fisherman's Wharf. They had lunch at the American Bistro.

It was Saturday, a perfect San Francisco day for monogrammed leather briefcases and power ties, dark suits and discreetly monogrammed shirts, a day for power lunches and penthouses. A lawyer's day.

* * *

David and Sandra had met three years earlier at a small dinner party. David had gone to the party with the daughter of a client of the firm. Sandra was a paralegal, working for a rival firm. At dinner, Sandra and David had gotten into an argument about a decision that had been rendered in a political case in Washington. As the others at the dinner table watched, the argument between the two of them had become more and more heated. And in the middle of it, David and Sandra realized that neither of them cared about the court's decision. They were showing off for each other, engaged in a verbal mating dance.

David telephoned Sandra the next day. "I'd like to finish discussing that decision," David said. "I think it's important."

"So do I," Sandra agreed.

"Could we talk about it at dinner tonight?"

Sandra hesitated. She had already made a dinner date for that evening. "Yes," she said. "Tonight will be fine."

They were together from that night on. One year from the day they met, they were married.

Joseph Kincaid, the firm's senior partner, had given David the weekend off.

David's salary at Kincaid, Turner, Rose & Ripley was $45,000 a year. Sandra kept her job as a paralegal. But now, with the baby coming, their expenses were about to go up.

"I'll have to give up my job in a few months," Sandra said. "I don't want a nanny bringing up our baby, darling. I want to be here for him." The sonogram had shown that the baby was a boy.

"We'll be able to handle it," David assured her. The partnership was going to transform their lives.

David had begun to put in even longer hours. He wanted to make sure that he was not overlooked on partnership day.

Thursday morning, as David got dressed, he was watching the news on television.

An anchorman was saying breathlessly, "We have a breaking story. . . . Ashley Patterson, the daughter of the prominent San Francisco doctor Steven Patterson, has been arrested as the suspected serial killer the police and the FBI have been searching for. . . ."

David stood in front of the television set, frozen.

". . . last night Santa Clara County Sheriff Matt Dowling announced Ashley Patterson's arrest for a series of murders that included bloody castrations. Sheriff Dowling told reporters, 'There's no doubt that we have the right person. The evidence is conclusive.' "

Dr. Steven Patterson. David's mind went back, remembering the past. . . .

He was twenty-one years old and just starting law school. He came home from class one day to find his mother on the bedroom floor, unconscious. He called 911, and an ambulance took his mother to San Francisco Memorial Hospital. David waited outside the emergency room until a doctor came to talk to him.

"Is she—Is she going to be all right?"

The doctor hesitated. "We had one of our cardiologists examine her. She has a ruptured cord in her mitral valve."

"What does that mean?" David demanded.

"I'm afraid there's nothing we can do for her. She's too weak to have a transplant, and mini heart surgery is new and too risky."

David felt suddenly faint. "How—how long can she—?"

"I'd say a few more days, maybe a week. I'm sorry, son."

David stood there, panicky. "Isn't there *anyone* who can help her?"

"I'm afraid not. The only one who might have been able to help is Steven Patterson, but he's a very—"

"Who's Steven Patterson?"

"Dr. Patterson pioneered minimally invasive heart surgery. But between his schedule and his research, there's no chance that—"

David was gone.

He called Dr. Patterson's office from a pay phone in the hospital corridor. "I'd like to make an appointment with Dr. Patterson. It's for my mother. She—"

"I'm sorry. We're not accepting any new appointments. The first available time would be six months from now."

"She doesn't have six months," David shouted.

"I'm sorry. I can refer you to—"

David slammed down the phone.

The following morning David went to Dr. Patterson's office. The waiting room was crowded. David walked up to the receptionist. "I'd like to make an appointment to see Dr. Patterson. My mother's very ill and—"

She looked up at him and said, "You called yesterday, didn't you?"

"Yes."

"I told you then. We don't have any appointments open, and we're not making any just now."

"I'll wait," David said stubbornly.

"You can't wait. The doctor is—"

David took a seat. He watched the people in the waiting room being called into the inner office one by one until finally he was the only one left.

At six o'clock, the receptionist said, "There's no point in waiting any longer. Dr. Patterson has gone home."

David went to visit his mother in intensive care that evening.

"You can only stay a minute," a nurse warned him. "She's very weak."

David stepped inside the room, and his eyes filled with tears. His mother was attached to a respirator with tubes running into her arms and through her nose. She looked whiter than the sheets she lay on. Her eyes were closed.

David moved close to her and said, "It's me, Mom. I'm not going to let anything happen to you. You're going to be fine." Tears were running down his cheeks. "Do you hear me? We're going to fight this thing. Nobody can lick the two of us, not as long as we're together. I'm going to get you the best doctor in the world. You just hang in there. I'll be back tomorrow." He bent down and gently kissed her cheek.

Will she be alive tomorrow?

The following afternoon, David went to the garage in the basement of the building where Dr. Patterson had his offices. An attendant was parking cars.

He came up to David. "May I help you?"

"I'm waiting for my wife," David said. "She's seeing Dr. Patterson."

The attendant smiled. "He's a great guy."

"He was telling us about some fancy car that he owns." David paused, trying to remember. "Was it a Cadillac?"

The attendant shook his head. "Naw." He pointed to a Rolls-Royce parked in the corner. "It's that Rolls over there."

David said, "Right. I think he said he has a Cadillac, too."

"Wouldn't surprise me," the attendant said. He hurried off to park an incoming car.

David walked casually toward the Rolls. When he was sure no one was watching, he opened the door, slipped into the backseat and got down on the floor. He lay there, cramped and uncomfortable, willing Dr. Patterson to come out.

At 6:15, David felt a slight jar as the front door of the car opened and someone moved into the driver's seat. He heard the engine start, and then the car began to move.

"Good night, Dr. Patterson."

"Good night, Marco."

The car left the garage, and David felt it turn a corner. He waited for two minutes, then took a deep breath and sat up.

Dr. Patterson saw him in the rearview mirror. He said calmly, "If this is a holdup, I have no cash with me."

"Turn onto a side street and pull over to the curb."

Dr. Patterson nodded. David watched warily as the doctor turned the car onto a side street, pulled over to the curb and stopped.

"I'll give you what cash I have on me," Dr. Patterson said. "You can take the car. There's no need for violence. If—"

David had slid into the front seat. "This isn't a holdup. I don't want the car."

Dr. Patterson was looking at him with annoyance. "What the hell do you want?"

"My name is Singer. My mother's dying. I want you to save her."

There was a flicker of relief on Dr. Patterson's face, replaced by a look of anger.

"Make an appointment with my—"

"There's no time to make a goddamn appointment." David was yelling. "She's going to *die*, and I'm not going to let that happen." He was fighting to control himself. "Please. The other doctors told me you're the only hope we have."

Dr. Patterson was watching him, still wary. "What's her problem?"

"She has a—a ruptured cord in her mitral valve. The doctors are afraid to operate. They say that you're the only one who can save her life."

Dr. Patterson shook his head. "My schedule—"

"I don't give a shit about your schedule! This is my mother. You've got to save her! She's all I have. . . ."

There was a long silence. David sat there, his eyes tightly shut. He heard Dr. Patterson's voice.

"I won't promise a damn thing, but I'll see her. Where is she?"

David turned to look at him. "She's in the intensive care unit at San Francisco Memorial Hospital."

"Meet me there at eight o'clock tomorrow morning."

David had difficulty finding his voice. "I don't know how to—"

"Remember, I'm not promising anything. And I don't appreciate being scared out of my wits, young man. Next time, try the telephone."

David sat there, rigid.

Dr. Patterson looked at him. "What?"

"There's another problem."

"Oh, really?"

"I—I don't have any money. I'm a law student, and I'm working my way through law school."

Dr. Patterson was staring at him.

David said passionately, "I swear I'll find a way to pay you back. If it takes all my life, I'll see that you get paid. I know how expensive you are, and I—"

"I don't think you do, son."

"I have no one else to turn to, Dr. Patterson. I—I'm begging you."

There was another silence.

"How many years of law school have you had?"

"None. I'm just starting."

"But you expect to be able to pay me back?"

"I swear it."

"Get the hell out."

When David got home, he was certain he was going to be picked up by the police for kidnapping, threatening bodily harm, God only knew what. But nothing happened. The question in his mind was whether Dr. Patterson was going to show up at the hospital.

When David walked into the intensive care ward the next morning, Dr. Patterson was there, examining David's mother.

David watched, his heart pounding, his throat dry.

Dr. Patterson turned to one of a group of doctors standing there. "Get her up to the operating room, Al. Stat!"

As they started to slide David's mother onto a gurney, David said hoarsely, "Is she—?"

"We'll see."

Six hours later, David was in the waiting room when Dr. Patterson approached him.

David jumped to his feet. "How is—?" He was afraid to finish the question.

"She's going to be fine. Your mother's a strong lady."

David stood there, filled with an overpowering sense of relief. He breathed a silent prayer. *Thank you, God.*

Dr. Patterson was watching him. "I don't even know your first name."

"David, sir."

"Well, David sir, do you know why I decided to do this?"

"No . . ."

"Two reasons. Your mother's condition was a challenge for me. I like challenges. The second reason was you."

"I—I don't understand."

"What you did was the kind of thing I might have done myself when I was younger. You showed imagination. Now"—his tone changed—"you said you were going to repay me."

David's heart sank. "Yes, sir. One day—"

"How about now?"

David swallowed. *"Now?"*

"I'll make you a deal. Do you know how to drive?"

"Yes, sir . . ."

"All right. I get tired of driving that big car around. You drive me to work every morning and pick me up at six or seven o'clock every evening for one year. At the end of that time, I'll consider my fee paid. . . ."

That was the deal. David drove Dr. Patterson to the office and back home every day, and in exchange, Dr. Patterson saved the life of David's mother.

During that year, David learned to revere Dr. Patterson. Despite the doctor's occasional outbursts of temper, he was the most self-less man David had ever known. He was heavily involved in charity work and donated his spare time to free clinics. Driving to and from the office or hospital, he and David had long talks.

"What kind of law are you studying, David?"

"Criminal law."

"Why? So you can help the damn scoundrels get off scot-free?"
"No, sir. There are a lot of honest people caught up in the law who need help. I want to help them."
When the year was up, Dr. Patterson shook David's hand and said, "We're even. . . ."

David had not seen Steven Patterson in years, but he kept coming across his name.
"Dr. Steven Patterson opened a free clinic for babies with AIDS. . . ."
"Dr. Steven Patterson arrived in Kenya today to open the Patterson Medical Center. . . ."
"Work on the Patterson Charity Shelter began today. . . ."
He seemed to be everywhere, donating his time and his money to those who needed him.
Sandra's voice shook David out of his reverie. "David. Are you all right?"
He turned away from the television set. "They've just arrested Steven Patterson's daughter for those serial killings."
Sandra said, "That's terrible! I'm so sorry, darling."
"He gave Mother seven more years of a wonderful life. It's unfair that anything like that should happen to a man like him. He's the greatest gentleman I've ever known, Sandra. He doesn't deserve this. How could he have a monster like that for a daughter?" He looked at his watch. "Damn! I'm going to be late."
"You haven't had breakfast."
"I'm too upset to eat." He glanced toward the television set. "This . . . and today's partnership day. . . ."
"You're going to get it. There's no question about it."
"There's *always* a question about it, honey. Every year, someone who's supposed to be a shoo-in winds up in the loser's box."
She hugged him and said, "They'll be lucky to have you."
He leaned over and kissed her. "Thanks, baby. I don't know what I'd do without you."
"You'll never have to. You'll call me as soon as you get the news, won't you, David?"
"Of course I will. We'll go out and celebrate." And the words reverberated in his mind. Years ago, he had said to someone else, *"We'll go out and celebrate."*
And he had killed her.

*   *   *

The offices of Kincaid, Turner, Rose & Ripley occupied three floors in the TransAmerica Pyramid in downtown San Francisco. When David Singer walked through the doors, he was greeted with knowing smiles. It seemed to him that there was even a different quality in the "good mornings." They knew they were addressing a future partner in the firm.

On the way to his small office, David passed the newly decorated office that would belong to one of the chosen partners, and he could not resist looking inside. It was a large, beautiful office with a private washroom, a desk and chairs facing a picture window with a magnificent view of the Bay. He stood there a moment, drinking it in.

When David walked into his office, his secretary, Holly, said, "Good morning, Mr. Singer." There was a lilt in her voice.

"Good morning, Holly."

"I have a message for you."

"Yes?"

"Mr. Kincaid would like to see you in his office at five o'clock." She broke into a broad smile.

So it was really happening. "Great!"

She moved closer to David and said, "I think I should also tell you, I had coffee with Dorothy, Mr. Kincaid's secretary, this morning. She says you're at the top of the list."

David grinned. "Thanks, Holly."

"Would you like some coffee?"

"Love it."

"Hot and strong, coming up."

David walked over to his desk. It was heaped with briefs and contracts and files.

Today was the day. Finally. *"Mr. Kincaid would like to see you in his office at five o'clock. . . . You're at the top of the list."*

He was tempted to telephone Sandra with the news. Something held him back. *I'll wait until it happens,* he thought.

David spent the next two hours dealing with the material on his desk. At eleven o'clock, Holly came in. "There's a Dr. Patterson here to see you. He has no app—"

He looked up in surprise. "Dr. Patterson is *here?*"

"Yes."

David rose. "Send him in."

Steven Patterson came in, and David tried to conceal his reaction. The doctor looked old and tired.

"Hello, David."

"Dr. Patterson. Please, sit down." David watched him slowly take a chair. "I saw the news this morning. I—I can't tell you how very sorry I am."

Dr. Patterson nodded wearily. "Yes. It's been quite a blow." He looked up. "I need your help, David."

"Of course," David said eagerly. "Anything I can do. *Anything.*"

"I want you to represent Ashley."

It took a moment for the words to sink in. "I—I can't do that. I'm not a criminal defense lawyer."

Dr. Patterson looked him in the eye and said, "Ashley's not a criminal."

"I—You don't understand, Dr. Patterson. I'm a corporate lawyer. I can recommend an excellent—"

"I've already had calls from half a dozen top criminal de-fense lawyers. They all want to represent her." He leaned forward in his chair. "But they're not interested in my daughter, David. This is a high-profile case, and they're looking for the limelight. They don't give a damn about her. I do. She's all I have."

"I want you to save my mother's life. She's all I have." David said, "I really want to help you, but—"

"When you got out of law school, you went to work for a criminal law firm."

David's heart began to beat faster. "That's true, but—"

"You were a criminal defense lawyer for several years."

David nodded. "Yes, but I—I gave it up. That was a long time ago and—"

"Not that long ago, David. And you told me how much you loved it. Why did you quit and go into corporate law?"

David sat there, silent for a moment. "It's not important."

Dr. Patterson took out a handwritten letter and handed it to David. David knew what it said, without reading it.

Dear Dr. Patterson,
  There are no words that can ever express how much I owe you and how much I appreciate your great generosity. If there's ever anything at all that I can do for you, all you have to do is ask me, and it shall be done without question.

David stared at the letter without seeing it.
"David, will you talk to Ashley?"
David nodded. "Yes, of course I'll talk to her, but I—"
Dr. Patterson rose. "Thank you."
David watched him walk out the door.

"Why did you quit and go into corporate law?"
Because I made a mistake, and an innocent woman I loved is dead. I swore I would never take anyone's life in my hands again. Ever.
I can't defend Ashley Patterson.
David pressed down the intercom button. "Holly, would you ask Mr. Kincaid if he can see me now?"
"Yes, sir."

Thirty minutes later, David was walking into the elaborate offices of Joseph Kincaid. Kincaid was in his sixties, a gray monochrome of a man, physically, mentally and emotionally.
"Well," he said as David walked in the door, "you're an anxious young fellow, aren't you? Our meeting wasn't supposed to be until five o'clock."
David approached the desk. "I know. I came here to discuss something else, Joseph."
Years ago, David had made the mistake of calling him Joe, and the old man had had a fit. *"Don't you ever call me Joe."*
"Sit down, David."
David took a seat.
"Cigar? They're from Cuba."
"No, thanks."
"What's on your mind?"
"Dr. Steven Patterson was just in to see me."
Kincaid said, "He was on the news this morning. Damned shame. What did he want with you?"
"He asked me to defend his daughter."
Kincaid looked at David, surprised. "You're not a criminal defense lawyer."
"I told him that."
"Well, then." Kincaid was thoughtful for a moment. "You know, I'd like to get Dr. Patterson as a client. He's very influential. He could bring a lot of business to this firm. He has connections with several medical organizations that—"

"There's more."

Kincaid looked at David, quizzically. "Oh?"

"I promised him I'd talk to his daughter."

"I see. Well, I suppose there's no harm in that. Talk to her, and then we'll find a good defense attorney to represent her."

"That's my plan."

"Good. We'll be building up some points with him. You go ahead." He smiled. "I'll see you at five o'clock."

"Right. Thank you, Joseph."

As David walked back to his office, he wondered to himself, *Why in the world would Dr. Patterson insist on having me represent his daughter?*

Chapter Twelve

At the Santa Clara County Jail, Ashley Patterson sat in her cell, too traumatized to try to make sense of how she got there. She was fiercely glad that she was in jail because the bars would keep out whoever was doing this to her. She wrapped the cell around herself like a blanket, trying to ward off the awful, inexplicable things that were happening to her. Her whole life had become a screaming nightmare. Ashley thought of all the mysterious events that had been happening: Someone breaking into her apartment and playing tricks on her . . . the trip to Chicago . . . the writing on her mirror . . . and now the police accusing her of unspeakable things she knew nothing about. There was some terrible conspiracy against her, but she had no idea who could be behind it or why.

Early that morning one of the guards had come to Ashley's cell. "Visitor."

The guard had led Ashley to the visitors' room, where her father was waiting for her.

He stood there, looking at her, his eyes grief stricken. "Honey . . . I don't know what to say."

Ashley whispered, "I didn't do any of the terrible things they said I did."

"I know you didn't. Someone's made an awful mistake, but we're going to straighten everything out."

Ashley looked at her father and wondered how she could have ever thought he was the guilty one.

". . . don't you worry," he was saying. "Everything's going to be fine. I am getting a lawyer for you. David Singer. He's one of the brightest young men I know. He'll be coming to see you. I want you to tell him everything.''

Ashley looked at her father and said hopelessly, "Father, I—I don't know what to tell him. I don't know what's happening.''

"We'll get to the bottom of this, baby. I'm not going to let anyone hurt you. No one! Ever! You mean too much to me. You're all I have, honey.''

"And you're all I have,'' Ashley whispered.

Ashley's father stayed for another hour. When he left, Ashley's world narrowed down to the small cell she was confined in. She lay on her cot, forcing herself not to think about anything. *This will be over soon, and I'll find that this is only a dream. . . . Only a dream . . . Only a dream . . .* She slept.

The voice of a guard awakened her. "You have a visitor.''

She was taken to the visitors' room, and Shane Miller was there, waiting.

He rose as Ashley entered. "Ashley . . .''

Her heart began to pound. "Oh, Shane!'' She had never been so glad to see anyone in her life. Somehow she had known that he would come and free her, that he would arrange for them to let her go.

"Shane, I'm so glad to see you!''

"I'm glad to see you,'' Shane said awkwardly. He looked around the drab visitors' room. "Although I must say, not under these circumstances. When I heard the news, I—I couldn't believe it. What happened? What made you do it, Ashley?''

The color slowly drained from her face. "What made me—? Do you think that I—?''

"Never mind,'' Shane said quickly. "Don't say any more. You shouldn't talk to anyone but your attorney.''

Ashley stood there, staring at him. He believed she was guilty. "Why did you come here?''

"Well, I—I hate to do this now, but under—under the circumstances, I—the company—is terminating you. I mean . . . naturally, we can't afford to be connected with anything like this. It's bad enough that the newspapers have already mentioned that you work for Global. You understand, don't you? There's nothing personal in this.''

* * *

Driving down to San Jose, David Singer decided what he was going to say to Ashley Patterson. He would find out what he could from her and then turn the information over to Jesse Quiller, one of the best criminal defense lawyers in the country. If anyone could help Ashley, it was Jesse.

David was ushered into the office of Sheriff Dowling. He handed the sheriff his card. "I'm an attorney. I'm here to see Ashley Patterson and—"

"She's expecting you."

David looked at him in surprise. "She is?"

"Yeah." Sheriff Dowling turned to a deputy and nodded.

The deputy said to David, "This way." He led David into the visitors' room, and a few minutes later, Ashley was brought in from her cell.

Ashley Patterson was a complete surprise to David. He had met her once years ago, when he was in law school, chauffeuring her father. She had struck David as being an attractive, intelligent young girl. Now, he found himself looking at a beautiful young woman with frightened eyes. She took a seat across from him.

"Hello, Ashley. I'm David Singer."

"My father told me you would be coming." Her voice was shaky.

"I just came to ask a few questions."

She nodded.

"Before I do, I want you to know that anything you tell me is privileged. It will just be between the two of us. But I need to know the truth." He hesitated. He had not intended to go this far, but he wanted to be able to give Jesse Quiller all the information he could, to persuade him to take the case. "Did you kill those men?"

"No!" Ashley's voice rang with conviction. "I'm innocent!"

David pulled a sheet of paper from his pocket and glanced at it. "Were you acquainted with a Jim Cleary?"

"Yes. We—we were going to be married. I would have had no reason to harm Jim. I loved him."

David studied Ashley a moment, then looked at the sheet of paper again. "What about Dennis Tibble?"

"Dennis worked at the company I worked for. I saw him the night he was murdered, but I had nothing to do with that. I was in Chicago."

David was watching Ashley's face.

"You have to believe me. I—I had no reason to kill him."

David said, "All right." He glanced at the sheet again. "What was your relationship with Jean Claude Parent?"

"The police asked me about him. I had never even heard of him. How could I have killed him when I didn't even know him?" She looked at David pleadingly. "Don't you see? They have the wrong person. They've arrested the wrong person." She began to weep. "I haven't killed anyone."

"Richard Melton?"

"I don't know who he is either."

David waited while Ashley regained control of herself. "What about Deputy Blake?"

Ashley shook her head. "Deputy Blake stayed at my apartment that night to watch over me. Someone had been stalking me and threatening me. I slept in my bedroom, and he slept on the couch in the living room. They—they found his body in the alley." Her lips were trembling. "Why would I kill him? He was *helping* me!"

David was studying Ashley, puzzled. *Something's very wrong here,* David thought. *Either she's telling the truth or she's one hell of an actress.* He stood up. "I'll be back. I want to talk to the sheriff."

Two minutes later, he was in the sheriff's office.

"Well, did you talk to her?" Sheriff Dowling asked.

"Yes. I think you've gotten yourself in a box, Sheriff."

"What does that mean, Counselor?"

"It means you might have been too eager to make an arrest. Ashley Patterson doesn't even know two of the people you're accusing her of killing."

A small smile touched Sheriff Dowling's lips. "She fooled you, too, huh? She sure as hell fooled us."

"What are you talking about?"

"I'll show you, mister." He opened a file folder on his desk and handed David some papers. "These are copies of coroner's reports, FBI reports, DNA reports and Interpol reports on the five men who were murdered and castrated. Each victim had had sex with a woman before he was murdered. There were vaginal traces and fingerprints at each of the murder scenes. There were supposed to have been three different women involved. Well, the FBI collated all this evidence, and guess what they came up with? The three women turned out to be Ashley Patterson. Her DNA and fingerprints are positive on every one of the murders.''

David was staring at him in disbelief. "Are—are you sure?''

"Yeah. Unless you want to believe that Interpol, the FBI and five different coroner's offices are out to frame your client. It's all there, mister. One of the men she killed was my brother-in-law. Ashley Patterson's going to be tried for first-degree murder, and she's going to be convicted. Anything else?''

"Yes.'' David took a deep breath. "I'd like to see Ashley Patterson again.''

They brought her back to the visitors' room. When she walked inside, David asked angrily, "Why did you lie to me?''

"What? I didn't lie to you. I'm innocent. I—''

"They have enough evidence against you to burn you a dozen times over. I told you I wanted the truth.''

Ashley looked at him for a full minute, and when she spoke, she said in a quiet voice, "I told you the truth. I have nothing more to say.''

Listening to her, David thought, *She really believes what she's saying. I'm talking to a nut case. What am I going to tell Jesse Quiller?*

"Would you talk to a psychiatrist?''

"I don't—Yes. If you want me to.''

"I'll arrange it.''

On his way back to San Francisco, David thought, *I kept my end of the bargain. I talked to her. If she really thinks she's telling the truth, then she's crazy. I'll get her to Jesse, who will plead insanity, and that will be the end of it.*

His heart went out to Steven Patterson.

At San Francisco Memorial Hospital, Dr. Patterson was receiving the condolences of his fellow doctors.

"It's a damn shame, Steven. You sure don't deserve anything like this. . . .''

"It must be a terrible burden for you. If there's anything I can do . . .''

"I don't know what gets into kids these days. Ashley always seemed so normal. . . .''

And behind each expression of condolence was the thought: *Thank God it's not my kid.*

*   *   *

When David returned to the law firm, he hurried in to see Joseph Kincaid.

Kincaid looked up and said, "Well, it's after six o'clock, David, but I waited for you. Did you see Dr. Patterson's daughter?"

"Yes, I did."

"And did you find an attorney to defend her?"

David hesitated. "Not yet, Joseph. I'm arranging for a psychiatrist to see her. I'll be going back in the morning to talk to her again."

Joseph Kincaid looked at David, puzzled. "Oh? Frankly, I'm surprised that you're getting this involved. Naturally, we can't have this firm associated with anything as ugly as this trial is going to be."

"I'm not really involved, Joseph. It's just that I owe a great deal to her father. I made him a promise."

"There's nothing in writing, is there?"

"No."

"So it's only a moral obligation?"

David studied him a moment, started to say something, then stopped. "Yes. It's only a moral obligation."

"Well, when you're through with Miss Patterson, come back and we'll talk."

Not a word about the partnership.

When David got home that evening, the apartment was in darkness.

"Sandra?"

There was no answer. As David started to turn on the lights in the hallway, Sandra suddenly appeared from the kitchen, carrying a cake with lit candles.

"Surprise! We're having a celebration—" She saw the look on David's face and stopped. "Is something wrong, darling? Didn't you get it, David? Did they give it to someone else?"

"No, no," he said reassuringly. "Everything's fine."

Sandra put down the cake and moved closer to him. "Something's wrong."

"It's just that there's been a . . . a delay."

"Wasn't your meeting with Joseph Kincaid today?"

"Yes. Sit down, honey. We have to talk."

They sat down on the couch, and David said, "Something unexpected has come up. Steven Patterson came to see me this morning.''

"He did? What about?"

"He wants me to defend his daughter."

Sandra looked at him in surprise. "But, David . . . you're not—"

"I know. I tried to tell him that. But I *have* practiced criminal law."

"But you're not doing that anymore. Did you tell him you're about to become a partner in your firm?"

"No. He was very insistent that I was the only one who could defend his daughter. It doesn't make any sense, of course. I tried to suggest someone like Jesse Quiller, but he wouldn't even listen."

"Well, he'll have to get someone else."

"Of course. I promised to talk to his daughter, and I did."

Sandra sat back on the couch. "Does Mr. Kincaid know about this?"

"Yes. I told him. He wasn't thrilled." He mimicked Kincaid's voice. " 'Naturally, we can't have this firm associated with anything as ugly as this trial is going to be.' "

"What's Dr. Patterson's daughter like?"

"In medical terms, she's a fruitcake."

"I'm not a doctor," Sandra said. "What does that mean?"

"It means that she really believes she's innocent."

"Isn't that possible?"

"The sheriff in Cupertino showed me the file on her. Her DNA and fingerprints are all over the murder scenes."

"What are you going to do now?"

"I've called Royce Salem. He's a psychiatrist that Jesse Quiller's office uses. I'm going to have him examine Ashley and turn the report over to her father. Dr. Patterson can bring in another psychiatrist if he likes, or turn the report over to whichever attorney is going to handle the case."

"I see." Sandra studied her husband's troubled face. "Did Mr. Kincaid say anything about the partnership, David?"

He shook his head. "No."

Sandra said brightly, "He will. Tomorrow's another day."

Dr. Royce Salem was a tall, thin man with a Sigmund Freud beard. *Maybe that's just a coincidence,* David told himself. *Surely he's not trying to look like Freud.*

"Jesse talks about you often," Dr. Salem said. "He's very fond of you."

"I'm fond of him, Dr. Salem."

"The Patterson case sounds very interesting. Obviously the work of a psychopath. You're planning an insanity plea?"

"Actually," David told him, "I'm not handling the case. Before I get an attorney for her, I'd like to get an evaluation of her mental state." David briefed Dr. Salem on the facts as he knew them. "She claims she's innocent, but the evidence shows she committed the crimes."

"Well, let's have a look at the lady's psyche, shall we?"

The hypnotherapy session was to take place in the Santa Clara County Jail, in an interrogation room. The furniture in the room consisted of a rectangular wooden table and four wooden chairs.

Ashley, looking pale and drawn, was led into the room by a matron.

"I'll wait outside," the matron said, and withdrew.

David said, "Ashley, this is Dr. Salem. Ashley Patterson."

Dr. Salem said, "Hello, Ashley."

She stood there, nervously looking from one to the other, without speaking. David had the feeling that she was ready to flee the room.

"Mr. Singer tells me that you have no objection to being hypnotized."

Silence.

Dr. Salem went on. "Would you let me hypnotize you, Ashley?"

Ashley closed her eyes for a second and nodded. "Yes."

"Why don't we get started?"

"Well, I'll be running along," David said. "If—"

"Just a moment." Dr. Salem walked over to David. "I want you to stay."

David stood there, frustrated. He regretted now that he had gone this far. *I'm not going to get in any deeper,* David resolved. *This will be the end of it.*

"All right," David said reluctantly. He was eager to have it over with so he could get back to the office. The coming meeting with Kincaid loomed large in his mind.

Dr. Salem said to Ashley, "Why don't you sit in this chair?"

Ashley sat down.

"Have you ever been hypnotized before, Ashley?"
She hesitated an instant, then shook her head. "No."
"There's nothing to it. All you have to do is relax and listen to
the sound of my voice. You have nothing to worry about. No one's
going to hurt you. Feel your muscles relax. That's it. Just relax
and feel your eyes getting heavy. You've been through a lot. Your
body is tired, very tired. All you want to do is to go to sleep. Just
close your eyes and relax. You're getting very sleepy . . . very
sleepy. . . ."

It took ten minutes to put her under. Dr. Salem walked over to
Ashley. "Ashley, do you know where you are?"

"Yes. I'm in jail." Her voice sounded hollow, as though coming from a distance.

"Do you know why you're in jail?"

"People think I did something bad."

"And is it true? Did you do something bad?"

"No."

"Ashley, did you ever kill anyone?"

"No."

David looked at Dr. Salem in surprise. *Weren't people supposed
to tell the truth under hypnosis?*

"Do you have any idea who could have committed those murders?"

Suddenly, Ashley's face contorted and she began breathing
hard, in short, raspy breaths. The two men watched in astonishment as her persona started changing. Her lips tightened and her
features seemed to shift. She sat up straight, and there was a sudden liveliness in her face. She opened her eyes, and they were
sparkling. It was an amazing transformation. Unexpectedly, she
began to sing, in a sultry voice with an English accent:

> *"Half a pound of tupenny rice,*
> *Half a pound of treacle,*
> *Mix it up and make it nice,*
> *Pop! goes the weasel."*

David listened in astonishment. *Who does she think she's fooling? She's pretending to be someone else.*

"I want to ask you some more questions, Ashley."

She tossed her head and said in an English accent, "I'm not
Ashley."

Dr. Salem exchanged a look with David, then turned back to Ashley. "If you're not Ashley, who are you?"

"Toni. Toni Prescott."

And Ashley is doing this with a straight face, David thought. *How long is she going to go on with this stupid charade?* She was wasting their time.

"Ashley," said Dr. Salem.

"Toni."

She's determined to keep it up, David thought.

"All right, Toni. What I'd like is—"

"Let me tell you what *I'd* like. I'd like to get out of this bloody place. Can you get us out of here?"

"That depends," Dr. Salem said. "What do you know about—?"

"—those murders that little Goody Two-shoes is in here for? I can tell you things that—"

Ashley's expression suddenly started to change again. As David and Dr. Salem watched, Ashley seemed to shrink in her chair, and her face began to soften and go through an incredible metamorphosis until she seemed to become another distinct personality.

She said in a soft voice with an Italian accent, "Toni . . . don't say any more, *per piacere.*"

David was watching in bewilderment.

"Toni?" Dr. Salem edged closer.

The soft voice said, "I apologize for the interruption, Dr. Salem."

Dr. Salem asked, "Who are you?"

"I am Alette. Alette Peters."

My God, it's not an act, David thought. *It's real.* He turned to Dr. Salem.

Dr. Salem said quietly, "They're alters."

David stared at him, totally confused. "They're what?"

"I'll explain later."

Dr. Salem turned back to Ashley. "Ashley . . . I mean Alette . . . How—how many of you are in there?"

"Beside Ashley, only Toni and me," Alette answered.

"You have an Italian accent."

"Yes. I was born in Rome. Have you ever been to Rome?"

"No, I've never been to Rome."

I can't believe I'm hearing this conversation, David thought.

"*È molto bello.*"

"I'm sure. Do you know Toni?"

"*Sì, naturalmente.*"

"She has an *English* accent."

"Toni was born in London."

"Right. Alette, I want to ask you about these murders. Do you have any idea who—?"

And David and Dr. Salem watched as Ashley's face and personality changed again before their eyes. Without her saying a word, they knew that she had become Toni.

"You're wasting your time with her, luv."

There was that English accent.

"Alette doesn't know anything. I'm the one you're going to have to talk to."

"All right, Toni. I'll talk to you. I have some questions for you."

"I'm sure you do, but I'm tired." She yawned. "Miss Tight Ass has kept us up all night. I've got to get some sleep."

"Not now, Toni. Listen to me. You have to help us to—"

Her face hardened. "Why should I help you? What has Miss Goody Two-shoes done for Alette or me? All she ever does is keep us from having fun. Well, I'm sick of it, and I'm sick of her. Do you hear me?" She was screaming, her face contorted.

Dr. Salem said, "I'm going to bring her out of it."

David was perspiring. "Yes."

Dr. Salem leaned close to Ashley. "Ashley . . . Ashley . . . Everything is fine. Close your eyes now. They're very heavy, very heavy. You're completely relaxed. Ashley, your mind is at peace. Your body is relaxed. You're going to wake up at the count of five, completely relaxed. One . . ." He looked over at David and then back at Ashley. "Two . . ."

Ashley began to stir. They watched her expression start to change.

"Three . . ."

Her face softened.

"Four . . ."

They could sense her returning, and it was an eerie feeling.

"Five."

Ashley opened her eyes. She looked around the room. "I feel— Was I asleep?"

David stood there, staring at her, stunned.

"Yes," Dr. Salem said.

Ashley turned to David. "Did I say anything? I mean . . . was I helpful?"

My God, David thought. *She doesn't know! She really doesn't know!* David said, "You did fine, Ashley. I'd like to talk to Dr. Salem alone."

"All right."

"I'll see you later."

The men stood there, watching the matron lead Ashley away.

David sank into a chair. "What—what the hell was that all about?"

Dr. Salem took a deep breath. "In all the years that I've been practicing, I've never seen a more clear-cut case."

"A case of *what*?"

"Have you ever heard of multiple personality disorder?"

"What is it?"

"It's a condition where there are several completely different personalities in one body. It's also known as dissociative identity disorder. It's been in the psychiatric literature for more than two hundred years. It usually starts because of a childhood trauma. The victim shuts out the trauma by creating another identity. Sometimes a person will have dozens of different personalities or alters."

"And they know about each other?"

"Sometimes, yes. Sometimes, no. Toni and Alette know each other. Ashley is obviously not aware of either of them. Alters are created because the host can't stand the pain of the trauma. It's a way of escape. Every time a fresh shock occurs, a new alter can be born. The psychiatric literature on the subject shows that alters can be totally different from one another. Some alters are stupid, while others are brilliant. They can speak different languages. They have varied tastes and personalities."

"How—how common is this?"

"Some studies suggest that one percent of the entire population suffers from multiple personality disorder, and that up to twenty percent of all patients in psychiatric hospitals have it."

David said, "But Ashley seems so normal and—"

"People with MPD *are* normal . . . until an alter takes over. The host can have a job, raise a family and live a perfectly ordinary life, but an alter can take over at any time. An alter can be in control for an hour, a day or even weeks, and then the host suffers a fugue, a loss of time and memory, for the period that the alter is in charge.''

"So Ashley—the host—would have no recollection of anything that the alter does?"

"None."

David listened, spellbound.

"The most famous case of multiple personality disorder was Bridey Murphy. That's what first brought the subject to the public's attention. Since then, there have been an endless number of cases, but none as spectacular or as well publicized."

"It—it seems so incredible."

"It's a subject that's fascinated me for a long time. There are certain patterns that almost never change. For instance, frequently, alters use the same initials as their host—Ashley Patterson . . . Alette Peters . . . Toni Prescott. . . ."

"Toni—?" David started to ask. Then he realized, "Antoinette?"

"Right. You've heard the expression 'alter ego.' "

"Yes."

"In a sense, we all have alter egos, or multiple personalities. A kind person can commit acts of cruelty. Cruel people can do kind things. There's no limit to the incredible range of human emotions. *Dr. Jekyll and Mr. Hyde* is fiction, but it's based on fact."

David's mind was racing. "If Ashley committed the murders . . ."

"She would not be aware of it. It was done by one of her alters."

"My God! How can I explain that in court?"

Dr. Salem looked at David curiously. "I thought you said you weren't going to be her attorney."

David shook his head. "I'm not. I mean, I don't know. I—At this point, I'm a multiple personality myself." David was silent for a moment. "Is this curable?"

"Often, yes."

"And if it can't be cured, what happens?"

There was a pause. "The suicide rate is quite high."

"And Ashley knows nothing about this?"

"No."

"Would—would you explain it to her?"

"Yes, of course."

*   *   *

"No!" It was a scream. She was cowering against the wall of her cell, her eyes filled with terror. "You're lying! It's not true!"

Dr. Salem said, "Ashley, it is. You have to face it. I've explained to you that what happened to you is not your fault. I—"

"Don't come near me!"

"No one's going to hurt you."

"I want to die. Help me die!" She began sobbing uncontrollably.

Dr. Salem looked at the matron and said, "You'd better give her a sedative. And put a suicide watch on her."

David telephoned Dr. Patterson. "I need to talk to you."

"I've been waiting to hear from you, David. Did you see Ashley?"

"Yes. Can we meet somewhere?"

"I'll wait in my office for you."

Driving back to San Francisco, David thought, *There's no way that I can take this case. I have too much to lose.*

I'll find her a good criminal attorney and that will be the end of it.

Dr. Patterson was waiting for David in his office. "You talked to Ashley?"

"Yes."

"Is she all right?"

How do I answer that question? David took a deep breath. "Have you ever heard of multiple personality disorder?"

Dr. Patterson frowned. "Vaguely ..."

"It's when one or more personalities—or alters—exist in a person and take control from time to time, and that person is not aware of it. Your daughter has multiple personality disorder."

Dr. Patterson was looking at him, stunned. "*What?* I—I can't believe it. Are you sure?"

"I listened to Ashley while Dr. Salem had her under hypnosis. She has two alters. At various times, they possess her." David was talking more rapidly now. "The sheriff showed me the evidence against your daughter. There's no doubt that she committed the murders."

Dr. Patterson said. "Oh, my God! Then she's—she's guilty?"

"No. Because I don't believe she was aware that she committed the murders. She was under the influence of one of the alters. Ashley had no reason to commit those crimes. She had no motive, and she was not in control of herself. I think the state may have a difficult time proving motive or intent.''

''Then your defense is going to be that—''

David stopped him. ''I'm not going to defend her. I'm going to get you Jesse Quiller. He's a brilliant trial lawyer. I used to work with him, and he's the most—''

''No.'' Dr. Patterson's voice was sharp. ''You must defend Ashley.''

David said patiently, ''You don't understand. I'm not the right one to defend her. She needs—''

''I told you before that you're the only one I trust. My daughter means everything in the world to me, David. You're going to save her life.''

''I can't. I'm not qualified to—''

''Of course you are. You were a criminal attorney.''

''Yes, but I—''

''I won't have anyone else.'' David could see that Dr. Patterson was trying to keep his temper under control.

This makes no sense, David thought. He tried again. ''Jesse Quiller is the best—''

Dr. Patterson leaned forward, the color rising in his face. ''David, your mother's life meant a lot to you. Ashley's life means as much to me. You asked for my help once, and you put your mother's life in my hands. I'm asking for your help now, and I'm putting Ashley's life in your hands. I want you to defend Ashley. You owe me that.''

He won't listen, David thought despairingly. *What's the matter with him?* A dozen objections flashed through David's mind, but they all faded before that one line: *''You owe me that.''* David tried one last time. ''Dr. Patterson—''

''Yes or no, David.''

Chapter Thirteen

WHEN David got home, Sandra was waiting for him.
"Good evening, darling."

He took her in his arms and thought, *My God, she's lovely. What idiot said that pregnant women weren't beautiful?*

Sandra said excitedly, "The baby kicked again today." She took David's hand and put it on her belly. "Can you feel him?"

After a few moments, David said, "No. He's a stubborn little devil."

"By the way, Mr. Crowther called."

"Crowther?"

"The real estate broker. The papers are ready to be signed."

David felt a sudden sinking feeling. "Oh."

"I want to show you something," Sandra said eagerly. "Don't go away."

David watched her hurry into the bedroom and thought, *What am I going to do? I have to make a decision.*

Sandra came back into the room holding up several samples of blue wallpaper. "We're doing the nursery in blue, and we'll do the living room of the apartment in blue and white, your favorite colors. Which color wallpaper do you like, the lighter shade or the darker?"

David forced himself to concentrate. "The lighter looks good."

"I like it, too. The only problem is that the rug is going to be a dark blue. Do you think they should match?"

I can't give up the partnership. I've worked too hard for it. It means too much.

"David. Do you think they should match?"

He looked at her. "What? Oh. Yes. Whatever you think, honey."

"I'm so excited. It's going to be beautiful."

There's no way we can afford it if I don't get the partnership.

Sandra looked around the little apartment. "We can use some of this furniture, but I'm afraid we're going to need a lot of new things." She looked at him anxiously. "We can handle it, can't we, darling? I don't want to go overboard."

"Right," David said absently.

She snuggled against his shoulder. "It's going to be like a whole new life, isn't it? The baby and the partnership and the penthouse. I went by there today. I wanted to see the playground and the school. The playground's beautiful. It has slides and swings and jungle gyms. I want you to come with me Saturday to look at it. Jeffrey's going to adore it."

Maybe I can convince Kincaid that this would be a good thing for the firm.

"The school looks nice. It's just a couple blocks from our condo, and it's not too large. I think that's important."

David was listening to her now and thought, *I can't let her down. I can't take away her dreams. I'll tell Kincaid in the morning that I'm not taking the Patterson case. Patterson will have to find someone else.*

"We'd better get ready, darling. We're due at the Quillers' at eight o'clock."

This was the moment of truth. David felt himself tense. "There's something we have to talk about."

"Yes?"

"I went to see Ashley Patterson this morning."

"Oh? Tell me about it. Is she guilty? Did she do those terrible things?"

"Yes and no."

"Spoken like a lawyer. What does that mean?"

"She committed the murders . . . but she's not guilty."

"David—!"

"Ashley has a medical condition called multiple personality disorder. Her personality is split, so that she does things without knowing she's doing them."

Sandra was staring at him. "How horrible."

"There are two other personalities. I've heard them."

"You've *heard* them?"

"Yes. And they're real. I mean, she's not faking."

"And she has no idea that she—?"

"None."

"Then is she innocent or guilty?"

"That's for the courts to decide. Her father won't talk to Jesse Quiller, so I'll have to find some other attorney."

"But Jesse's perfect. Why won't he talk to him?"

David hesitated. "He wants me to defend her."

"But you told him you can't, of course."

"Of course."

"Then—?"

"He won't listen."

"What did he say, David?"

He shook his head. "It doesn't matter."

"What did he say?"

David replied slowly, "He said that I trusted him enough to put my mother's life in his hands, and he saved her, and now he was trusting me enough to put his daughter's life in my hands, and he is asking me to save her."

Sandra was studying his face. "Do you think you could?"

"I don't know. Kincaid doesn't want me to take the case. If I did take it, I could lose the partnership."

"Oh."

There was a long silence.

When he spoke, David said, "I have a choice. I can say no to Dr. Patterson and become a partner in the firm, or I can defend his daughter and probably go on an unpaid leave, and see what happens afterward."

Sandra was listening quietly.

"There are people much better qualified to handle Ashley's case, but for some damn reason, her father won't hear of anyone else. I don't know why he's so stubborn about it, but he is. If I take the case and I don't get the partnership, we'll have to forget about moving. We'll have to forget about a lot of our plans, Sandra."

Sandra said softly, "I remember before we were married, you told me about him. He was one of the busiest doctors in the world, but he found time to help a penniless young boy. He was your hero, David. You said that if we ever had a son, you would want him to grow up to be like Steven Patterson."

David nodded.

"When do you have to decide?"

"I'm seeing Kincaid first thing in the morning."

Sandra took his hand and said, "You don't need that much time. Dr. Patterson saved your mother. You're going to save his daughter." She looked around and smiled. "Anyway, we can always do this apartment over in blue and white."

Jesse Quiller was one of the top criminal defense attorneys in the country. He was a tall, rugged man with a homespun touch that made jurors identify with him. They felt that he was one of them, and they wanted to help him. That was one of the reasons he seldom lost a case. The other reasons were that he had a photographic memory and a brilliant mind.

Instead of vacationing, Quiller used his summers to teach law, and years earlier David had been one of his pupils. When David graduated, Quiller invited him to join his criminal law firm, and two years later, David had become a partner. David loved practicing criminal law and excelled at it. He made sure that at least 10 percent of his cases were pro bono. Three years after becoming a partner, David had abruptly resigned and gone to work for Kincaid, Turner, Rose & Ripley to practice corporate law.

Over the years, David and Quiller had remained close friends. They, and their wives, had dinner together once a week.

Jesse Quiller had always fancied tall, sylphlike, sophisticated blondes. Then he had met Emily and fallen in love with her. Emily was a prematurely gray dumpling of a woman, from an Iowa farm—the exact opposite of other women Quiller had dated. She was a caretaker, mother earth. They made an unlikely couple, but the marriage worked because they were deeply in love with each other.

Every Tuesday, the Singers and the Quillers had dinner and then played a complicated card game called Liverpool.

When Sandra and David arrived at the Quillers' beautiful home on Hayes Street, Jesse met them at the door.

He gave Sandra a hug and said, "Come in. We've got the champagne on ice. It's a big day for you, huh? The new penthouse and the partnership. Or is it the partnership and the penthouse?"

David and Sandra looked at each other.

"Emily's in the kitchen fixing a celebration dinner." He looked at their faces. "I *think* it's a celebration dinner. Am I missing something?"

David said, "No, Jesse. It's just that we may have a—a little problem."

"Come on in. Fix you a drink?" He looked at Sandra.

"No, thanks. I don't want the baby to get into bad habits."

"He's a lucky kid, having parents like you," Quiller said warmly. He turned to David. "What can I get for you?"

"I'm fine," David said.

Sandra started toward the kitchen. "I'll go see if I can help Emily."

"Sit down, David. You look serious."

"I'm in a dilemma," David admitted.

"Let me guess. Is it the penthouse or the partnership?"

"Both."

"Both?"

"Yes. You know about the Patterson case?"

"Ashley Patterson? Sure. What's that got to do with—?" He stopped. "Wait a minute. You told me about Steven Patterson, in law school. He saved your mother's life."

"Yes. He wants me to defend his daughter. I tried to turn the case over to you, but he won't hear of anyone but me defending her."

Quiller frowned. "Does he know you're not practicing criminal law anymore?"

"Yes. That's what's so damn strange. There are dozens of lawyers who can do a hell of a lot better job than I can."

"He knows that you *were* a criminal defense lawyer?"

"Yes."

Quiller said carefully, "How does he feel about his daughter?"

What a strange question, David thought. "She means more to him than anything in the world."

"Okay. Suppose you took her case. The downside is that—"

"The downside is that Kincaid doesn't want me to take it. If I do, I have a feeling that I'll lose the partnership."

"I see. And that's where the penthouse comes in?"

David said angrily, "That's where my whole goddamn future comes in. It would be stupid for me to do this, Jesse. I mean really *stupid!*"

"What are you getting mad about?"

David took a deep breath. "Because I'm going to do it."

Quiller smiled. "Why am I not surprised?"

David ran his hand across his forehead. "If I turned him down, and his daughter was convicted and executed, and I did nothing to help, I—I couldn't live with myself."

"I understand. How does Sandra feel about this?"

David managed a smile. "You know Sandra."

"Yeah. She wants you to go ahead with it."

"Right."

Quiller leaned forward. "I'll do everything I can to help you, David."

David sighed. "No. That's part of my bargain. I have to handle this alone."

Quiller frowned. "That doesn't make any sense."

"I know. I tried to explain that to Dr. Patterson, but he wouldn't listen."

"Have you told Kincaid about this yet?"

"I'm having a meeting with him in the morning."

"What do you think will happen?"

"I know what's going to happen. He's going to advise me not to take the case and, if I insist, he'll ask me to take a leave of absence without pay."

"Let's have lunch tomorrow. Rubicon, one o'clock."

David nodded. "Fine."

Emily came in from the kitchen wiping her hands on a kitchen towel. David and Quiller rose.

"Hello, David." Emily bustled up to him, and he gave her a kiss on the cheek.

"I hope you're hungry. Dinner's almost ready. Sandra's in the kitchen helping me. She's such a dear." She picked up a tray and hurried back into the kitchen.

Quiller turned to David. "You mean a great deal to Emily and me. I'm going to give you some advice. You've got to let go."

David sat there, saying nothing.

"That was a long time ago, David. And what happened wasn't your fault. It could have happened to anyone."

David looked at Quiller. "It happened to me, Jesse. I killed her."

It was déjà vu. All over again. And again. David sat there, transported back to another time and another place.

It had been a pro bono case, and David had said to Jesse Quiller, "I'll handle it."

Helen Woodman was a lovely young woman accused of murdering her wealthy stepmother. There had been bitter public quarrels between the two, but all the evidence against Helen was circumstantial. After David had gone to the jail and met with her, he was convinced she was innocent. With each meeting, he had become more emotionally involved. In the end, he had broken a basic rule: Never fall in love with a client.

The trial had gone well. David had refuted the prosecutor's evidence bit by bit, and he had won the jury over to his client's side. And unexpectedly, a disaster had occurred. Helen's alibi was that at the time of the murder she had been at the theater with a friend. Under questioning in court, her friend admitted that the alibi was a lie, and a witness had come forward to say that he had seen Helen at her stepmother's apartment at the time of the murder. Helen's credibility was completely gone. The jury convicted her of first-degree murder, and the judge sentenced her to be executed. David was devastated.

"How could you have done this, Helen?" he demanded. "Why did you lie to me?"

"I didn't kill my stepmother, David. When I got to her apartment, I found her on the floor, dead. I was afraid you wouldn't believe me, so I—I made up the story about being at the theater."

He stood there, listening, a cynical expression on his face.

"I'm telling you the truth, David."

"Are you?" He turned and stormed out.

Sometime during the night, Helen committed suicide.

One week later, an ex-convict caught committing a burglary confessed to the murder of Helen's stepmother.

The next day, David quit Jesse Quiller's firm. Quiller had tried to dissuade him.

"It wasn't your fault, David. She lied to you and—"

"That's the point. I let her. I didn't do my job. I didn't make sure she was telling me the truth. I wanted to believe her, and because of that, I let her down."

Two weeks later, David was working for Kincaid, Turner, Rose & Ripley.

"I'll never be responsible for another person's life," David had sworn.

And now he was defending Ashley Patterson.

Chapter Fourteen

A T ten o'clock the following morning, David walked into Joseph Kincaid's office. Kincaid was signing some papers and he glanced up as David entered.

"Ah. Sit down, David. I'll be through in a moment."

David sat down and waited.

When Kincaid had finished, he smiled and said, "Well! You have some good news, I trust?"

Good news for whom? David wondered.

"You have a very bright future here, David, and I'm sure you wouldn't want to do anything to spoil that. The firm has big plans for you."

David was silent, trying to find the right words.

Kincaid said, "Well? Have you told Dr. Patterson that you'd find another lawyer for him?"

"No. I've decided that I'm going to defend her."

Kincaid's smile faded. "Are you really going to defend that woman, David? She's a vicious, sick murderer. Anyone who defends her will be tarred with the same brush."

"I'm not doing this because I want to, Joseph. I'm obligated. I owe Dr. Patterson a great deal, and this is the only way I can ever repay him."

Kincaid sat there, silent. When he finally spoke, he said, "If you've really decided to go ahead with this, then I suggest that it would be appropriate for you to take a leave of absence. Without pay, of course."

Good-bye, partnership.

"After the trial, naturally, you'll come back to us and the partnership will be waiting for you."

David nodded. "Naturally."

"I'll have Collins take over your workload. I'm sure you'll want to begin concentrating on the trial."

Thirty minutes later, the partners of Kincaid, Turner, Rose & Ripley were in a meeting.

"We can't afford to have this firm be involved in a trial like that," Henry Turner objected.

Joseph Kincaid was quick to respond. "We're not really involved, Henry. We're giving the boy a leave of absence."

Albert Rose spoke up. "I think we should cut him loose."

"Not yet. That would be shortsighted. Dr. Patterson could be a cash cow for us. He knows everybody, and he'll be grateful to us for letting him borrow David. No matter what happens at the trial, it's a win-win situation. If it goes well, we get the doctor as a client and make Singer a partner. If the trial goes badly, we'll drop Singer and see if we can't keep the good doctor. There's really no downside."

There was a moment of silence, then John Ripley grinned. "Good thinking, Joseph."

When David left Kincaid's office, he went to see Steven Patterson. He had telephoned ahead, and the doctor was waiting for him.

"Well, David?"

My answer is going to change my life, David thought. *And not for the better.* "I'm going to defend your daughter, Dr. Patterson."

Steven Patterson took a deep breath. "I knew it. I would have bet my life on it." He hesitated a moment. "I'm betting my daughter's life on it."

"My firm has given me a leave of absence. I'm going to get help from one of the best trial lawyers in the—"

Dr. Patterson raised a hand. "David, I thought I made it clear to you that I don't want anyone else involved in this case. She's in your hands and your hands only."

"I understand," David said. "But Jesse Quiller is—"

Dr. Patterson got to his feet. "I don't want to hear anything more about Jesse Quiller or any of the rest of them. I know trial lawyers, David. They're interested in the money and the publicity. This isn't about money or publicity. This is about Ashley."

David started to speak, then stopped. There was nothing he could say. The man was fanatic on the subject. *I can use all the help I can get,* David thought. *Why won't he let me?*

"Have I made myself clear?"

David nodded. "Yes."

"I'll take care of your fee and your expenses, of course."

"No. This is pro bono."

Dr. Patterson studied him a moment, then nodded. "Quid pro quo?"

"Quid pro quo." David managed a smile. "Do you drive?"

"David, if you're on a leave of absence, you'll need some expense money to keep you going. I insist."

"As you wish," David said.

At least we'll eat during the trial.

Jesse Quiller was waiting for David at Rubicon.

"How did it go?"

David sighed. "It was predictable. I'm on a leave of absence, no salary."

"Those bastards. How can they—?"

"I can't blame them," David interrupted. "They're a very conservative firm."

"What are you going to do now?"

"What do you mean?"

"What do I *mean*? You're handling the trial of the century. You don't have an office to work in anymore; you don't have access to research files or case files, criminal law books or a fax machine, and I've seen that outdated computer that you and Sandra have. It won't be able to run the legal software you'll need or get you on the Internet."

"I'll be all right," David said.

"You're damn right you will. There's an empty office in my suite that you're going to use. You'll find everything you need there."

It took David a moment to find his voice. "Jesse, I can't—"

"Yes, you can." Quiller grinned. "You'll find a way to pay me back. You always pay people back, don't you, Saint David?" He picked up a menu. "I'm starved." He looked up. "By the way, lunch is on you."

*　　*　　*

David went to visit Ashley in the Santa Clara County Jail.

"Good morning, Ashley."

"Good morning." She looked even paler than usual. "Father was here this morning. He told me that you're going to get me out of here."

I wish I were that optimistic, David thought. He said carefully, "I'm going to do everything I can, Ashley. The trouble is that not many people are familiar with the problem you have. We're going to let them know about it. We're going to get the finest doctors in the world to come here and testify for you."

"It scares me," Ashley whispered.

"What does?"

"It's as though two different people are living inside me, and I don't even know them." Her voice was trembling. "They can take over anytime they want to, and I have no control over them. I'm so frightened." Her eyes filled with tears.

David said quietly, "They're not people, Ashley. They're in your mind. They're part of you. And with the proper treatment, you're going to be well."

When David got home that evening, Sandra gave him a hug and said, "Did I ever tell you how proud I am of you?"

"Because I'm out of a job?" David asked.

"That, too. By the way, Mr. Crowther called. The real estate broker. He said the papers are ready to sign. They want the down payment of sixty thousand dollars. I'm afraid we'll have to tell him we can't afford—"

"Wait! I have that much in the company pension plan. With Dr. Patterson giving us some expense money, maybe we can still swing this."

"It doesn't matter, David. We don't want to spoil the baby with a penthouse, anyway."

"Well, I have some good news. Jesse is going to let me—"

"I know. I talked to Emily. We're moving into Jesse's offices."

David said, *"We?"*

"You forget, you married a paralegal. Seriously, darling, I can be very helpful. I'll work with you until"—she touched her stomach—"Jeffrey comes along, and then we'll see."

"Mrs. Singer, do you have any idea how much I love you?"

"No. But take your time. Dinner's not for another hour."

"An hour isn't enough time," David told her.

She put her arms around him and murmured, "Why don't you get undressed, Tiger?"

"What?" He pulled back and looked at her, worried. "What about the—What does Dr. Bailey say?"

"The doctor says if you don't get undressed in a hurry, I should attack you."

David grinned. "His word's good enough for me."

The following morning, David moved into the back office of Jesse Quiller's suite. It was a serviceable office, part of a five-office suite.

"We've expanded a little since you were here," Jesse explained to David. "I'm sure you'll find everything. The law library is next door; you've got faxes, computers, everything you need. If there's anything you don't see, just ask."

"Thanks," David said. "I—I can't tell you how much I appreciate this, Jesse."

Jesse smiled. "You're going to pay me back. Remember?"

Sandra arrived a few minutes later. "I'm ready," she said. "Where do we begin?"

"We begin by looking up every case we can find on multiple personality trials. There's probably a ton of stuff on the Internet. We'll try the California Criminal Law Observer, the Court TV site and some other criminal law links, and we'll gather whatever useful information we can get from Westlaw and Lexis-Nexis. Next, we get hold of doctors who specialize in multiple personality problems, and we contact them as possible expert witnesses. We'll need to interview them and see if we can use their testimony to strengthen our case. I'll have to brush up on criminal court procedures and get ready for voir dire. We've also got to get a list of the district attorney's witnesses and the witnesses' statements. I want his whole discovery package."

"And we have to send him ours. Are you going to call Ashley to the stand?"

David shook his head. "She's much too fragile. The prosecution would tear her apart." He looked up at Sandra. "This is going to be a hard one to win."

Sandra smiled. "But you're going to win it. I know you are."

David put in a call to Harvey Udell, the accountant at Kincaid, Turner, Rose & Ripley.

"Harvey. David Singer."

"Hello, David. I hear you're leaving us for a little while."

"Yes."

"That's an interesting case you're taking on. The papers are full of it. What can I do for you?"

David said, "I have sixty thousand dollars in my pension plan there, Harvey. I wasn't going to take it out this early, but Sandra and I just bought a penthouse, and I'm going to need the money for a down payment."

"A penthouse. Well, congratulations."

"Thanks. How soon can I get the money?"

There was a brief hesitation. "Can I get back to you?"

"Of course." David gave him his telephone number.

"I'll call you right back."

"Thanks."

Harvey Udell replaced the receiver and then picked up the telephone again. "Tell Mr. Kincaid I'd like to see him."

Thirty minutes later he was in Joseph Kincaid's office. "What is it, Harvey?"

"I got a call from David Singer, Mr. Kincaid. He's bought a penthouse, and he needs the sixty thousand he has in his pension fund for a down payment. In my opinion, we're not obligated to give him the money now. He's on leave, and he's not—"

"I wonder if he knows how expensive it is to maintain a penthouse?"

"Probably not. I'll just tell him we can't—"

"Give him the money."

Harvey looked at him in surprise. "But we don't have to—"

Kincaid leaned forward in his chair. "We're going to help him dig a hole for himself, Harvey. Once he puts a down payment on that penthouse . . . we own him."

Harvey Udell telephoned David. "I've good news for you, David. That money you have in the pension plan, you're taking it out early, but there's no problem. Mr. Kincaid says to give you anything you want."

"Mr. Crowther. David Singer."

"I've been waiting to hear from you, Mr. Singer."

"The down payment on the penthouse is on its way. You'll have it tomorrow."

"Wonderful. As I told you, we have some other folks who are anxious to get it, but I have the feeling that you and your wife are the right owners for it. You're going to be very happy there."

All it will take, David thought, *is a few dozen miracles.*

Ashley Patterson's arraignment took place in the Superior Court of the County of Santa Clara on North First Street in San Jose. The legal wrangling about jurisdiction had gone on for weeks. It had been complicated, because the murders had taken place in two countries and two different states. A meeting was held in San Francisco, attended by Officer Guy Fontaine from the Quebec Police Department, Sheriff Dowling from Santa Clara County, Detective Eagan from Bedford, Pennsylvania, Captain Rudford from the San Francisco Police Department, and Roger Toland, the chief of police in San Jose.

Fontaine said, "We would like to try her in Quebec because we have absolute evidence of her guilt. There's no way she can win a trial there."

Detective Eagan said, "For that matter, so do we, Officer Fontaine. Jim Cleary's was the first murder she committed, and I think that should take precedence over the others."

Captain Rudford of the San Francisco police said, "Gentlemen, there's no doubt that we can all prove her guilt. But three of these murders took place in California, and she should be tried here for all of them. That gives us a much stronger case."

"I agree," Sheriff Dowling said. "And two of them took place in Santa Clara County, so this is where the jurisdiction should lie."

They spent the next two hours arguing the merits of their positions, and in the end, it was decided that the trial for the murders of Dennis Tibble, Richard Melton and Deputy Sam Blake would be held at the Hall of Justice in San Jose. They agreed that the murders in Bedford and Quebec would be put on hold.

On the day of arraignment, David stood at Ashley's side.

The judge on the bench said, "How do you plead?"

"Not guilty and not guilty by reason of insanity."

The judge nodded. "Very well."

"Your Honor, we're requesting bail at this time."

The attorney from the prosecutor's office jumped in. "Your

Honor, we strongly object. The defendant is accused of three savage murders and faces the death penalty. If she were given the opportunity, she would flee the country.''

"That's not true," David said. "There's no—"

The judge interrupted. "I've reviewed the file and the prosecutor's affidavit in support of no bail. Bail denied. This case is assigned to Judge Williams for all purposes. The defendant will be held in custody at the Santa Clara County Jail until trial."

David sighed. "Yes, Your Honor." He turned to Ashley. "Don't worry. Everything's going to work out. Remember . . . you're not guilty."

When David returned to the office, Sandra said, "Have you seen the headlines? The tabloids are calling Ashley 'the Butcher Bitch.' The story is all over television."

"We knew this was going to be rough," David said. "And this is only the beginning. Let's go to work."

The trial was eight weeks away.

The next eight weeks were filled with feverish activity. David and Sandra worked all day and far into the night, digging up transcripts of trials of defendants with multiple personality disorder. There were dozens of cases. The various defendants had been tried for murder, rape, robbery, drug dealing, arson. . . . Some had been convicted, some had been acquitted.

"We're going to get Ashley acquitted," David told Sandra.

Sandra gathered the names of prospective witnesses and telephoned them.

"Dr. Nakamoto, I'm working with David Singer. I believe you testified in *The State of Oregon Versus Bohannan.* Mr. Singer is representing Ashley Patterson. . . . Oh, you did? Yes. Well, we would like you to come to San Jose and testify in her behalf. . . .''

"Dr. Booth, I'm calling from David Singer's office. He's defending Ashley Patterson. You testified in the *Dickerson* case. We're interested in your expert testimony. . . . We would like you to come to San Jose and testify for Miss Patterson. We need your expertise. . . .''

"Dr. Jameson, this is Sandra Singer. We need you to come to . . .''

And so it went, from morning until midnight. Finally, a list of a dozen witnesses was compiled. David looked at it and said, "It's pretty impressive. Doctors, a dean ... heads of law schools." He looked up at Sandra and smiled. "I think we're in good shape."

From time to time, Jesse Quiller came into the office David was using. "How are you getting along?" he asked. "Anything I can do to help?"
"I'm fine."
Quiller looked around the office. "Do you have everything you need?"
David smiled. "Everything, including my best friend."

On a Monday morning, David received a package from the prosecutor's office listing the state's discovery. As David read it, his spirits sank.
Sandra was watching him, concerned. "What is it?"
"Look at this. He's bringing in a lot of heavyweight medical experts to testify against MPD."
"How are you going to handle that?" Sandra asked.
"We're going to admit that Ashley was at the scenes when the murders took place, but that the murders were actually committed by an alter ego." *Can I persuade a jury to believe that?*

Five days before the trial was to begin, David received a telephone call saying that Judge Williams wanted to meet with him.
David walked into Jesse Quiller's office. "Jesse, what can you tell me about Judge Williams?"
Jesse leaned back in his chair and laced his fingers behind his head. "Tessa Williams ... Were you ever a Boy Scout, David?"
"Yes ..."
"Do you remember the Boy Scout motto,—'be prepared'?"
"Sure."
"When you walk into Tessa Williams's courtroom, be prepared. She's brilliant. She came up the hard way. Her folks were Mississippi sharecroppers. She went through college on a scholarship, and the people in her hometown were so proud of her, they raised the money to put her through law school. There's a rumor that she turned down a big appointment in Washington because she likes it where she is. She's a legend."
"Interesting," David said.
"The trial is going to be in Santa Clara County?"

"Yes."

"Then you'll have my old friend Mickey Brennan prosecuting."

"Tell me about him."

"He's a feisty Irishman, tough on the inside, tough on the outside. Brennan comes from a long line of overachievers. His father runs a huge publishing business; his mother's a doctor; his sister is a college professor. Brennan was a football star in his college days, and he was at the top of his law class." He leaned forward. "He's good, David. Be careful. His trick is to disarm witnesses and then move in for the kill. He likes to blindside them. . . . Why does Judge Williams want to see you?"

"I have no idea. The call just said she wants to discuss the Patterson case with me."

Jesse Quiller frowned. "That's unusual. When are you meeting with her?"

"Wednesday morning."

"Watch your back."

"Thanks, Jesse. I will."

The superior courthouse in Santa Clara County is a white, four-story building on North First Street. Directly inside the courthouse entrance is a desk manned by a uniformed guard; there is a metal detector, a railing alongside and an elevator. There are seven courtrooms in the building, each one presided over by a judge and staff.

At ten o'clock Wednesday morning, David Singer was ushered into the chambers of Judge Tessa Williams. In the room with her was Mickey Brennan. The leading prosecutor from the district attorney's office was in his fifties, a short, burly man with a slight brogue. Tessa Williams was in her late forties, a slim, attractive African-American woman with a crisp, authoritative manner.

"Good morning, Mr. Singer. I'm Judge Williams. This is Mr. Brennan."

The two men shook hands.

"Sit down, Mr. Singer. I want to talk about the Patterson case. According to the records, you've filed a plea of not guilty and not guilty by reason of insanity?"

"Yes, Your Honor."

Judge Williams said, "I brought you two together because I think we can save a lot of time and save the state a great deal of expense. I'm usually against plea bargaining, but in this case, I think it's justified."

David was listening, puzzled.

The judge turned to Brennan. "I've read the preliminary hearing transcript, and I see no reason for this case to go to trial. I'd like the state to waive the death penalty and accept a guilty plea with no chance of parole."

David said, "Wait a minute. That's out of the question!"

They both turned to look at him.

"Mr. Singer—"

"My client is not guilty. Ashley Patterson passed a lie detector test that proves—"

"That doesn't prove anything, and as you well know it's not admissible in court. Because of all the publicity, this is going to be a long and messy trial."

"I'm sure that—"

"I've been practicing law a long time, Mr. Singer. I've heard the whole basket of legal pleas. I've heard pleas of self-defense— that's an acceptable plea; murder by reason of temporary insanity—that's a reasonable plea; diminished capacity. . . . But I'll tell you what I don't believe in, Counselor. 'Not guilty because I didn't commit the crime, my alter ego did it.' To use a term you might not find in *Blackstone,* that's 'bullshit.' Your client either committed the crimes or she didn't. If you change your plea to guilty, we can save a lot of—"

"No, Your Honor, I won't."

Judge Williams studied David a moment. "You're very stubborn. A lot of people find that an admirable quality." She leaned forward in her chair. "I don't."

"Your Honor—"

"You're forcing us into a trial that's going to last at least three months—maybe longer."

Brennan nodded. "I agree."

"I'm sorry that you feel—"

"Mr. Singer, I'm here to do you a favor. If we try your client, she's going to die."

"Hold on! You're prejudging this case without—"

"Prejudging it? Have you seen the evidence?"

"Yes, I—"

"For God's sake, Counselor, Ashley Patterson's DNA and fingerprints are at every crime scene. I've never seen a more clearcut case of guilt. If you insist on going ahead with this, it could turn into a circus. Well, I'm not going to let that happen. I don't like circuses in my court. Let's dispose of this case here and now. I'm going to ask you once more, will you plead your client to life without parole?''

David said stubbornly, "No."

She was glaring at him. "Right. I'll see you next week."

He had made an enemy.

Chapter Fifteen

SAN Jose had quickly taken on the atmosphere of a carnival town. Media from all over the world were pouring in. Every hotel was booked, and some of the members of the press were forced to take rooms in the outlying towns of Santa Clara, Sunnyvale and Palo Alto. David was besieged by reporters.

"Mr. Singer, tell us about the case. Are you pleading your client not guilty . . . ?"

"Are you going to put Ashley Patterson on the stand . . . ?"

"Is it true that the district attorney was willing to plea-bargain?"

"Is Dr. Patterson going to testify for his daughter . . . ?"

"My magazine will pay fifty thousand dollars for an interview with your client. . . ."

Mickey Brennan was also pursued by the media.

"Mr. Brennan, would you say a few words about the trial?"

Brennan turned and smiled at the television cameras. "Yes. I can sum up the trial in five words. 'We're going to win it.' No further comment."

"Wait! Do you think she's insane . . . ?"

"Is the state going to ask for the death penalty . . . ?"

"Did you call it an open-and-shut case . . . ?"

David rented an office in San Jose close to the courthouse, where he could interview his witnesses and prepare them for the trial. He had decided that Sandra would work out of Quiller's office in

San Francisco until the trial started. Dr. Salem had arrived in San Jose.

"I want you to hypnotize Ashley again," David said. "Let's get all the information we can from her and the alters before the trial starts."

They met Ashley in a holding room at the county detention center. She was trying hard to conceal her nervousness. To David, she looked like a deer trapped in the headlights of a juggernaut.

"Morning, Ashley. You remember Dr. Salem?"

Ashley nodded.

"He's going to hypnotize you again. Will that be all right?"

Ashley said, "He's going to talk to the . . . the others?"

"Yes. Do you mind?"

"No. But I—I don't want to talk to them."

"That's all right. You don't have to."

"I hate this!" Ashley burst out angrily.

"I know," David said soothingly. "Don't worry. It's going to be over soon." He nodded to Dr. Salem.

"Make yourself comfortable, Ashley. Remember how easy this was. Close your eyes and relax. Just try to clear your mind. Feel your body relaxing. Listen to the sound of my voice. Let everything else go. You're getting very sleepy. Your eyes are getting very heavy. You want to go to sleep. . . . Go to sleep. . . ."

In ten minutes, she was under. Dr. Salem signaled to David. David walked over to Ashley.

"I'd like to talk to Alette. Are you in there, Alette?"

And they watched Ashley's face soften and go through the same transformation they had seen earlier. And then, that soft, mellifluous Italian accent.

"Buon giorno".

"Good morning, Alette. How do you feel?"

"Male. This is a very difficult time."

"It's difficult for all of us," David assured her, "but everything's going to be all right."

"I hope so."

"Alette, I'd like to ask you a few questions."

"Sì . . ."

"Did you know Jim Cleary?"

"No."

"Did you know Richard Melton?"

"Yes." There was a deep sadness in her voice. "It was . . . it was terrible what happened to him."

David looked over at Dr. Salem. "Yes, it was terrible. When was the last time you saw him?"

"I visited him in San Francisco. We went to a museum and then had dinner. Before I left, he asked me to go to his apartment with him."

"And did you go?"

"No. I wish I had," Alette said regretfully. "I might have saved his life." There was a short silence. "We said good-bye, and I drove back to Cupertino."

"And that was the last time you saw him?"

"Yes."

"Thank you, Alette."

David moved closer to Ashley and said, "Toni? Are you there, Toni? I'd like to talk to you."

As they watched, Ashley's face went through another remarkable transformation. Her persona changed before their eyes. There was a new assurance, a sexual awareness. She began to sing in that clear, throaty voice:

> *"Up and down the city road,*
> *In and out of the Eagle.*
> *That's the way the money goes,*
> *Pop! goes the weasel."*

She looked at David. "Do you know why I like to sing that song, luv?"

"No."

"Because my mother hated it. She hated me."

"Why did she hate you?"

"Well, we can't ask her now, can we?" Toni laughed. "Not where she is. I couldn't do anything right for her. What kind of mother did you have, David?"

"My mother was a wonderful person."

"You're lucky then, aren't you? It's really the luck of the draw, I suppose. God plays games with us, doesn't he?"

"Do you believe in God? Are you a religious person, Toni?"

"I don't know. Maybe there's a God. If there is, he has a strange sense of humor, doesn't he? Alette is the religious one. She goes to church regularly, that one."

"And do you?"

Toni gave a short laugh. "Well, if she's there, I'm there."

"Toni, do you believe it's right to kill people?"

"No, of course not."

"Then—"

"Not unless you have to."

David and Dr. Salem exchanged a look.

"What do you mean by that?"

Her tone of voice changed. She suddenly sounded defensive. "Well, you know, like if you have to protect yourself. If someone's hurting you." She was getting agitated. "If some git is trying to do dirty things to you." She was becoming hysterical.

"Toni—"

She started sobbing. "Why can't they leave me alone? Why did they have to—?" She was screaming.

"Toni—"

Silence.

"Toni . . ."

Nothing.

Dr. Salem said, "She's gone. I'd like to wake Ashley up."

David sighed. "All right."

A few minutes later, Ashley was opening her eyes.

"How do you feel?" David asked.

"Tired. Did it . . . did it go all right?"

"Yes. We talked to Alette and Toni. They—"

"I don't want to know."

"All right. Why don't you go rest now, Ashley? I'll be back to see you this afternoon."

They watched a female jailer lead her away.

Dr. Salem said, "You have to put her on the stand, David. That will convince any jury in the world that—"

"I've given it a lot of thought," David said. "I don't think I can."

Dr. Salem looked at him a moment. "Why not?"

"Brennan, the prosecuting attorney, is a killer. He would tear her apart. I can't take that chance."

David and Sandra were having dinner with the Quillers two days before the preliminaries of the trial were to begin.

"We've checked into the Wyndham Hotel," David said. "The

manager did me a special favor. Sandra's coming down with me. The town is crowded beyond belief.''

"And if it's that bad now,'' Emily said, "imagine what it's going to be like when the trial starts.''

Quiller looked at David. "Anything I can do to help?''

David shook his head. "I have a big decision to make. Whether to put Ashley on the stand or not.''

"It's a tough call,'' Jesse Quiller said. "You're damned if you do and damned if you don't. The problem is that Brennan is going to build Ashley Patterson up as a sadistic, murdering monster. If you don't put her on the stand, that's the image the jurors will carry in their minds when they go into the jury room to reach a verdict. On the other hand, from what you tell me, if you do put Ashley on the stand, Brennan can destroy her.''

"Brennan's going to have all his medical experts there to discredit multiple personality disorder.''

"You've got to convince them that it's real.''

"And I intend to,'' David said. "Do you know what bothers me, Jesse? The jokes. The latest one going around is that I wanted to ask for a change of venue, but I decided not to because there are no places left where Ashley hasn't murdered someone. Do you remember when Johnny Carson was on television? He was funny and he always remained a gentleman. Now, the hosts on the late-night shows are all malicious. Their humor at the expense of other people is savage.''

"David?''

"Yes.''

Jesse Quiller said quietly, "It's going to get worse.''

David Singer was unable to sleep the night before he was to go into court. He could not stem the negative thoughts swirling through his head. When he finally fell asleep, he heard a voice saying, *You let your last client die. What if you let this one die?*

He sat up in bed, bathed in perspiration.

Sandra opened her eyes. "Are you all right?''

"Yes. No. What the hell am I doing here? All I had to do was say no to Dr. Patterson.''

Sandra squeezed his arm and said softly, "Why didn't you?''

He grunted. "You're right. I couldn't.''

"All right then. Now, how about getting some sleep so you'll be nice and fresh in the morning?''

"Great idea."

He was awake the rest of the night.

Judge Williams had been correct about the media. The reporters were relentless. Journalists were swarming in from around the world, avid to cover the story of a beautiful young woman being tried as a serial killer who sexually mutilated her victims.

The fact that Mickey Brennan was forbidden to bring the names of Jim Cleary or Jean Claude Parent into the trial had been frustrating, but the media had solved the problem for him. Television talk shows, magazines and newspapers all carried lurid stories of the five murders and castrations. Mickey Brennan was pleased.

When David arrived at the courtroom, the press was out in full force. David was besieged.

"Mr. Singer, are you still employed by Kincaid, Turner, Rose & Ripley . . . ?"

"Look this way, Mr. Singer. . . ."

"Is it true you were fired for taking this case . . . ?"

"Can you tell us about Helen Woodman? Didn't you handle her murder trial . . . ?"

"Did Ashley Patterson say why she did it . . . ?"

"Are you going to put your client on the stand . . . ?"

"No comment," David said curtly.

When Mickey Brennan drove up to the courthouse, he was instantly surrounded by the media.

"Mr. Brennan, how do you think the trial is going to go . . . ?"

"Have you ever tried an alter ego defense before . . . ?"

Brennan smiled genially. "No. I can't wait to talk to all the defendants." He got the laugh that he wanted. "If there are enough of them, they can have their own ball club." Another laugh. "I've got to get inside. I don't want to keep any of the defendants waiting."

The voir dire started with Judge Williams asking general questions of the potential jurors. When she had finished, it was the defense's turn and then the prosecution's.

To laymen, the selection of a jury seems simple: *Choose the prospective juror who seemed friendly and dismiss the others.* In fact, voir dire was a carefully planned ritual. Skilled trial lawyers did not ask direct questions that would bring yes or no answers. They asked general questions that would encourage the jurors to talk and reveal something of themselves and their true feelings.

Mickey Brennan and David Singer had different agendas. In this case, Brennan wanted a preponderance of men on the jury, men who would be disgusted and shocked at the idea of a woman stabbing and castrating her victims. Brennan's questions were meant to pinpoint people who were traditional in their thinking, who would be less likely to believe in spirits and goblins and people who claimed they were inhabited by alters. David took the opposite approach.

"Mr. Harris, is it? I'm David Singer. I'm representing the defendant. Have you ever served on a jury before, Mr. Harris?"

"No."

"I appreciate your taking the time and trouble to do this."

"It should be interesting, a big murder trial like this."

"Yes. I think it will be."

"In fact, I've been looking forward to it."

"Have you?"

"Yeah."

"Where do you work, Mr. Harris?"

"At United Steel."

"I imagine you and your fellow workers have talked about the Patterson case."

"Yes. As a matter of fact, we have."

David said, "That's understandable. Everyone seems to be talking about it. What's the general opinion? Do your fellow workers think Ashley Patterson is guilty?"

"Yeah. I have to say they do."

"And do you think so?"

"Well, it sure looks like it."

"But you're willing to listen to the evidence before making up your mind?"

"Yeah. I'll listen to it."

"What do you like to read, Mr. Harris?"

"I'm not a big reader. I like to camp out and hunt and fish."

"An outdoorsman. When you're camping out at night and you look at the stars, do you ever wonder if there are other civilizations up there?"

"You mean that crazy UFO stuff? I don't believe in all that nonsense."

David turned to Judge Williams. "Pass for cause, Your Honor."

Another juror interrogation:

"What do you like to do in your spare time, Mr. Allen?"

"Well, I like to read and watch television."

"I like to do the same things. What do you watch on television?"

"There's some great shows on Thursday nights. It's hard to choose. The damn networks put all the good shows on at the same time."

"You're right. It's a shame. Do you ever watch the *X-Files*?"

"Yeah. My kids love it."

"What about *Sabrina, the Teenage Witch*?"

"Yeah. We watch that. That's a good show."

"What do you like to read?"

"Anne Rice, Stephen King . . ."

Yes.

Another juror interrogation:

"What do you like to watch on television, Mr. Mayer?"

"*Sixty Minutes*, the *NewsHour* with Jim Lehrer, documentaries . . ."

"What do you like to read?"

"Mainly history and political books."

"Thank you."

No.

Judge Tessa Williams sat on the bench, listening to the questioning, her face betraying nothing. But David could feel her disapproval every time she looked at him.

When the last juror was finally selected, the panel consisted of seven men and five women. Brennan glanced at David triumphantly. *This is going to be a slaughter.*

Chapter Sixteen

EARLY on the morning the trial of Ashley Patterson was to begin, David went to see Ashley at the detention center. She was near hysteria.

"I can't go through with this. I can't! Tell them to leave me alone."

"Ashley, it's going to be all right. We're going to face them, and we're going to win."

"You don't know—You don't know what this is like. I feel as though I'm in some kind of hell."

"We're going to get you out of it. This is the first step."

She was trembling. "I'm afraid they're—they're going to do something terrible to me."

"I won't let them," David said firmly. "I want you to believe in me. Just remember, you're not responsible for what happened. You haven't done anything wrong. They're waiting for us."

She took a deep breath. "All right. I'm going to be fine. I'm going to be fine. I'm going to be fine."

Seated in the spectators' section was Dr. Steven Patterson. He had responded to the barrage of reporters' questions outside the courtroom with one answer: "My daughter is innocent."

Several rows away were Jesse and Emily Quiller, there for moral support.

At the prosecutor's table were Mickey Brennan and two associates, Susan Freeman and Eleanor Tucker.

Sandra and Ashley were seated at the defendant's table, with David between them. The two women had met the previous week.

"David, you can *look* at Ashley and know she's innocent."

"Sandra, you can look at the evidence she left on her victims and know she killed them. But killing them and being guilty are two different things. Now all I have to do is convince the jury."

Judge Williams entered the courtroom and moved to the bench. The court clerk announced, "All rise. Court is now in session. The Honorable Judge Tessa Williams presiding."

Judge Williams said, "You may be seated. This is the case of *The People of the State of California Versus Ashley Patterson.* Let's get started." Judge Williams looked at Brennan. "Would the prosecutor like to make an opening statement?"

Mickey Brennan rose. "Yes, Your Honor." He turned to the jury and moved toward them. "Good morning. As you know, ladies and gentlemen, the defendant is on trial, accused of committing three bloody murders. Murderers come in many disguises." He nodded toward Ashley. "Her disguise is that of an innocent, vulnerable young woman. But the state will prove to you beyond a reasonable doubt that the defendant willfully and knowingly murdered and mutilated three innocent men.

"She used an alias to commit one of these murders, hoping not to get caught. She knew exactly what she was doing. We're talking calculated, cold-blooded murder. As the trial goes on, I will show you all the strands, one by one, that tie this case to the defendant sitting there. Thank you."

He returned to his seat.

Judge Williams looked at David. "Does the defense have an opening statement?"

"Yes, Your Honor." David stood and faced the jury. He took a deep breath. "Ladies and gentlemen, in the course of this trial, I will prove to you that Ashley Patterson is not responsible for what happened. She had no motive for any of the murders, nor any knowledge of them. My client is a victim. She is a victim of MPD—multiple personality disorder, which in the course of this trial will be explained to you."

He glanced at Judge Williams and said firmly, "MPD is an established medical fact. It means that there are other personalities, or alters, that take over their hosts and control their actions. MPD has a long history. Benjamin Rush, a physician and signer of the Declaration of Independence, discussed case histories of MPD in his lectures. Many incidents of MPD were reported throughout the nineteenth century and in this century of people taken over by alters.''

Brennan was listening to David, a cynical smile on his face.

''We will prove to you that it was an alter who took command and committed the murders that Ashley Patterson had absolutely no reason to commit. None. She had no control over what happened, and therefore is not responsible for what happened. During the course of the trial, I will bring in eminent doctors who will explain in greater detail about MPD. Fortunately, it is curable.''

He looked into the faces of the jurors. ''Ashley Patterson had no control over what she did, and in the name of justice, we ask that Ashley Patterson not be convicted of crimes for which she is not responsible.''

David took his seat.

Judge Williams looked at Brennan. ''Is the state ready to proceed?''

Brennan rose. ''Yes, Your Honor.'' He flashed a smile at his associates and moved in front of the jury box. Brennan stood there a moment and deliberately let out a loud burp. The jurors were staring at him, surprised.

Brennan looked at them a moment as though puzzled and then his face cleared. ''Oh, I see. You were waiting for me to say 'excuse me.' Well, I didn't say it because I didn't do that. My alter ego, Pete, did it.''

David was on his feet, furious. ''Objection. Your Honor, this is the most outrageous—''

''Sustained.''

But the damage had already been done.

Brennan gave David a patronizing smile and then turned back to the jury. ''Well, I guess there hasn't been a defense like this since the Salem witch trials three hundred years ago.'' He turned to look at Ashley. ''I didn't do it. No, sir. The devil made me do it.''

David was on his feet again. ''Objection. The—''

''Overruled.''

David slammed back into his seat.

Brennan stepped closer to the jury box. ''I promised you that I was going to prove that the defendant willfully and cold-bloodedly murdered and mutilated three men—Dennis Tibble, Richard Melton and Deputy Samuel Blake. *Three men!* In spite of what the defense says''—he turned and pointed to Ashley again—''there's only *one* defendant sitting there, and she's the one who committed the murders. What did Mr. Singer call it? Multiple personality disorder? Well, I'm going to bring some prominent doctors here who will tell you, under oath, that there is no such thing! But first, let's hear from some experts who are going to tie the defendant to the crimes."

Brennan turned to Judge Williams. "I would like to call my first witness, Special Agent Vincent Jordan."

A short bald man stood up and moved toward the witness box. The clerk said, "Please state your full name and spell it for the record."

"Special Agent Vincent Jordan, *J-o-r-d-a-n*."

Brennan waited until he was sworn in and took a seat. "You are with the Federal Bureau of Investigation in Washington, D.C.?"

"Yes, sir."

"And what do you do with the FBI, Special Agent Jordan?"

"I'm in charge of the fingerprints section."

"How long have you had that job?"

"Fifteen years."

"Fifteen years. In all that time have you ever come across a duplicate set of fingerprints from different people?"

"No, sir."

"How many sets of fingerprints are currently on file with the FBI?"

"At last count, just over two hundred and fifty million, but we receive over thirty-four thousand fingerprint cards a day."

"And none of them matches any others?"

"No, sir."

"How do you identify a fingerprint?"

"We use seven different fingerprint patterns for identification purposes. Fingerprints are unique. They're formed before birth and last throughout one's life. Barring accidental or intentional mutilation, no two patterns are alike."

"Special Agent Jordan, you were sent the fingerprints found at the scenes of the three victims who the defendant is accused of murdering?"

"Yes, sir. We were."

"And you were also sent the fingerprints of the defendant, Ashley Patterson?"

"Yes, sir."

"Did you personally examine those prints?"

"I did."

"And what was your conclusion?"

"That the prints left at the murder scenes and the prints that were taken from Ashley Patterson were identical."

There was a loud buzz in the courtroom.

"Order! Order!"

Brennan waited until the courtroom quieted down. "They were identical? Is there any doubt in your mind, Agent Jordan? Could there be any mistake?"

"No, sir. All the prints were clear and easily identifiable."

"Just to clarify this . . . we're talking about the fingerprints left at the murder scenes of Dennis Tibble, Richard Melton and Deputy Samuel Blake?"

"Yes, sir."

"And the fingerprints of the defendant, Ashley Patterson, were found at all the scenes of the murders?"

"That is correct."

"And what would you say was the margin of error?"

"None."

"Thank you, Agent Jordan." Brennan turned to David Singer. "Your witness."

David sat there a moment, then rose and walked over to the witness box. "Agent Jordan, when you examine fingerprints, do you ever find that some have been deliberately smudged, or damaged in some way, in order for the felon to conceal his crime?"

"Yes, but we're usually able to correct them with high-intensity laser techniques."

"Did you have to do that in the case of Ashley Patterson?"

"No, sir."

"Why was that?"

"Well, like I said . . . the fingerprints were all clear."

David glanced at the jury. "So what you're saying is that the defendant made no attempt to erase or disguise her fingerprints?"

"That is correct."

"Thank you. No further questions." He turned to the jury. "Ashley Patterson made no attempt to conceal her prints because she was innocent and—"

Judge Williams snapped, "That's enough, Counselor! You'll have your chance to plead your case later."

David resumed his seat.

Brennan turned to Special Agent Jordan. "You're excused." The FBI agent stepped down.

Brennan said, "I would like to call as my next witness, Stanley Clarke."

A young man with long hair was ushered into the courtroom. He walked toward the witness stand. The courtroom was still as he was sworn in and took his seat.

Brennan said, "What is your occupation, Mr. Clarke?"

"I'm with National Biotech Laboratory. I work with deoxyribonucleic acid."

"More commonly known to us simple nonscientists as DNA?"

"Yes, sir."

"How long have you worked at National Biotech Laboratory?"

"Seven years."

"And what is your position?"

"I'm a supervisor."

"So, in that seven years, I assume that you've had a lot of experience with testing DNA?"

"Sure. I do it every day."

Brennan glanced at the jury. "I think we're all familiar with the importance of DNA." He pointed to the spectators. "Would you say that perhaps half a dozen people in this courtroom have identical DNA?"

"Hell no, sir. If we took a profile of DNA strands and assigned it a frequency based on collected databases, only one in five hundred billion unrelated Caucasians would have the same DNA profile."

Brennan looked impressed. "One in five hundred billion. Mr. Clarke, how do you obtain DNA from a crime scene?"

"Lots of ways. We find DNA in saliva or semen or vaginal discharge, blood, a strand of hair, teeth, bone marrow . . ."

"And from any *one* of those things you can match it to a specific person?"

"That's correct."

"Did you personally compare the DNA evidence in the murders of Dennis Tibble, Richard Melton and Samuel Blake?"

"I did."

"And were you later given several strands of hair from the defendant, Ashley Patterson?"

"I was."

"When you compared the DNA evidence from the various murder scenes with the strands of hair from the defendant, what was your conclusion?''

"They were identical.''

This time the reaction from the spectators was even noisier.

Judge Williams slammed down her gavel. "Order! Be quiet, or I'll have the courtroom cleared.''

Brennan waited until the room was still. "Mr. Clarke, did you say that the DNA taken from every one of the three murder scenes and the DNA of the accused were *identical?*'' Brennan leaned on the word.

"Yes, sir.''

Brennan glanced over at the table where Ashley was sitting, then turned back to the witness. "What about contamination? We're all aware of a famous criminal trial where the DNA evidence was supposedly contaminated. Could the evidence in this case have been mishandled so that it was no longer valid or—?''

"No, sir. The DNA evidence in these murder cases was very carefully handled and sealed.''

"So there's no doubt about it. The defendant murdered the three—?''

David was on his feet. "Objection, Your Honor. The defendant is leading the witness and—''

"Sustained.''

David took his seat.

"Thank you, Mr. Clarke.'' Brennan turned to David. "Nothing further.''

Judge Williams said, "Your witness, Mr. Singer.''

"No questions.''

The jurors were staring at David.

Brennan acted surprised. *"No questions?''* He turned to the witness. "You may step down.''

Brennan looked at the jurors and said, "I'm amazed that the defense is not questioning the evidence, because it proves beyond a doubt that the defendant murdered and castrated three innocent men and—''

David was on his feet. "Your Honor—''

"Sustained. You're stepping over the boundaries, Mr. Brennan!''

"Sorry, Your Honor. No more questions.''

Ashley was looking at David, frightened.

He whispered, "Don't worry. It will be our turn soon.''

*   *   *

The afternoon consisted of more witnesses for the prosecution, and their testimony was devastating.

"The building superintendent summoned you to Dennis Tibble's apartment, Detective Lightman?"

"Yes."

"Would you tell us what you found there?"

"It was a mess. There was blood all over the place."

"What was the condition of the victim?"

"He had been stabbed to death and castrated."

Brennan glanced at the jury, a look of horror on his face. "Stabbed to death and castrated. Did you find any evidence at the scene of the crime?"

"Oh, yes. The victim had had sex before he died. We found some vaginal discharge and fingerprints."

"Why didn't you arrest someone immediately?"

"The fingerprints we found didn't match any that we had on record. We were waiting for a match on the prints we had."

"But when you finally got Ashley Patterson's fingerprints and her DNA, it all came together?"

"It sure did. It all came together."

Dr. Steven Patterson was at the trial every day. He sat in the spectators' section just behind the defendant's table. Whenever he entered or left the courtroom, he was besieged by reporters.

"Dr. Patterson, how do you think the trial is going?"

"It's going very well."

"What do you think is going to happen?"

"My daughter is going to be found innocent."

Late one afternoon when David and Sandra got back to the hotel, there was a message waiting for them. "Please call Mr. Kwong at your bank."

David and Sandra looked at each other. "Is it time for another payment already?" Sandra asked.

"Yes. Time flies when you're having fun," he said dryly. David was thoughtful for a moment. "The trial's going to be over soon, honey. We have enough left in our bank account to give them this month's payment."

Sandra looked at him, worried. "David, if we can't make all the payments . . . do we lose everything we've put in?"

"We do. But don't worry. Good things happen to good people."
And he thought about Helen Woodman.

Brian Hill was sitting in the witness box after being sworn in.
Mickey Brennan gave him a friendly smile.

"Would you tell us what you do, Mr. Hill?"

"Yes, sir. I'm a guard at the De Young Museum in San Francisco."

"That must be an interesting job."

"It is, if you like art. I'm a frustrated painter."

"How long have you worked there?"

"Four years."

"Do a lot of the same people visit the museum? That is, do people come again and again?"

"Oh, yes. Some people do."

"So I suppose that over a period of time, they would become familiar to you, or at least they would be familiar faces?"

"That's true."

"And I'm told that artists are permitted to come in to copy some of the museum's paintings?"

"Oh, yes. We have a lot of artists."

"Did you ever meet any of them, Mr. Hill?"

"Yes, we—You kind of become friendly after a while."

"Did you ever meet a man named Richard Melton?"

Brian Hill sighed. "Yes. He was very talented."

"So talented, in fact, that you asked him to teach you to paint?"

"That's right."

David got to his feet. "Your Honor, this is fascinating, but I don't see what it has to do with the trial. If Mr. Brennan—"

"It's relevant, Your Honor. I'm establishing that Mr. Hill could identify the victim by sight and by name and tell us who the victim associated with."

"Objection overruled. You may go ahead."

"And did he teach you to paint?"

"Yes, he did, when he had time."

"When Mr. Melton was at the museum, did you ever see him with any young ladies?"

"Well, not in the beginning. But then he met somebody he was kind of interested in, and I used to see him with her."

"What was her name?"

"Alette Peters."

Brennan looked puzzled. "Alette Peters? Are you sure you have the right name?"

"Yes, sir. That's the way he introduced her."

"You don't happen to see her in this courtroom right now, do you, Mr. Hill?"

"Yes, sir." He pointed to Ashley. "That's her sitting there."

Brennan said, "But that's not Alette Peters. That's the defendant, Ashley Patterson."

David was on his feet. "Your Honor, we have already said that Alette Peters is a part of this trial. She is one of the alters who controls Ashley Patterson and—"

"You're getting ahead of yourself, Mr. Singer. Mr. Brennan, please continue."

"Now, Mr. Hill, you're sure that the defendant, who's here under the name of Ashley Patterson, was known to Richard Melton as Alette Peters?"

"That's right."

"And there's no doubt that this is the same woman?"

Brian Hill hesitated. "Well . . . Yeah, it's the same woman."

"And you saw her with Richard Melton the day that Melton was murdered?"

"Yes, sir."

"Thank you." Brennan turned to David. "Your witness."

David got up and slowly walked over to the witness box. "Mr. Hill, I would think it's a big responsibility being a guard in a place where so many hundreds of millions of dollars' worth of art was being exhibited."

"Yes, sir. It is."

"And to be a good guard, you have to be on the alert all the time."

"That's right."

"You have to be aware of what's going on all the time."

"You bet."

"Would you say that you're a trained observer, Mr. Hill?"

"Yes, I would."

"I ask that because I noticed when Mr. Brennan asked you if you had any doubts about whether Ashley Patterson was the woman who was with Richard Melton, you hesitated. Weren't you sure?"

There was a momentary pause. "Well, she looks a lot like the same woman, but in a way she seems different."

"In what way, Mr. Hill?"

"Alette Peters was more Italian, and she had an Italian accent
... and she seemed younger than the defendant."

"That's exactly right, Mr. Hill. The person you saw in San
Francisco was an alter of Ashley Patterson. She was born in Rome,
she was eight years younger—"

Brennan was on his feet, furious. "Objection."

David turned to Judge Williams. "Your Honor, I was—"

"Will counsel approach the bench, please?" David and Brennan
walked over to Judge Williams. "I don't want to have to tell you
this again, Mr. Singer. The defense will have its chance when the
prosecution rests. Until then, stop pleading your case."

Bernice Jenkins was on the stand.

"Would you tell us your occupation, Miss Jenkins?"

"I'm a waitress."

"And where do you work?"

"The café at the De Young Museum."

"What was your relationship with Richard Melton?"

"We were good friends."

"Could you elaborate on that?"

"Well, at one time we had a romantic relationship and then
things kind of cooled off. Those things happen."

"I'm sure they do. And then what?"

"Then we became like brother and sister. I mean, I—I told him
about all my problems, and he told me about all his problems."

"Did he ever discuss the defendant with you?"

"Well, yeah, but she called herself by a different name."

"And that name was?"

"Alette Peters."

"But he knew her name was really Ashley Patterson?"

"No. He thought her name was Alette Peters."

"You mean she deceived him?"

David sprang to his feet, furious. "Objection."

"Sustained. You will stop leading the witness, Mr. Brennan."

"Sorry, Your Honor." Brennan turned back to the witness box.
"He spoke to you about this Alette Peters, but did you ever see
the two of them together?"

"Yes, I did. He brought her into the restaurant one day and
introduced us."

"And you're speaking of the defendant, Ashley Patterson?"

"Yeah. Only she called herself Alette Peters."

Gary King was on the stand.

Brennan asked, "You were Richard Melton's roommate?"

"Yes."

"Were you also friends? Did you go out with him socially?"

"Sure. We double-dated a lot together."

"Was Mr. Melton interested in any young lady in particular?"

"Yeah."

"Do you know her name?"

"She called herself Alette Peters."

"Do you see her in this courtroom?"

"Yeah. She's sitting over there."

"For the record, you are pointing to the defendant, Ashley Patterson?"

"Right."

"When you came home on the night of the murder, you found Richard Melton's body in the apartment?"

"I sure did."

"What was the condition of the body?"

"Bloody."

"The body had been castrated?"

A shudder. "Yeah. Man, it was awful."

Brennan looked over at the jury for their reaction. It was exactly what he hoped for.

"What did you do next, Mr. King?"

"I called the police."

"Thank you." Brennan turned to David. "Your witness."

David rose and walked over to Gary King.

"Tell us about Richard Melton. What kind of man was he?"

"He was great."

"Was he argumentative? Did he like to get into fights?"

"Richard? No. Just the opposite. He was very quiet, laid back."

"But he liked to be around women who were tough and kind of physical?"

Gary was looking at him strangely. "Not at all. Richard liked nice, quiet women."

"Did he and Alette have a lot of fights? Did she yell at him a lot?"

Gary was puzzled. "You've got it all wrong. They never yelled at each other. They were great together."

"Did you ever see anything that would lead you to believe that Alette Peters would do anything to harm—?"

"Objection. He's leading the witness."

"Sustained."

"No more questions," David said.

When David sat down, he said to Ashley, "Don't worry. They're building up our case for us."

He sounded more confident than he felt.

David and Sandra were having dinner at San Fresco, the restaurant in the Wyndham Hotel, when the maître d' came up to David and said, "There's an urgent telephone call for you, Mr. Singer."

"Thank you." David said to Sandra, "I'll be right back."

He followed the maître d' to a telephone. "This is David Singer."

"David—Jesse. Go up to your room and call me back. The goddamn roof is falling in!"

Chapter Seventeen

"**J**ESSE —?"

"David, I know I'm not supposed to interfere, but I think you should ask for a mistrial."

"What's happened?"

"Have you been on the Internet in the past few days?"

"No. I've been a little busy."

"Well, the trial is all over the damned Internet. That's all they're talking about in the chat rooms."

"That figures," David said. "But what's the—?"

"It's all negative, David. They're saying that Ashley is guilty and that she should be executed. And they're saying it in very colorful ways. You can't believe how vicious they are."

David, suddenly realizing, said, "Oh, my God! If any of the jurors are on the Internet—"

"The odds are pretty good that some of them are, and they'll be influenced. I would ask for a mistrial, or at the very least, to have the jurors sequestered."

"Thanks, Jesse. Will do." David replaced the receiver. When he returned to the restaurant where Sandra was waiting, she asked, "Bad?"

"Bad."

Before court convened the following morning, David asked to see Judge Williams. He was ushered into her chambers, along with Mickey Brennan.

"You asked to see me?"

"Yes, Your Honor. I learned last night that this trial is the number one subject on the Internet. It's what all the chat rooms are discussing, and they've already convicted the defendant. It's very prejudicial. And since I'm sure that some of the jurors have computers with on-line access, or talk to friends who have on-line access, it could seriously damage the defense. Therefore, I'm making a motion for a mistrial."

She was thoughtful for a moment. "Motion denied."

David sat there, fighting to control himself. "Then I make a motion to immediately sequester the jury so that—"

"Mr. Singer, every day the press is at this courtroom in full force. This trial is the number one topic on television, on radio and in the newspapers all over the world. I warned you that this was going to turn into a circus, and you wouldn't listen." She leaned forward. "Well, it's *your* circus. If you wanted the jury sequestered, you should have made that motion before the trial. And I probably would not have granted it. Is there anything else?"

David sat there, his stomach churning. "No, Your Honor."

"Then let's get into the courtroom."

Mickey Brennan was questioning Sheriff Dowling.

"Deputy Sam Blake called to tell you that he was going to spend the night at the defendant's apartment in order to protect her? She told him that someone was threatening her life?"

"That is correct."

"When did you hear from Deputy Blake again?"

"I—I didn't. I got a call in the morning that his—his body had been found in the alley in back of Miss Patterson's apartment building."

"And of course you went there immediately?"

"Of course."

"And what did you find?"

He swallowed. "Sam's body was wrapped in a bloody sheet. He had been stabbed to death and castrated like the other two victims."

"Like the *other* two victims. So all those murders were carried out in a similar fashion?"

"Yes, sir."

"As though they were killed by the same person?"

David was on his feet. "Objection!"

"Sustained."

"I'll withdraw that. What did you do next, Sheriff?"

"Well, up until that time, Ashley Patterson wasn't a suspect. But after this happened, we took her in and had her fingerprints taken."

"And then?"

"We sent them to the FBI, and we got a positive make on her."

"Would you explain to the jury what you mean by a positive make?"

Sheriff Dowling turned to the jury. "Her fingerprints matched other fingerprints on file that they were trying to identify from the previous murders."

"Thank you, Sheriff." Brennan turned to David. "Your witness."

David got up and walked over to the witness box. "Sheriff, we've heard testimony in this courtroom that a bloody knife was found in Miss Patterson's kitchen."

"That's right."

"How was it hidden? Wrapped up in something? Stashed away where it couldn't be found?"

"No. It was right out in the open."

"Right out in the open. Left there by someone who had nothing to hide. Someone who was innocent because—"

"Objection!"

"Sustained."

"No more questions."

"The witness is dismissed."

Brennan said, "If it pleases the court . . ." He signaled someone at the back of the courtroom, and a man in overalls came in, carrying the mirror from Ashley Patterson's medicine cabinet. On it, in red lipstick, was written YOU WILL DIE.

David rose. "What is this?"

Judge Williams turned to Mickey Brennan. "Mr. Brennan?"

"This is the bait the defendant used to get Deputy Blake to come to her apartment so she could murder him. I would like this marked as exhibit D. It came from the medicine chest of the defendant."

"Objection, Your Honor. It has no relevance."

"I will prove that there is a relevance."

"We'll see. In the meantime, you may proceed."

Brennan placed the mirror in full view of the jury. "This mirror was taken from the defendant's bathroom." He looked at the jurors. "As you can see, scrawled across it is 'You Will Die.' This was the defendant's pretext for having Deputy Blake come to her apartment that night to protect her." He turned to Judge Williams. "I would like to call my next witness, Miss Laura Niven."

A middle-aged woman walking with a cane approached the witness box and was sworn in.

"Where do you work, Miss Niven?"

"I'm a consultant for the County of San Jose."

"And what do you do?"

"I'm a handwriting expert."

"How long have you worked for the county, Miss Niven?"

"Twenty-two years."

Brennan nodded toward the mirror. "You have been shown this mirror before?"

"Yes."

"And you've examined it?"

"I have."

"And you've been shown an example of the defendant's handwriting?"

"Yes."

"And had a chance to examine that?"

"Yes."

"And you've compared the two?"

"I have."

"And what is your conclusion?"

"They were written by the same person."

There was a collective gasp from the courtroom.

"So what you're saying is that Ashley Patterson wrote this threat to herself?"

"That is correct."

Mickey Brennan looked over at David. "Your witness."

David hesitated. He glanced at Ashley. She was staring down at the table, shaking her head. "No questions."

Judge Williams was studying David. "No questions, Mr. Singer?"

David rose to his feet. "No. All this testimony is meaningless." He turned to the jury. "The prosecution will have to prove that Ashley Patterson knew the defendants and had a motive to—"

Judge Williams said angrily, "I've warned you before. It is not your place to instruct the jury on the law. If—"

"Someone has to," David exploded. "You're letting him get away with—"

"That's enough, Mr. Singer. Approach the bench."

David walked to the bench.

"I'm citing you for contempt of court and sentencing you to a night here in our nice jail the day this trial is over."

"Wait, Your Honor. You can't—"

She said grimly, "I've sentenced you to one night. Would you like to try for two?"

David stood there, glaring at her, taking deep breaths. "For the sake of my client, I'll—I'll keep my feelings to myself."

"A wise decision," Judge Williams said curtly. "Court is adjourned." She turned to a bailiff. "When this trial is ended, I want Mr. Singer taken into custody."

"Yes, Your Honor."

Ashley turned to Sandra. "Oh, my God! What's happening?"

Sandra squeezed her arm. "Don't worry. You have to trust David."

Sandra telephoned Jesse Quiller.

"I heard," he said. "It's all over the news, Sandra. I don't blame David for losing his temper. She's been goading him from the beginning. What did David do to get her so down on him?"

"I don't know, Jesse. It's been horrible. You should see the faces of the jurors. They hate Ashley. They can't wait to convict her. Well, it's the defense's turn next. David will change their minds."

"Hold the thought."

"Judge Williams hates me, Sandra, and it's harming Ashley. If I don't do something about this, Ashley is going to die. I can't let that happen."

"What can you do?" Sandra asked.

David took a deep breath. "Resign from the case."

Both of them knew what that meant. The media would be full of his failure.

"I never should have agreed to take on the trial," David said bitterly. "Dr. Patterson trusted me to save his daughter's life, and I've—" He could not go on.

Sandra put her arms around him and held him close. "Don't worry, darling. Everything's going to turn out fine."

I've let everyone down, David thought. *Ashley, Sandra . . . I'm*

going to be kicked out of the firm, I won't have a job and the baby is due soon. "Everything's going to turn out fine."
Right.

In the morning, David asked to see Judge Williams in her chambers. Mickey Brennan was there.

Judge Williams said, "You asked to see me, Mr. Singer?"

"Yes, Your Honor. I want to resign from the case."

Judge Williams said, "On what grounds?"

David spoke carefully. "I don't believe I'm the right lawyer for this trial. I think I'm hurting my client. I would like to be replaced."

Judge Williams said quietly, "Mr. Singer, if you think I'm going to let you walk away from this and then have to start this trial all over again and waste even more time and money, you're quite mistaken. The answer is no. Do you understand me?"

David closed his eyes for an instant, forcing himself to stay calm. He looked up and said, "Yes, Your Honor. I understand you."

He was trapped.

Chapter Eighteen

MORE than three months had gone by since the beginning of the trial, and David could not remember when he had last had a full night's sleep.

One afternoon, when they returned from the courtroom, Sandra said, "David, I think I should go back to San Francisco."

David looked at her in surprise. "Why? We're right in the middle of—Oh, my God." He put his arms around her. "The baby. Is it coming?"

Sandra smiled. "Anytime now. I'd feel safer if I were back there, closer to Dr. Bailey. Mother said she'd come and stay with me."

"Of course. You have to go back," David said. "I lost track of time. He's due in three weeks, isn't he?"

"Yes."

He grimaced. "And I can't be there with you."

Sandra took his hand. "Don't be upset, darling. This trial's going to be over soon."

"This goddamn trial is ruining our lives."

"David, we're going to be fine. My old job's waiting for me. After the baby comes, I can—"

David said, "I'm so sorry, Sandra. I wish—"

"David, don't ever be sorry for doing something you believe is right."

"I love you."

"I love you."

He stroked her stomach. "I love you both." He sighed. "All

right. I'll help you pack. I'll drive you back to San Francisco tonight and—"

"No," Sandra said firmly. "You can't leave here. I'll ask Emily to come and pick me up."

"Ask her if she can join us here for dinner tonight."

"All right."

Emily had been delighted. "Of course I'll come to pick you up." And she had arrived in San Jose two hours later.

The three of them had dinner that evening at Chai Jane.

"It's terrible timing," Emily said. "I hate to see you two away from each other right now."

"The trial's almost over," David said hopefully. "Maybe it will end before the baby comes."

Emily smiled. "We'll have a double celebration."

It was time to go. David held Sandra in his arms. "I'll talk to you every night," he said.

"Please don't worry about me. I'll be fine. I love you very much." Sandra looked at him and said, "Take care of yourself, David. You look tired."

It wasn't until Sandra left that David realized how utterly alone he was.

Court was in session.

Mickey Brennan rose and addressed the court. "I would like to call Dr. Lawrence Larkin as my next witness."

A distinguished gray-haired man was sworn in and took the stand.

"I want to thank you for being here, Dr. Larkin. I know your time is very valuable. Would you tell us a little about your background?"

"I have a successful practice in Chicago. I'm a past president of the Chicago Psychiatric Association."

"How many years have you been in practice, Doctor?"

"Approximately thirty years."

"And as a psychiatrist, I imagine you've seen many cases of multiple personality disorder?"

"No."

Brennan frowned. "When you say no, you mean you haven't seen a lot of them? Maybe a dozen?"

"I've never seen one case of multiple personality disorder."

Brennan looked at the jury in mock dismay, then back at the doctor. "In thirty years of working with mentally disturbed patients, you have never seen a *single* case of multiple personality disorder?"

"That's correct."

"I'm amazed. How do you explain that?"

"It's very simple. I don't think that multiple personality disorder exists."

"Well, I'm puzzled, Doctor. Haven't cases of multiple personality disorder been reported?"

Dr. Larkin snorted. "Being reported doesn't mean they're real. You see, what some doctors believe is MPD, they're confusing with schizophrenia, depressions and various other anxiety disorders."

"That's very interesting. So in your opinion, as an expert psychiatrist, you don't believe that multiple personality disorder even exists?"

"That is correct."

"Thank you, Doctor." Mickey Brennan turned to David. "Your witness."

David rose and walked over to the witness box. "You are a past president of the Chicago Psychiatric Association, Dr. Larkin?"

"Yes."

"You must have met a great many of your peers."

"Yes. I'm proud to say that I have."

"Do you know Dr. Royce Salem?"

"Yes. I know him very well."

"Is he a good psychiatrist?"

"Excellent. One of the best."

"Did you ever meet Dr. Clyde Donovan?"

"Yes. Many times."

"Would you say that he's a good psychiatrist?"

"I would use him"—a small chuckle—"if I needed one."

"And what about Dr. Ingram? Do you know him?"

"Ray Ingram? Indeed, I do. Fine man."

"Competent psychiatrist?"

"Oh, yes."

"Tell me, do all psychiatrists agree on every mental condition?"

"No. Of course we have some disagreements. Psychiatry is not an exact science."

"That's interesting, Doctor. Because Dr. Salem, Dr. Donovan and Dr. Ingram are going to come here and testify that they have treated cases of multiple personality disorder. Perhaps none of them is as competent as you are. That's all. Dismissed."

Judge Williams turned to Brennan. "Redirect?"

Brennan got to his feet and walked over to the witness box.

"Dr. Larkin, do you believe that because these other doctors disagree with your opinion about MPD that that makes them right and you wrong?"

"No. I could produce dozens of psychiatrists who don't believe in MPD."

"Thank you, Doctor. No more questions."

Mickey Brennan said, "Dr. Upton, we've heard testimony that sometimes what is thought to be multiple personality disorder is really confused with other disorders. What are the tests that prove multiple personality disorder isn't one of those other conditions?"

"There is no test."

Brennan's mouth dropped open in surprise as he glanced at the jury. "There *is* no test? Are you saying that there's *no* way to tell whether someone who claims he has MPD is lying or malingering or using it to excuse some crime he or she doesn't want to be held responsible for?"

"As I said, there is no test."

"So it's simply a matter of opinion? Some psychiatrists believe in it and some don't?"

"That's right."

"Let me ask you this, Doctor. If you hypnotize someone, surely you can tell whether they really have MPD or they're pretending to have it?"

Dr. Upton shook his head. "I'm afraid not. Even under hypnosis or with sodium amytal, there is no way of exposing someone if he or she is faking."

"That's very interesting. Thank you, Doctor. No more questions." Brennan turned to David. "Your witness."

David rose and walked over to the witness box. "Dr. Upton, have you ever had patients come to you, having been diagnosed by other doctors as having MPD?"

"Yes. Several times."

"And did you treat those patients?"

"No, I didn't."

"Why not?"

"I can't treat conditions that don't exist. One of the patients was an embezzler who wanted me to testify that he wasn't responsible because he had an alter who did it. Another patient was a housewife who was arrested for beating her children. She says that someone inside her made her do it. There were a few more like that with different excuses, but they were all trying to hide from something. In other words, they were faking."

"You seem to have a very definite opinion about this, Doctor."

"I do. I know I'm right."

David said, "You know you're right?"

"Well, I mean—"

"—that everyone else must be wrong? All the doctors who believe in MPD are all wrong?"

"I didn't mean that—"

"And you're the only one who's right. Thank you, Doctor. That's all."

Dr. Simon Raleigh was on the stand. He was a short, bald man in his sixties.

Brennan said, "Thank you for coming here, Doctor. You've had a long and illustrious career. You're a doctor, you're a professor, you went to school at—"

David stood up. "The defense will stipulate to the witness's distinguished background."

"Thank you." Brennan turned back to the witness. "Dr. Raleigh, what does *iatrogenicity* mean?"

"That's when there's an existing illness, and medical treatment of psychotherapy aggravates it."

"Would you be more specific, Doctor?"

"Well, in psychotherapy, very often the therapist influences the patient with his questions or attitude. He might make the patient feel that he has to meet the expectations of the therapist."

"How would that apply to MPD?"

"If the psychiatrist is questioning the patient about different personalities within him, the patient might make up some in order to please the therapist. It's a very tricky area. Amytal and hypnosis can mimic MPD in patients who are otherwise normal."

"So what you're saying is that under hypnosis the psychiatrist himself can alter the condition of the patient so that the patient believes something that is not true?''

"That has happened, yes."

"Thank you, Doctor." He looked at David. "Your witness."

David said, "Thank you." He rose and walked over to the witness box. David said disarmingly, "Your credentials are very impressive. You're not only a psychiatrist, but you teach at a university."

"Yes."

"How long have you been teaching, Doctor?"

"More than fifteen years."

"That's wonderful. How do you divide your time? By that I mean, do you spend half of your time teaching and the other half working as a doctor?"

"Now, I teach full-time."

"Oh? How long has it been since you actually practiced medicine?"

"About eight years. But I keep up on all the current medical literature."

"I have to tell you, I find that admirable. So you read up on everything. That's how you're so familiar with iatrogenicity?"

"Yes."

"And in the past, a lot of patients came to you claiming they had MPD?"

"Well, no . . ."

"Not a lot? In the years you were practicing as a doctor, would you say you had a dozen cases who claimed they had MPD?"

"No."

"Six?"

Dr. Raleigh shook his head.

"Four?"

There was no answer.

"Doctor, have you *ever* had a patient who came to you with MPD?"

"Well, it's hard to—"

"Yes or no, Doctor?"

"No."

"So all you really know about MPD is what you've read? No further questions."

*   *   *

The prosecution called six more witnesses, and the pattern was the same with each. Mickey Brennan had assembled nine top psychiatrists from around the country, all united in their belief that MPD did not exist.

The prosecution's case was winding to a close.

When the last witness on the prosecution's list had been excused, Judge Williams turned to Brennan. "Do you have any more witnesses to call, Mr. Brennan?"

"No, Your Honor. But I would like to show the jury police photographs of the death scenes from the murders of—"

David said furiously, "Absolutely not."

Judge Williams turned to David. "What did you say, Mr. Singer?"

"I said"—David caught himself—"objection. The prosecution is trying to inflame the jury by—"

"Objection overruled. The foundation was laid in a pretrial motion." Judge Williams turned to Brennan. "You may show the photographs."

David took his seat, furious.

Brennan walked back to his desk and picked up a stack of photographs and handed them out to the jurors. "These are not pleasant to look at, ladies and gentlemen, but this is what the trial is about. It's not about words or theories or excuses. It's not about mysterious alter egos killing people. It's about three real people who were savagely and brutally murdered. The law says that someone has to pay for those murders. It's up to each one of you to see that justice is done."

Brennan could see the horror on the faces of the jurors as they looked at the photographs.

He turned to Judge Williams. "The prosecution rests."

Judge Williams looked at her watch. "It's four o'clock. The court will recess for the day and begin again at ten o'clock Monday morning. Court adjourned."

Chapter Nineteen

ASHLEY Patterson was on the gallows being hanged, when a policeman ran up and said, "Wait a minute. She's supposed to be electrocuted."

The scene changed, and she was in the electric chair. A guard reached up to pull the switch, and Judge Williams came running in screaming, "No. We're going to kill her with a lethal injection."

David woke up and sat upright in bed, his heart pounding. His pajamas were wet with perspiration. He started to get up and was suddenly dizzy. He had a pounding headache, and he felt feverish. He touched his forehead. It was hot.

As David started to get out of bed, he was overcome by a wave of dizziness. "Oh, no," he groaned. "Not today. Not now."

This was the day he had been waiting for, the day the defense would begin to present its case. David stumbled into the bathroom and bathed his face in cold water. He looked in the mirror. "You look like hell."

When David arrived in court, Judge Williams was already on the bench. They were all waiting for him.

"I apologize for being late," David said. His voice was a croak. "May I approach the bench?"

"Yes."

David walked up to the bench, with Mickey Brennan close behind him. "Your Honor," David said, "I'd like to ask for a one-day stay."

"On what grounds?"

"I—I'm not feeling very well, Your Honor. I'm sure a doctor can give me something and tomorrow I'll be fine."

Judge Williams said, "Why don't you have your associate take over for you?"

David looked at her in surprise. "I don't have an associate."

"Why don't you, Mr. Singer?"

"Because . . ."

Judge Williams leaned forward. "I've never seen a murder trial conducted like this. You're a one-man show looking for glory, aren't you? Well, you won't find it in this court. I'll tell you something else. You probably think I should recuse myself because I don't believe in your devil-made-me-do-it defense, but I'm not recusing myself. We're going to let the jury decide whether they think your client is innocent or guilty. Is there anything else, Mr. Singer?"

David stood there looking at her, and the room was swimming. He wanted to tell her to go fuck herself. He wanted to get on his knees and beg her to be fair. He wanted to go home to bed. He said in a hoarse voice, "No. Thank you, Your Honor."

Judge Williams nodded. "Mr. Singer, you're on. Don't waste any more of this court's time."

David walked over to the jury box, trying to forget about his headache and fever. He spoke slowly.

"Ladies and gentlemen, you have listened to the prosecution ridiculing the facts of multiple personality disorder. I'm sure that Mr. Brennan wasn't being deliberately malicious. His statements were made out of ignorance. The fact is that he obviously knows nothing about multiple personality disorder, and the same is true of some of the witnesses he has put on the stand. But I'm going to have some people talk to you who *do* know about it. These are reputable doctors, who are experts in this problem. When you have heard their testimony, I'm sure that it will cast a whole different light on what Mr. Brennan has had to say.

"Mr. Brennan has talked about my client's guilt in committing these terrible crimes. That's a very important point. *Guilt.* For murder in the first degree to be proved, there must be not only a guilty act, but a guilty intention. I will show you that there was no guilty intention, because Ashley Patterson was not in control at the time the crimes occurred. She was totally unaware that they were taking place. Some eminent doctors are going to testify that

Ashley Patterson has two additional personalities, or alters, one of them a controlling one.''

David looked into the faces of the jurors. They seemed to be swaying in front of him. He squeezed his eyes shut for an instant.

"The American Psychiatric Association recognizes multiple personality disorder. So do prominent physicians around the world who have treated patients with this problem. One of Ashley Patterson's personalities committed murder, but it was a *personality*— an *alter*—over which she had no control.'' His voice was getting stronger. "To see the problem clearly, you must understand that the law does not punish an innocent person. So there is a paradox here. Imagine that a Siamese twin is being tried for murder. The law says that you cannot punish the guilty one because you would then have to punish the innocent one.'' The jury was listening intently.

David nodded toward Ashley. "In this case, we have not two but three personalities to deal with.''

He turned to Judge Williams. "I would like to call my first witness. Dr. Joel Ashanti.''

"Dr. Ashanti, where do you practice medicine?''

"At Madison Hospital in New York.''

"And did you come here at my request?''

"No. I read about the trial, and I wanted to testify. I've worked with patients who have multiple personality disorder, and I wanted to be helpful, if I could. MPD is much more common than the public realizes, and I want to try to clear up any misunderstandings about it.''

"I appreciate that, Doctor. In cases like these, is it usual to find a patient with two personalities or alters?''

"In my experience, people with MPD usually have many more alters, sometimes as many as a hundred.''

Eleanor Tucker turned to whisper something to Mickey Brennan. Brennan smiled.

"How long have you been dealing with multiple personality disorder, Dr. Ashanti?''

"For the past fifteen years.''

"In a patient with MPD, is there usually one alter who dominates?''

"Yes.''

Some of the jurors were making notes.

"And is the host—the person who has those personalities within him or her—aware of the other alters?"

"It varies. Sometimes some of the alters know all the other alters, sometimes they know only some of them. But the host is usually not aware of them, not until psychiatric treatment."

"That's very interesting. Is MPD curable?"

"Often, yes. It requires psychiatric treatment over long periods. Sometimes up to six or seven years."

"Have you ever been able to cure MPD patients?"

"Oh, yes."

"Thank you, Doctor."

David turned to study the jury for a moment. *Interested, but not convinced,* he thought.

He looked over at Mickey Brennan. "Your witness."

Brennan rose and walked over to the witness box. "Dr. Ashanti, you testified that you flew here all the way from New York because you wanted to be helpful?"

"That's correct."

"Your coming here couldn't have anything to do with the fact that this is a high-profile case and that the publicity would be beneficial to—"

David was on his feet. "Objection. Argumentative."

"Overruled."

Dr. Ashanti said calmly, "I stated why I came here."

"Right. Since you've been practicing medicine, Doctor, how many patients would you say you've treated for mental disorders?"

"Oh, perhaps two hundred."

"And of those cases, how many would you say suffered from multiple personality disorder?"

"A dozen . . ."

Brennan looked at him in feigned astonishment. "Out of two hundred patients?"

"Well, yes. You see—"

"What I don't see, Dr. Ashanti, is how you can consider yourself an expert if you've dealt with only those few cases. I would appreciate it if you would give us some evidence that would prove or disprove the existence of multiple personality disorder."

"When you say proof—"

"We're in a court of law, Doctor. The jury is not going to make decisions based on theory and 'what if.' What if, for example, the defendant hated the men she murdered, and after killing them, decided to use the excuse of an alter inside her so that she—''

David was on his feet. "Objection! That's argumentative and leading the witness."

"Overruled."

"Your Honor—"

"Sit down, Mr. Singer."

David glared at Judge Williams and angrily took his seat.

"So what you're telling us, Doctor, is that there's no evidence that will prove or disprove the existence of MPD?"

"Well, no. But—"

Brennan nodded. "That's all."

Dr. Royce Salem was on the witness stand.

David said, "Dr. Salem, you examined Ashley Patterson?"

"I did."

"And what was your conclusion?"

"Miss Patterson is suffering from MPD. She has two alters who call themselves Toni Prescott and Alette Peters."

"Does she have any control over them?"

"None. When they take over, she is in a state of fugue amnesia."

"Would you explain that, Dr. Salem?"

"Fugue amnesia is a condition where the victim loses consciousness of where he is, or what he is doing. It can last for a few minutes, days or sometimes weeks."

"And during that time would you say that that person is responsible for his or her actions?"

"No."

"Thank you, Doctor." He turned to Brennan. "Your witness."

Brennan said, "Dr. Salem, you are a consultant at several hospitals and you give lectures all around the world?"

"Yes, sir."

"I assume that your peers are gifted, capable doctors?"

"Yes, I would say they are."

"So, they all agree about multiple personality disorder?"

"No."

"What do you mean, no?"

"Some of them don't agree."

"You mean, they don't believe it exists?"

"Yes."

"But they're wrong and you're right?"

"I've treated patients, and I *know* that there is such a thing. When—"

"Let me ask you something. If there *were* such a thing as multiple personality disorder, would one alter always be in charge of telling the host what to do? The alter says, 'Kill,' and the host does it?"

"It depends. Alters have various degrees of influence."

"So the host *could* be in charge?"

"Sometimes, of course."

"The majority of times?"

"No."

"Doctor, where is the proof that MPD exists?"

"I have witnessed complete physical changes in patients under hypnosis, and I know—"

"And that's a basis of truth?"

"Yes."

"Dr. Salem, if I hypnotized you in a warm room and told you that you were at the North Pole naked in a snowstorm, would your body temperature drop?"

"Well, yes, but—"

"That's all."

David walked over to the witness stand. "Dr. Salem, is there any doubt in your mind that these alters exist in Ashley Patterson?"

"None. And they are absolutely capable of taking over and dominating her."

"And she would not be aware of it?"

"She would not be aware of it."

"Thank you."

"I would like to call Shane Miller to the stand." David watched him being sworn in. "What do you do, Mr. Miller?"

"I'm a supervisor at Global Computer Graphics Corporation."

"And how long have you worked there?"

"About seven years."

"And was Ashley Patterson employed there?"

"Yes."

"And did she work under your supervision?"

"She did."

"So you got to know her pretty well?"

"That's right."

"Mr. Miller, you've heard doctors testify that some of the symptoms of multiple personality disorder are paranoia, nervousness, distress. Have you ever noticed any of those symptoms in Miss Patterson?"

"Well, I—"

"Didn't Miss Patterson tell you that she felt someone was stalking her?"

"Yes. She did."

"And that she had no idea who it could be or why anyone would do that?"

"That's right."

"Didn't she once say that someone used her computer to threaten her with a knife?"

"Yes."

"And didn't things get so bad that you finally sent her to the psychologist who works at your company, Dr. Speakman?"

"Yes."

"So Ashley Patterson did exhibit the symptoms we're talking about?"

"That's right."

"Thank you, Mr. Miller." David turned to Mickey Brennan. "Your witness."

"How many employees do you have directly under you, Mr. Miller?"

"Thirty."

"And out of thirty employees, Ashley Patterson is the only one you've ever seen get upset?"

"Well, no . . ."

"Oh, really?"

"Everyone gets upset sometimes."

"You mean other employees had to go and see your company psychologist?"

"Oh, sure. They keep him pretty busy."

Brennan seemed impressed. "Is that so?"

"Yeah. A lot of them have problems. Hey, they're all human."

"No further questions."

"Redirect."

David approached the witness stand. "Mr. Miller, you said that some of the employees under you had problems. What kind of problems?"

"Well, it could be about an argument with a boyfriend or a husband. . . ."

"Yes?"

"Or it could be about a financial problem. . . ."

"Yes?"

"Or their kids bugging them. . . ."

"In other words, the ordinary kinds of domestic problems that any of us might face?"

"Yes."

"But no one went to see Dr. Speakman because they thought they were being stalked or because they thought someone was threatening to kill them?"

"No."

"Thank you."

The trial was recessed for lunch.

David got into his car and drove through the park, depressed. The trial was going badly. The doctors couldn't make up their minds whether MPD existed or not. *If they can't agree,* David thought, *how am I going to get a jury to agree? I can't let anything happen to Ashley. I can't.* He was approaching Harold's Café, a restaurant near the courthouse. He parked the car and went inside. The hostess smiled at him.

"Good afternoon, Mr. Singer."

He was famous. *Infamous?*

"Right this way, please." He followed her to a booth and sat down. The hostess handed him the menu, gave him a lingering smile and walked away, her hips moving provocatively. *The perks of fame,* David thought wryly.

He was not hungry, but he could hear Sandra's voice saying, "You have to eat to keep up your strength."

There were two men and two women seated in the booth next to him. One of the men was saying, "She's a hell of a lot worse than Lizzie Borden. Borden killed only two people."

The other man added, "And *she* didn't castrate them."

"What do you think they'll do to her?"

"Are you kidding? She'll get the death sentence."

"Too bad the Butcher Bitch can't get three death sentences."

That's the public speaking, David thought. He had the depressing feeling that if he walked around the restaurant, he would hear variations of the same comments. Brennan had built her up as a monster. He could hear Quiller's voice. *"If you don't put her on the stand, that's the image the jurors will carry in their minds when they go into the jury room to reach a verdict."*

I've got to take the chance. I've got to let the jurors see for themselves that Ashley's telling the truth.

The waitress was at his side. "Are you ready to order, Mr. Singer?"

"I've changed my mind," David said. "I'm not hungry." As he got up and walked out of the restaurant, he could feel baleful eyes following him. *I hope they're not armed,* David thought.

Chapter Twenty

WHEN David returned to the courthouse, he visited Ashley in her cell. She was seated on the little cot, staring at the floor.

"Ashley."

She looked up, her eyes filled with despair.

David sat next to her. "We have to talk."

She watched him, silent.

"These terrible things they're saying about you . . . none of them are true. But the jurors don't know that. They don't know you. We've got to let them see what you're really like."

Ashley looked at him and said dully, "What am I really like?"

"You're a decent human being who has an illness. They'll sympathize with that."

"What do you want me to do?"

"I want you to get on the witness stand and testify."

She was staring at him, horrified. "I—I can't. I don't know anything. I can't tell them anything."

"Let me handle that. All you have to do is answer my questions."

A guard came up to the cell. "Court's coming into session."

David rose and squeezed Ashley's hand. "It's going to work. You'll see."

"All rise. Court is now in session. The Honorable Judge Tessa Williams presiding in the case of *The People of the State of California Versus Ashley Patterson*."

Judge Williams took her seat on the bench.

David said, "May I approach the bench?"

"You may."

Mickey Brennan walked to the bench with David.

"What is it, Mr. Singer?"

"I'd like to call a witness who's not on the discovery list."

Brennan said, "It's awfully late in the trial to introduce new witnesses."

"I would like to call Ashley Patterson as my next witness."

Judge Williams said, "I don't—"

Mickey Brennan said quickly, "The state has no objection, Your Honor."

Judge Williams looked at the two attorneys. "Very well. You may call your witness, Mr. Singer."

"Thank you, Your Honor." He walked over to Ashley and held out his hand. "Ashley . . ."

She sat there in a panic.

"You must."

She rose, her heart palpitating, and slowly made her way to the witness stand.

Mickey Brennan whispered to Eleanor, "I was praying that he'd call her."

Eleanor nodded. "It's over."

Ashley Patterson was being sworn in by the court clerk. "You do solemnly swear to tell the truth, the whole truth and nothing but the truth, so help you God?"

"I do." Her voice was a whisper. Ashley took her seat in the witness box.

David walked over to her. He said gently, "I know this is very difficult for you. You've been accused of horrible crimes that you did not commit. All I want is for the jury to know the truth. Do you have any memory of committing any of those crimes?"

Ashley shook her head. "No."

David glanced at the jury, then went on. "Did you know Dennis Tibble?"

"Yes. We worked together at Global Computer Graphics Corporation."

"Did you have any reason to kill Dennis Tibble?"

"No." It was difficult for her to speak. "I—I went to his apartment to give him some advice that he had asked me for, and that was the last time I saw him."

"Did you know Richard Melton?"

"No . . ."

"He was an artist. He was murdered in San Francisco. The police found evidence of your DNA and fingerprints there."

Ashley was shaking her head from side to side. "I—I don't know what to say. I didn't know him!"

"You knew Deputy Sam Blake?"

"Yes. He was helping me. I didn't kill him!"

"Are you aware that you have two other personalities, or alters, within you, Ashley?"

"Yes." Her voice was strained.

"When did you learn this?"

"Before the trial. Dr. Salem told me about it. I couldn't believe it. I—I still can't believe it. It's—it's too awful."

"You had no previous knowledge of these alters."

"No."

"You had never heard of Toni Prescott or Alette Peters?"

"No!"

"Do you believe now that they exist within you?"

"Yes . . . I have to believe it. They must have done all these—these horrible things. . . ."

"So you have no recollection of ever having met Richard Melton, you had no motive for killing Dennis Tibble or for killing Deputy Sam Blake, who was at your apartment to protect you?"

"That's right." Her eyes swept over the crowded courtroom, and she felt a sense of panic.

"One last question," David said. "Have you ever been in trouble with the law?"

"Never."

David put his hand on hers. "That's all for now." He turned to Mickey Brennan. "Your witness."

Brennan rose, a big smile on his face. "Well, Miss Patterson, we finally get to talk to all of you. Did you ever, at any time, have sexual intercourse with Dennis Tibble?"

"No."

"Did you ever have sexual intercourse with Richard Melton?"

"No."

"Did you ever, at any time, have sexual intercourse with Deputy Samuel Blake?"

"No."

"That's very interesting." Brennan glanced at the jury. "Because traces of a vaginal discharge were found on the bodies of all three men. The DNA tests matched your DNA."

"I . . . I don't know anything about that."

"Maybe you've been framed. Maybe some fiend got hold of it—"

"Objection! It's argumentative."

"Overruled."

"—and planted it on those three mutilated bodies. Do you have any enemies who would do such a thing to you?"

"I . . . don't know."

"The FBI's fingerprint lab checked the fingerprints the police found at the scenes of the crimes. And I'm sure this will surprise you—"

"Objection."

"Sustained. Be careful, Mr. Brennan."

"Yes, Your Honor."

Satisfied, David slowly sat down.

Ashley was on the verge of hysteria. "The alters must have—"

"The fingerprints at the scenes of the three murders were yours, and yours alone."

Ashley sat there, silent.

Brennan walked over to a table, picked up a butcher knife wrapped in cellophane and held it up. "Do you recognize this?"

"It—it could be one of . . . one of my—"

"One of your knives? It is. It has already been admitted into evidence. The stains on it match the blood of Deputy Blake. Your fingerprints are on this murder weapon."

Ashley was mindlessly shaking her head from side to side.

"I've never seen a clearer case of cold-blooded murder or a more feeble defense. Hiding behind two nonexistent, imaginary characters is the most—"

David was on his feet again. "Objection."

"Sustained. I've already warned you, Mr. Brennan."

"Sorry, Your Honor."

Brennan went on. "I'm sure that the jury would like to meet the characters you're talking about. You are Ashley Patterson, correct?"

"Yes . . ."

"Fine. I would like to talk to Toni Prescott."

"I . . . I can't bring her out."

Brennan looked at her in surprise. "You *can't*? *Really*? Well, then, how about Alette Peters?"

Ashley shook her head despairingly. "I . . . I don't control them."

"Miss Patterson, I'm trying to help you," Brennan said. "I want to show the jury your alters who killed and mutilated three innocent men. Bring them out!"

"I . . . I can't." She was sobbing.

"You can't because they don't exist! You're hiding behind phantoms. You're the only one sitting in that box, and you're the only one who's guilty. They don't exist, but *you* do, and I'll tell you what else exists—irrefutable, undeniable proof that you murdered three men and cold-bloodedly emasculated them." He turned to Judge Williams. "Your Honor, the state rests."

David turned to look at the jury. They were all staring at Ashley and their faces were filled with repulsion.

Judge Williams turned to David. "Mr. Singer?"

David rose. "Your Honor, I would like permission to have the defendant hypnotized so that—"

Judge Williams said curtly, "Mr. Singer, I warned you before that I will not have this trial turned into a sideshow. You can't hypnotize her in *my* courtroom. The answer is no."

David said fiercely, "You *have* to let me do this. You don't know how important—"

"That's enough, Mr. Singer." Her voice was ice. "I'm citing you a second time for contempt. Do you want to reexamine the witness or don't you?"

David stood there, frustrated. "Yes, Your Honor." He walked over to the witness box. "Ashley, you know you're under oath?"

"Yes." She was taking deep breaths, fighting to control herself.

"And everything you've said is the truth as you know it?"

"Yes."

"You know that there are two alters in your mind and body and soul who you have no control over?"

"Yes."

"Toni and Alette?"

"Yes."

"You didn't commit any of those terrible murders?"

"No."

"One of them did, and you're not responsible."

Eleanor looked at Brennan questioningly, but he smiled and shook his head. "Let him hang himself," he whispered.

"Helen—" David stopped, white-faced at his slip. "I mean, Ashley . . . I want you to have Toni come out."

Ashley looked at David and shook her head helplessly. "I—I can't," she whispered.

David said, "Yes, you can. Toni is listening to us right now. She's enjoying herself, and why shouldn't she? She got away with three murders." He raised his voice. "You're very clever, Toni. Come on out and take a bow. No one can touch you. They can't punish you because Ashley is innocent, and they'd have to punish her to get at you."

Everyone in the courtroom was staring at David. Ashley sat there, frozen.

David moved closer to her. "Toni! Toni, can you hear me? I want you to come out. *Now!*"

He waited a moment. Nothing happened. He raised his voice. "Toni! Alette! Come out! Come on out. We all know you're in there!"

There was not a sound in the courtroom.

David lost control. He was yelling, "Come out. Show your faces. . . . *Damn it! Now! Now!*"

Ashley dissolved in tears.

Judge Williams said furiously, "Approach the bench, Mr. Singer."

Slowly, David walked over to the bench.

"Are you through badgering your client, Mr. Singer? I'm going to send a report of your behavior to the state bar association. You're a disgrace to your profession, and I'm going to recommend that you're disbarred."

David had no answer.

"Do you have any more witnesses to call?"

David shook his head defeated. "No, Your Honor."

It was over. He had lost. Ashley was going to die.

"The defense rests."

Joseph Kincaid was seated in the last row of the courtroom, watching, his face grim. He turned to Harvey Udell. "Get rid of him." Kincaid got up and left.

Udell stopped David as he was leaving the courtroom.

"David . . ."

"Hello, Harvey."

"Sorry about the way this turned out."

"It's not—"

"Mr. Kincaid hates to do this, but, well, he thinks it would be better if you didn't come back to the firm. Good luck."

The moment David stepped outside the courtroom, he was surrounded by television cameras and shouting reporters.

"Do you have a statement, Mr. Singer . . . ?"

"We hear Judge Williams says you're going to be disbarred. . . ."

"Judge Williams says she's going to hold you for contempt of court. Do you think you—?"

"The experts feel you've lost this case. Do you plan to appeal . . . ?"

"Our network legal experts say that your client will get the death penalty. . . ."

"Have you made any plans for the future . . . ?"

David got into his car without a word and drove away.

Chapter Twenty-one

H E rewrote the scenes in his mind, over and over again, endlessly.

I saw the news this morning, Dr. Patterson. I can't tell you how very sorry I am.
Yes. It's been quite a blow. I need your help, David.
Of course. Anything I can do.
I want you to represent Ashley.
I can't do that. I'm not a criminal defense lawyer. But I can recommend a great attorney, Jesse Quiller.
That will be fine. Thank you, David. . . .

You're an anxious young fellow, aren't you? Our meeting wasn't supposed to be until five o'clock. Well, I have good news for you. We're making you a partner.

You asked to see me?
Yes, Your Honor. They're talking about this trial on the Internet, and they've already convicted the defendant. This could seriously damage the defense. Therefore, I'm making a motion for a mistrial.
I think those are excellent grounds for a mistrial, Mr. Singer. I'm going to grant it. . . .

The bitter-tasting game of "what if." . . .

The following morning, the court was in session.

"Is the prosecution ready to make its closing argument?" Brennan stood up. He walked over to the jury box and looked at the jurors one by one.

"You're in a position to make history here. If you believe that the defendant is really a lot of different people and she's not responsible for what she's done, for the terrible crimes she committed, and you let her go, then you're saying that anybody can get away with murder by simply claiming that they didn't do it, that some mysterious alter ego did it. They can rob, rape and kill, and are they guilty? No. 'I didn't do it. My alter ego did it.' Ken or Joe or Suzy or whatever they want to call themselves. Well, I think you're all too intelligent to fall for that fantasy. The reality is in those photographs you looked at. Those people weren't murdered by any alter egos. They were all deliberately, calculatedly, cruelly murdered by the defendant sitting at that table, Ashley Patterson. Ladies and gentlemen of the jury, what the defense has tried to do in this court has been tried before. In *Mann Versus Teller,* the decision was that a finding of MPD does not, per se, require a finding of acquittal. In *United States Versus Whirley,* a nurse who murdered a baby pleaded that she had MPD. The court found her guilty.

"You know, I almost feel sorry for the defendant. All those characters living in that poor girl. I'm sure none of us would want a bunch of crazy strangers moving around inside us, would we? Going around murdering and castrating men. I'd be scared."

He turned to look at Ashley. "The defendant doesn't seem scared, does she? Not too scared to put on a pretty dress and comb her hair nicely and apply makeup. She doesn't seem scared at all. She thinks you're going to believe her story and let her go. No one can prove whether this multiple personality disorder really exists at all, so we're going to have to make our own judgments.

"The defense claims that these characters come out and take over. Let's see—there's Toni; she was born in England. And Alette; she was born in Italy. They're all the same person. They were just born in different countries at different times. Does that confuse you? I know it confuses me. I offered the defendant a chance to let us see her alters, but she didn't take me up on it. I wonder why? Could it be because they don't exist . . . ? Does California law recognize MPD as a mental condition? No. Colorado law? No. Mississippi? No. Federal law? No. As a matter of fact, *no* state has a law confirming MPD as a legal defense. And why? Because it *isn't* a defense. Ladies and gentlemen, it's a fictitious alibi to escape punishment. . . ."

"What the defense is asking you to believe is that there are two people inside the defendant, so no one bears any responsibility for her criminal actions. But there is only one defendant sitting in this courtroom—Ashley Patterson. We have proved beyond a shadow of a doubt that she is a murderer. But she claims she didn't commit the crimes. That was done by someone else, someone who borrowed her body to kill innocent people—her alters. Wouldn't it be wonderful if we all had alters, someone to carry out anything we secretly wanted done that society doesn't permit? Or maybe not. Would you like to live in a world where people could go around murdering others and say, 'You can't touch me, my alter did it' and 'You can't punish my alter because my alter is really me'?

"But this trial is not about some mythical characters who don't exist. The defendant, Ashley Patterson, is on trial for three vicious, cold-blooded murders, and the state is asking the death penalty. Thank you."

Mickey Brennan returned to his seat.

"Is the defense ready to present its closing argument?"

David rose. He walked to the jury box and looked into the faces of the jurors, and what he saw there was disheartening. "I know that this has been a very difficult case for all of us. You've heard experts testify that they've treated multiple personality disorder, and you've heard other experts testify that there is no such thing. You're not doctors, so no one expects you to make your judgment based on medical knowledge. I want to apologize to all of you if my behavior yesterday seemed boorish. I yelled at Ashley Patterson only because I wanted to force her alters to come out. I've talked to those alters. I know they exist. There really is an Alette and a Toni, and they can control Ashley anytime they want to. She has no knowledge of committing any murders.

"I told you at the beginning of this trial that for someone to be convicted of first-degree murder, there has to be physical evidence and a motive. There is no motive here, ladies and gentlemen. None. And the law says that the prosecution must prove a defendant is guilty beyond a reasonable doubt. I'm sure you'll agree that in this case, there *is* a reasonable doubt.

"As far as proof is concerned, the defense does not question it. There are Ashley Patterson's fingerprints and traces of DNA at each of the crime scenes. But the very fact that they are there should give us pause. Ashley Patterson is an intelligent young woman. If she committed a murder and did not want to be caught, would she have been stupid enough to leave her fingerprints at each one of the scenes? The answer is no.''

David went on for another thirty minutes. At the end, he looked at their faces and was not reassured. He sat down.

Judge Williams turned to the jurors. ''I want to instruct you now on the applicable law to this case. I want you to listen carefully.'' She talked for the next twenty minutes, detailing what was admissible and allowable by law.

''If you have any questions, or want any part of the testimony read back to you, the court reporter will do so. The jury is excused to go deliberate. Court is adjourned until they return with their verdict.''

David watched the jury file out of the box and into the jury room. *The longer the jurors take, the better our chances,* David thought.

The jurors returned forty-five minutes later.

David and Ashley watched as the jurors filed in and took their seats in the jury box. Ashley was stone-faced. David found that he was perspiring.

Judge Williams turned to the jury foreman. ''Have the jurors reached a verdict?''

''We have, Your Honor.''

''Would you please hand it to the bailiff.''

The bailiff carried the piece of paper to the judge. Judge Williams unfolded it. There was not a sound in the courtroom.

The bailiff returned the paper to the jury foreman.

''Would you read the verdict, please?''

In a slow, measured tone, he read, ''In the case of *The People of the State of California Versus Ashley Patterson,* we, the jury, in the above entitled action, find the defendant, Ashley Patterson, guilty of the murder of Dennis Tibble, a violation of Penal Code Section 187.''

There was a gasp in the courtroom. Ashley shut her eyes tightly.

''In the case of *The People of the State of California Versus Ashley Patterson,* we, the jury, in the above entitled action, find the defendant, Ashley Patterson, guilty of the murder of Deputy Samuel Blake, a violation of Penal Code Section 187.

"In the case of *The People of the State of California Versus Ashley Patterson,* we, the jury, in the above entitled action, find the defendant, Ashley Patterson, guilty of the murder of Richard Melton, a violation of Penal Code Section 187. We, the jury, in all the verdicts, further fix the degree at first degree."

David was finding it difficult to breathe. He turned to Ashley, but he had no words. He leaned over and put his arms around her.

Judge Williams said, "I would like to have the jury polled."

One by one, each juror stood up.

"Was the verdict read, your verdict?"

And when each one had affirmed it, Judge Williams said, "The verdict will be recorded and entered into the minutes." She went on. "I want to thank the jury for their time and service in this case. You're dismissed. Tomorrow the court will take up the issue of sanity."

David sat there, numb, watching Ashley being led away.

Judge Williams got up and walked to her chambers without looking at David. Her attitude told David more clearly than words what her decision was going to be in the morning. Ashley was going to be sentenced to die.

Sandra called from San Francisco. "Are you all right, David?"

He tried to sound cheerful. "Yes, I'm great. How are you feeling?"

"I'm fine. I've been watching the news on television. The judge wasn't fair to you. She can't have you disbarred. You were only trying to help your client."

He had no answer.

"I'm so sorry, David. I wish I were with you. I could drive down and—"

"No," David said. "We can't take any chances. Did you see the doctor today?"

"Yes."

"What did he say?"

"Very soon now. Any day."

Happy birthday, Jeffrey.

Jesse Quiller called.

"I bungled it," David said.

"Like hell you did. You got the wrong judge. What did you ever do to get her so down on you?"

David said, "She wanted me to plea-bargain. She didn't want this to go to trial. Maybe I should have listened to her."

All the television channels were full of the news of his disgrace. He watched one of the network's legal experts discussing the case. "I've never heard of a defending attorney screaming at his own client before. I must tell you, the courtroom was stunned. It was one of the most outrageous—"

David switched off the station. *Where did it all go wrong? Life is supposed to have a happy ending. Because I've bungled everything, Ashley's going to die, I'm going to be disbarred, the baby's going to be born any minute and I don't even have a job.*

He sat in his hotel room in the middle of the night, staring into the darkness. It was the lowest moment of his life. Playing over and over again in his mind was the final courtroom scene. *"You can't hypnotize her in my courtroom. The answer is no."*

If only she had let me hypnotize Ashley on the stand, I know she would have convinced the jury. Too late. It's all over now.

And a small, nagging voice in his mind said, *Who says it's over? I don't hear the fat lady singing.*

There's nothing more I can do.

Your client is innocent. Are you going to let her die?

Leave me alone.

Judge Williams's words kept echoing in his mind. *"You can't hypnotize her in my courtroom."*

And three words kept repeating themselves—*in my courtroom."*

At five o'clock in the morning, David made two excited, urgent phone calls. As he finished, the sun was just beginning to appear over the horizon. *It's an omen,* David thought. *We're going to win.*

A little later, David hurried into an antiques store.

The clerk approached him. "May I help you, sir?" He recognized David. "Mr. Singer."

"I'm looking for a folding Chinese screen. Do you have something like that?"

"Yes, we do. We don't have any real antique screens, but—"

"Let's see what you have."

"Certainly." He led David over to the section where there were several Chinese folding screens. The clerk pointed to the first one. "Now, this one—"

"That's fine," David said.

"Yes, sir. Where shall I send it?"

"I'll take it with me."

David's next stop was at a hardware store, where he bought a Swiss Army knife. Fifteen minutes later, he was walking into the lobby of the courthouse carrying the screen. He said to the guard at the desk, "I made arrangements to interview Ashley Patterson. I have permission to use Judge Goldberg's chambers. He's not here today."

The guard said, "Yes, sir. It's all set. I'll have the defendant brought up. Dr. Salem and another man are already up there, waiting."

"Thank you."

The guard watched David carry the Chinese screen into the elevator. *Crazy as a loon,* he thought.

Judge Goldberg's chamber was a comfortable-looking room with a desk facing the window, a swivel chair, and near one wall a couch and several chairs. Dr. Salem and another man were standing in the room when David entered.

"Sorry I'm late," David said.

Dr. Salem said, "This is Hugh Iverson. He's the expert you asked for."

The two men shook hands. "Let's get set up fast," David said. "Ashley's on her way here."

He turned to Hugh Iverson and pointed to a corner of the room. "How's that for you?"

"Fine."

He watched Iverson go to work. A few minutes later, the door opened and Ashley entered with a guard.

"I'll have to stay in the room," the guard said.

David nodded. "That's all right." He turned to Ashley. "Sit down, please."

He watched her take a seat. "First of all, I want to tell you how terribly sorry I am about the way things went."

She nodded, almost dazed.

"But it's not over yet. We still have a chance."

She looked at him with disbelieving eyes.

"Ashley, I would like Dr. Salem to hypnotize you again."

"No. What's the point in—"

"Do it for me. Will you?"

She shrugged.

David nodded to Dr. Salem.

Dr. Salem said to Ashley, "We've done this before, so you know that all you have to do is close your eyes and relax. Just relax. Feel all the muscles in your body letting go of all the tension. All you want to do is sleep. You're getting very drowsy...."

Ten minutes later, Dr. Salem looked at David and said, "She's completely under."

David moved toward Ashley, and his heart was pounding. "I want to talk to Toni."

There was no reaction.

David raised his voice. "Toni. I want you to come out. Do you hear me? Alette ... I want you both to talk to me."

Silence.

David was yelling now. "What's the matter with you? Are you too frightened? That's what happened in the courtroom, isn't it? Did you hear what the jury said? Ashley's guilty. You were afraid to come out. You're a coward, Toni!"

They looked at Ashley. There was no reaction. David looked at Dr. Salem in despair. It was not going to work.

"Court is now in session. The Honorable Judge Tessa Williams presiding."

Ashley was seated at the defendant's table next to David. David's hand was wrapped in a large bandage.

David rose. "May I approach the bench, Your Honor?"

"You may."

David walked toward the bench. Brennan followed him.

David said, "I would like to present new evidence to this case."

"Absolutely not," Brennan objected.

Judge Williams turned to him and said, "Let me make that decision, Mr. Brennan." She turned back to David. "The trial is over. Your client has been convicted and—"

"This concerns the insanity plea," David said. "All I'm asking for is ten minutes of your time."

Judge Williams said angrily, "Time doesn't mean much to you, does it, Mr. Singer? You have already wasted a great deal of everyone's time." She made her decision. "All right. I hope this is the last request you'll ever be able to make in a court of law. The court is recessed for ten minutes."

David and Brennan followed the judge to her chambers.

She turned to David. "I'm giving you your ten minutes. What is it, Counselor?"

"I want to show you a piece of film, Your Honor."

Brennan said, "I don't see what this has to do with—"

Judge Williams said to Brennan, "I don't, either." She turned to David. "You now have nine minutes."

David hurried over to the door leading to the hallway and opened it. "Come in."

Hugh Iverson walked in, carrying a sixteen-millimeter projector and a portable screen. "Where should I set it up?"

David pointed to a corner of the room. "Over there."

They watched as the man set up the equipment and plugged in the projector.

"May I pull down the shades?" David asked.

It was all Judge Williams could do to hold back her anger. "Yes, you go right ahead, Mr. Singer." She looked at her watch. "You have seven minutes."

The projector was turned on. Judge Goldberg's chambers flickered onto the screen. David and Dr. Salem were watching Ashley, who was seated in a chair.

On the screen, Dr. Salem said, "She's completely under."

David walked up to Ashley. "I want to talk to Toni. . . . Toni, I want you to come out. Do you hear me? Alette . . . I want you both to talk to me."

Silence.

Judge Williams sat there, her face tight, watching the film.

David was yelling now. "What's the matter with you? Are you too frightened? That's what happened in the courtroom, isn't it? Did you hear what the jury said? Ashley's guilty. You were afraid to come out. You're a coward, Toni!"

Judge Williams got to her feet. "I've had enough of this! I've seen this disgusting performance before. Your time is up, Mr. Singer."

"Wait," David said. "You haven't—"

"It's finished," Judge Williams told him and started for the door.

Suddenly, a song began to fill the room.

"A penny for a spool of thread.
A penny for a needle.

That's the way the money goes,
Pop! goes the weasel."

Puzzled, Judge Williams turned around. She looked at the picture on the screen.

Ashley's face had completely changed. It was Toni.

Toni said angrily, "Too frightened to come out in court? Did you really think I would come out just because you ordered me to? What do you think I am, a trained pony?"

Judge Williams slowly moved back into the room, staring at the film.

"I listened to all those bloody gits making fools of themselves." She mimicked one of their voices. " 'I don't think that multiple personality disorder exists.' What idiots. I've never seen such—"

As they watched, Ashley's face changed again. She seemed to relax in her chair, and her face took on a shy look. In her Italian accent, Alette said, "Mr. Singer, I know you did the best you could. I wanted to appear in court and help you, but Toni wouldn't let me."

Judge Williams was watching, her face blank.

The face and voice changed again. "You're bleeding right I wouldn't," Toni said.

David said, "Toni, what do you think is going to happen to you if the judge gives Ashley the death sentence?"

"She's not going to give her the death sentence. Ashley didn't even know one of the men. Remember?"

David said, "But Alette knew them all. You committed those murders, Alette. You had sex with those men and then you stabbed them to death and castrated them. . . ."

Toni said, "You bloody idiot! You don't know anything, do you? Alette would never have had the nerve to do that. *I* did it. They deserved to die. All they wanted to do was have sex." She was breathing hard. "But I made them all pay for it, didn't I? And no one can ever prove I did it. Let little Miss Goody Two-shoes take the blame. We'll all go to a nice cozy asylum and—"

In the background, behind the Chinese screen in the corner, there was a loud click.

Toni turned. "What was that?"

"Nothing," David said quickly. "It was just—"

Toni rose and started running toward the camera until her face filled the screen. She pushed against something, and the scene tilted; part of the folding Chinese screen fell into the picture. A small hole had been cut in the center.

"You've got a fucking camera behind here," Toni screamed. She turned to David. "You son of a bitch, what are you trying to do? You tricked me!"

On the desk was a letter opener. Toni grabbed it and lunged at David, screaming, "I'm going to kill you. I'm going to kill you!"

David tried to hold her, but he was no match for her. The letter opener sliced into his hand.

Toni raised her arm to strike again, and the guard ran to her and tried to grab her. Toni knocked him to the floor. The door opened and a uniformed officer ran in. When he saw what was happening, he lunged at Toni. She kicked him in the groin, and he went down. Two more officers came running in. It took three of them to pin Toni to the chair, and all the time she was yelling and screaming at them.

Blood was pouring from David's hand. He said to Dr. Salem, "For God's sake, wake her up."

Dr. Salem said, "Ashley . . . Ashley . . . listen to me. You're going to come out now. Toni is gone. It's safe to come out now, Ashley. I'm going to count to three."

And as the group watched, Ashley's body became quiet and relaxed.

"Can you hear me?"

"Yes." It was Ashley's voice, sounding far away.

"You'll awaken at the count of three. One . . . two . . . three . . . How do you feel?"

Her eyes opened. "I feel so tired. Did I say anything?"

The screen in Judge Williams's office went blank. David walked over to the wall and turned on the lights.

Brennan said, "Well! What a performance. If they were giving out Oscars for the best—"

Judge Williams turned to him. "Shut up."

Brennan looked at her, in shock.

There was a momentary silence. Judge Williams turned to David. "Counselor."

"Yes?"

There was a pause. "I owe you an apology."

Seated on the bench, Judge Tessa Williams said, "Both counsels have agreed that they will accept the opinion of a psychiatrist who has already examined the defendant, Dr. Salem. The decision of this court is that the defendant is not guilty by reason of insanity. She will be ordered to a mental health facility, where she can be treated. The court is now adjourned.''

David stood up, drained. *It's over*, he thought. *It's finally over.* He and Sandra could start living their lives again.

He looked at Judge Williams and said happily, "We're having a baby.''

Dr. Salem said to David, "I would like to make a suggestion. I'm not sure it can be done, but if you can arrange it, I think it would be helpful to Ashley.''

"What is it?''

"The Connecticut Psychiatric Hospital back east has handled more cases of MPD than any other place in the country. A friend of mine, Dr. Otto Lewison, is in charge of it. If you could arrange for the court to have Ashley sent there, I think it would be very beneficial.''

"Thanks,'' David said. "I'll see what I can do.''

Dr. Steven Patterson said to David, "I—I don't know how to thank you.''

David smiled. "You don't have to. It was quid pro quo. Remember?''

"You did a brilliant job. For a while I was afraid—''

"So was I.''

"But justice has been served. My daughter's going to be cured.''

"I'm sure of it,'' David said. "Dr. Salem suggested a psychiatric hospital in Connecticut. Their doctors are trained in MPD.''

Dr. Patterson was silent for a moment. "You know, Ashley didn't deserve any of this. She's such a beautiful person.''

"I agree. I'll talk to Judge Williams and try to get the transfer.''

Judge Williams was in her chambers. "What can I do for you, Mr. Singer?''

"I'd like to ask a favor.''

She smiled. "I hope I can grant it. What is it?''

David explained to the judge what Dr. Salem had told him.

"Well, that's a rather unusual request. We have some fine psychiatric facilities right here in California.''

David said, "All right. Thank you, Your Honor." He turned to leave, disappointed.

"I haven't said no, Mr. Singer." David stopped. "It's an unusual request, but this has been an unusual case."

David waited.

"I think I can arrange for her to be transferred."

"Thank you, Your Honor. I appreciate it."

In her cell, Ashley thought, *They've sentenced me to death. A long death in an asylum filled with crazy people. It would have been kinder to kill me now.* She thought of the endless, hopeless years ahead of her, and she began to sob.

The cell door opened, and her father came in. He stood there a moment, looking at her, his face filled with anguish.

"Honey . . ." He sat down opposite her. "You're going to live," he said.

She shook her head. "I don't want to live."

"Don't say that. You have a medical problem, but it can be cured. And it's going to be. When you're better, you're going to come and live with me, and I'll take care of you. No matter what happens, we'll always have each other. They can't take that away from us."

Ashley sat there, saying nothing.

"I know how you're feeling right now, but believe me, that's going to change. My girl is going to come home to me, cured." He slowly got to his feet. "I'm afraid I have to get back to San Francisco." He waited for Ashley to say something.

She was silent.

"David told me that he thinks you're going to be sent to one of the best psychiatric centers in the world. I'll come and visit you. Would you like that?"

She nodded, dully. "Yes."

"All right, honey." He kissed her on the cheek and gave her a hug. "I'm going to see to it that you have the best care in the world. I want my little girl back."

Ashley watched her father leave, and she thought, *Why can't I die now? Why won't they let me die?*

One hour later, David came to see her.

"Well, we did it," he said. He looked at her in concern. "Are you all right?"

"I don't want to go to an insane asylum. I want to die. I can't stand living like this. Help me, David. Please help me."

"Ashley, you're going to get help. The past is over. You have a future now. The nightmare is going to be finished." He took her hand. "Look, you've trusted me this far. Keep trusting me. You're going to live a normal life again."

She sat there, silent.

"Say 'I believe you, David.' "

She took a deep breath. "I—I believe you, David."

He grinned. "Good girl. This is a new beginning for you."

The moment the ruling was made public, the media went crazy. Overnight, David was a hero. He had taken an impossible case and won it.

He called Sandra. "Honey, I—"

"I know, darling. I know. I just saw it on television. Isn't it wonderful? I'm so proud of you."

"I can't tell you how glad I am that it's over. I'll be coming back tonight. I can't wait to see—"

"David . . . ?"

"Yes?"

"David . . . oooh . . ."

"Yes? What's wrong, honey?"

". . . Oooh . . . We're having a baby. . . ."

"Wait for me!" David shouted.

Jeffrey Singer weighed eight pounds, ten ounces, and was the most beautiful baby David had ever seen.

"He looks just like you, David," Sandra said.

"He does, doesn't he?" David beamed.

"I'm glad everything turned out so well," Sandra said.

David sighed. "There were times when I wasn't so sure."

"I never doubted you."

David hugged Sandra and said, "I'll be back, honey. I have to clean out my things at the office."

When David arrived at the offices of Kincaid, Turner, Rose & Ripley, he was greeted warmly.

"Congratulations, David . . ."

"Good job . . ."

"You really showed them. . . ."

David walked into his office. Holly was gone. David started cleaning out his desk.

"David—"

David turned around. It was Joseph Kincaid.

Kincaid walked up to him and said, "What are you doing?"

"I'm cleaning out my office. I was fired."

Kincaid smiled. "Fired? Of course not. No, no, no. There was some kind of a misunderstanding." He beamed. "We're making you a partner, my boy. In fact, I've set up a press conference for you here this afternoon at three o'clock."

David looked at him. "Really?"

Kincaid nodded. "Absolutely."

David said, "You'd better cancel it. I've decided to go back into criminal law. I've been offered a partnership by Jesse Quiller. At least when you're dealing with that part of the law, you know who the criminals really are. So, Joey, baby, you take your partnership and shove it where the sun don't shine."

And David walked out of the office.

Jesse Quiller looked around the penthouse and said, "This is great. It really becomes you two."

"Thank you," Sandra said. She heard a sound from the nursery. "I'd better check on Jeffrey." She hurried off to the next room.

Jesse Quiller walked over to admire a beautiful sterling silver picture frame with Jeffrey's first photograph already in it. "This is lovely. Where did it come from?"

"Judge Williams sent it."

Jesse said, "I'm glad to have you back, partner."

"I'm glad to be back, Jesse."

"You'll probably want a little time to relax now. Rest up a little. . . ."

"Yes. We thought we'd take Jeffrey and drive up to Oregon to visit Sandra's parents and—"

"By the way, an interesting case came into the office this morning, David. This woman is accused of murdering her two children. I have a feeling she's innocent. Unfortunately, I'm going to Washington on another case, but I thought that you might just talk to her and see what you think. . . ."

Book Three

Chapter Twenty-two

THE Connecticut Psychiatric Hospital, fifteen miles north of Westport, was originally the estate of Wim Boeker, a wealthy Dutchman, who built the house in 1910. The forty lush acres contained a large manor house, a workshop, stable and swimming pool. The state had bought the property in 1925 and had refitted the manor house to accommodate a hundred patients. A tall chain-link fence had been erected around the property, with a manned guard post at the entrance. Metal bars had been placed on all the windows, and one section of the house had been fortified as a security area to hold dangerous inmates.

In the office of Dr. Otto Lewison, head of the psychiatric clinic, a meeting was taking place. Dr. Gilbert Keller and Dr. Craig Foster were discussing a new patient who was about to arrive.

Gilbert Keller was a man in his forties, medium height, blond hair and intense gray eyes. He was a renowned expert on multiple personality disorder.

Otto Lewison, the superintendent of the Connecticut Psychiatric Hospital, was in his seventies, a neat, dapper little man with a full beard and pince-nez glasses.

Dr. Craig Foster had worked with Dr. Keller for years and was writing a book on multiple personality disorder. All were studying Ashley Patterson's records.

Otto Lewison said, "The lady has been busy. She's only twenty-eight and she's murdered five men." He glanced at the paper again. "She also tried to murder her attorney."

"Everyone's fantasy," Gilbert Keller said dryly.

Otto Lewison said, "We're going to keep her in security ward A until we can get a full evaluation."

"When is she arriving?" Dr. Keller asked.

The voice of Dr. Lewison's secretary came over the intercom. "Dr. Lewison, they're bringing Ashley Patterson in. Would you like to have them bring her into your office?"

"Yes, please." Lewison looked up. "Does that answer your question?"

The trip had been a nightmare. At the end of her trial, Ashley Patterson had been taken back to her cell and held there for three days while arrangements were made to fly her back east.

A prison bus had driven her to the airport in Oakland, where a plane was waiting for her. It was a converted DC-6, part of the huge National Prisoner Transportation System run by the U.S. Marshals Service. There were twenty-four prisoners aboard, all manacled and shackled.

Ashley was wearing handcuffs, and when she sat down, her feet were shackled to the bottom of the seat.

Why are they doing this to me? I'm not a dangerous criminal. I'm a normal woman. And a voice inside her said, *Who murdered five innocent people.*

The prisoners on the plane were hardened criminals, convicted of murder, rape, armed robbery and a dozen other crimes. They were on their way to top security prisons around the country. Ashley was the only woman on board.

One of the convicts looked at her and grinned. "Hi, baby. How would you like to come over and warm up my lap?"

"Cool it," a guard warned.

"Hey! Don't you have any romance in your soul? This bitch ain't going to get laid for—What's your sentence, baby?"

Another convict said, "Are you horny, honey? How about me movin' into the seat next to you and slippin' you—?"

Another convict was staring at Ashley. "Wait a minute!" he said. "That's the broad who killed five men and castrated them."

They were all looking at Ashley now.

That was the end of the badgering.

On the way to New York, the plane made two landings to discharge or pick up passengers. It was a long flight, the air was turbulent and by the time they landed at La Guardia Airport, Ashley was airsick.

Two uniformed police officers were waiting for her on the tarmac when the plane landed. She was unshackled from the plane seat and shackled again in the interior of a police van. She had never felt so humiliated. The fact that she felt so normal made it all the more unbearable. Did they think she was going to try to escape or murder someone? All that was over, in the past. Didn't they know that? She was sure it would never happen again. She wanted to be away from there. Anywhere.

Sometime during the long, dreary drive to Connecticut, she dozed off. She was awakened by a guard's voice.

"We're here."

They had reached the gates of the Connecticut Psychiatric Hospital.

When Ashley Patterson was ushered into Dr. Lewison's office, he said, "Welcome to Connecticut Psychiatric Hospital, Miss Patterson."

Ashley stood there, pale and silent.

Dr. Lewison made the introductions and held out a chair. "Sit down, please." He looked at the guard. "Take off the handcuffs and shackles."

The restraints were removed, and Ashley took a seat.

Dr. Foster said, "I know this must be very difficult for you. We're going to do everything we can to make it as easy as possible. Our goal is to see that one day you will leave this place, cured."

Ashley found her voice. "How—how long could that take?"

Otto Lewison said, "It's too soon to answer that yet. If you *can* be cured, it could take five or six years."

Each word hit Ashley like a thunderbolt. *"If you* can *be cured, it could take five or six years. . . ."*

"The therapy is nonthreatening. It will consist of a combination of sessions with Dr. Keller—hypnotism, group therapy, art therapy. The important thing to remember is that we're not your enemies."

Gilbert Keller was studying her face. "We're here to help you, and we want you to help us do that."

There was nothing more to say.

Otto Lewison nodded to the attendant, and he walked over to Ashley and took her arm.

Craig Foster said, "He'll take you to your quarters now. We'll talk again later."

When Ashley had left the room, Otto Lewison turned to Gilbert Keller. "What do you think?"

"Well, there's one advantage. There are only two alters to work on."

Keller was trying to remember. "What's the most we've had?"

"The Beltrand woman—ninety alters."

Ashley had not known what to expect, but somehow she had envisioned a dark, dreary prison. The Connecticut Psychiatric Hospital was more like a pleasant clubhouse—with metal bars.

As the attendant escorted Ashley through the long, cheerful corridors, Ashley watched the inmates freely walking back and forth. There were people of every age, and all of them seemed normal. *Why are they here?* Some of them smiled at her and said, "Good morning," but Ashley was too bewildered to answer. Everything seemed surreal. She was in an insane asylum. *Am I insane?*

They reached a large steel door that closed off a part of the building. There was a male attendant behind the door. He pressed a red button and the huge door opened.

"This is Ashley Patterson."

The second attendant said, "Good morning, Miss Patterson." They made everything seem so normal. *But nothing is normal anymore*, Ashley thought. *The world is upside down.*

"This way, Miss Patterson." He walked her to another door and opened it. Ashley stepped inside. Instead of a cell, she was looking at a pleasant, medium-size room with pastel blue walls, a small couch and a comfortable-looking bed.

"This is where you'll be staying. They'll be bringing your things in a few minutes."

Ashley watched the guard leave and close the door behind him. *This is where you'll be staying.*

She began to feel claustrophobic. *What if I don't want to stay? What if I want to get out of here?*

She walked over to the door. It was locked. Ashley sat down

on the couch, trying to organize her thoughts. She tried to concentrate on the positive. *We're going to try to cure you.*
We're going to try to cure you.
We're going to cure you.

Chapter Twenty-three

DR. Gilbert Keller was in charge of Ashley's therapy. His specialty was treating multiple personality disorder, and while he had had failures, his success rate was high. In cases like this, there were no easy answers. His first job was to get the patient to trust him, to feel comfortable with him, and then to bring out the alters, one by one, so that in the end they could communicate with one another and understand why they existed, and finally, why there was no more need for them. That was the moment of blending, when the personality states came together as a single entity.

We're a long way from that, Dr. Keller thought.

The following morning, Dr. Keller had Ashley brought to his office. "Good morning, Ashley."

"Good morning, Dr. Keller."

"I want you to call me Gilbert. We're going to be friends. How do you feel?"

She looked at him and said, "They tell me I've killed five people. How should I feel?"

"Do you remember killing any of them?"

"No."

"I read the transcript of your trial, Ashley. You didn't kill them. One of your alters did. We're going to get acquainted with your alters, and in time, with your help, we'll make them disappear."

"I—I hope you can—"

"I can. I'm here to help you, and that's what I'm going to do. The alters were created in your mind to save you from an unbearable pain. We have to find out what caused that pain. I need to find out when those alters were born and why."

"How—how do you do that?"

"We'll talk. Things will come to you. From time to time, we'll use hypnotism or Sodium Amytal. You've been hypnotized before, haven't you?"

"Yes."

"No one's going to pressure you. We're going to take our time." He added reassuringly, "And when we're through, you're going to be well."

They talked for almost an hour. At the end of that time, Ashley felt much more relaxed. Back in her room, she thought, *I really think he can do it.* And she said a little prayer.

Dr. Keller had a meeting with Otto Lewison. "We talked this morning," Dr. Keller said. "The good news is that Ashley admits she has a problem, and she's willing to be helped."

"That's a beginning. Keep me informed."

"I will, Otto."

Dr. Keller was looking forward to the challenge ahead of him. There was something very special about Ashley Patterson. He was determined to help her.

They talked every day, and a week after Ashley arrived, Dr. Keller said, "I want you to be comfortable and relaxed. I'm going to hypnotize you." He moved toward her.

"No! Wait!"

He looked at her, surprised. "What's the matter?"

A dozen terrible thoughts flashed through Ashley's head. He was going to bring out her alters. She was terrified of the idea. "Please," she said. "I—I don't want to meet them."

"You won't," Dr. Keller assured her. "Not yet."

She swallowed. "All right."

"Are you ready?"

She nodded. "Yes."

"Good. Here we go."

It took fifteen minutes to hypnotize her. When she was under, Gilbert Keller glanced at a piece of paper on his desk. *Toni Prescott and Alette Peters.* It was time for switching, the process of changing from one dominating personality state to another.

He looked at Ashley, asleep in her chair, then leaned forward. "Good morning, Toni. Can you hear me?"

He watched Ashley's face transform, taken over by an entirely different personality. There was a sudden vivacity in her face. She began to sing:

> *"Half a pound of tupenny rice,*
> *Half a pound of treacle,*
> *Mix it up and make it nice,*
> *Pop! goes the weasel . . ."*

"That was very nice, Toni. I'm Gilbert Keller."

"I know who you are," Toni said.

"I'm glad to meet you. Did anyone ever tell you that you have a beautiful singing voice?"

"Sod off."

"I mean it. Did you ever take singing lessons? I'll bet you did."

"No, I didn't. As a matter of fact, I wanted to, but my"—*For God's sakes, will you stop that terrible noise! Whoever told you you could sing?*—"never mind."

"Toni, I want to help you."

"No, you don't, Dockie baby. You want to lay me."

"Why do you think that, Toni?"

"That's all you bloody men ever want to do. Ta."

"Toni . . . ? Toni . . . ?"

Silence.

Gilbert Keller looked at Ashley's face again. It was serene. Dr. Keller leaned forward. "Alette?"

There was no change in Ashley's expression.

"Alette . . . ?"

Nothing.

"I want to speak to you, Alette."

Ashley began to stir uneasily.

"Come out, Alette."

Ashley took a deep breath, and then there was a sudden explosion of words spoken in Italian.

"*C'è qualcuno che parla Italiano?*"

"Alette—"

"*Non so dove mi travo.*"

"Alette, listen to me. You're safe. I want you to relax."

"*Mi sento stanca. . . .* I'm tired."

"You've been through a terrible time, but all that is behind you.

Your future is going to be very peaceful. Do you know where you are?''

His voice was white.

"*Sì*. It's some kind of place for people who are *pazzo*." *That's why you're here, Doctor. You're the crazy one.*

"It's a place where you're going to be cured. Alette, when you close your eyes and visualize this place, what comes to your mind?''

"Hogarth. He painted insane asylums and scenes that are terrifying." *You're too ignorant ever to have heard of him.*

"I don't want you to think of this place as terrifying. Tell me about yourself, Alette. What do you like to do? What would you like to do while you're here?''

"I like to paint.''

"We'll have to get you some paints.''

"No!''

"Why?''

"I don't want to." *"What do you call that, child? It looks like an ugly blob to me."*

Leave me alone.

"Alette?" Gilbert Keller watched Ashley's face change again. Alette was gone. Dr. Keller awakened Ashley.

She opened her eyes and blinked. "Have you started?''

"We've finished.''

"How did I do?''

"Toni and Alette talked to me. We've made a good beginning, Ashley.''

The letter from David Singer read:

Dear Ashley,

Just a note to let you know that I'm thinking about you and hoping that you're making good progress. As a matter of fact, I think about you often. I feel as though we've gone through the wars together. It was a tough fight, but we won. And I have good news. I've been assured that the murder charges against you in Bedford and Quebec will be dropped. If there is anything I can do for you, let me know.

Warmest wishes,
David

The following morning, Dr. Keller was talking to Toni while Ashley was under hypnosis.

"What is it now, Dockie?"

"I just want to have a little chat with you. I'd like to help you."

"I don't need your bloody help. I'm doing fine."

"Well, I need *your* help, Toni. I want to ask you a question. What do you think of Ashley?"

"Miss *Tight Ass*? Don't get me started."

"You don't like her?"

"In spades."

"What don't you like about her?"

There was a pause. "She tries to keep everybody from having fun. If I didn't take over once in a while, our lives would be boring. *Boring*. She doesn't like to go to parties or travel or do any fun things."

"But you do?"

"You bet I do. That's what life's all about, isn't it, luv?"

"You were born in London, weren't you, Toni? Do you want to tell me about it?"

"I'll tell you one thing. I wish I were there now."

Silence.

"Toni . . . ? Toni . . . ?"

She was gone.

Gilbert Keller said to Ashley, "I'd like to speak to Alette." He watched the expression on Ashley's face change. He leaned forward and said softly, "Alette."

"*Sì.*"

"Did you hear my conversation with Toni?"

"Yes."

"Do you and Toni know each other?"

"Yes." *Of course we do, stupid.*

"But Ashley doesn't know either of you?"

"No."

"Do you like Ashley?"

"She's all right." *Why are you asking me all these foolish questions?*

"Why don't you talk to her?"

"Toni does not want me to."

"Does Toni always tell you what to do?"

"Toni is my friend." *It's none of your business.*

"I want to be your friend, Alette. Tell me about yourself. Where were you born?"

"I was born in Rome."

"Did you like Rome?"

Gilbert Keller watched the expression on Ashley's face change, and she began to weep.

Why? Dr. Keller leaned forward and said soothingly, "It's all right. You're going to awaken now, Ashley. . . ."

She opened her eyes.

"I talked to Toni and Alette. They're friends. I want you all to be friends."

While Ashley was at lunch, a male nurse walked into her room and saw a painting of a landscape on the floor. He studied it a moment, then took it to Dr. Keller's office.

There was a meeting in Dr. Lewison's office.

"How's it going, Gilbert?"

Dr. Keller said thoughtfully, "I've talked to the two alters. The dominant one is Toni. She has an English background and won't talk about it. The other one, Alette, was born in Rome, and she doesn't want to talk about it, either. So that's where I'm going to concentrate. That's where the traumas occurred. Toni is the more aggressive one. Alette is sensitive and withdrawn. She's interested in painting, but she's afraid to pursue it. I have to find out why."

"So you think Toni dominates Ashley?"

"Yes. Toni takes over. Ashley wasn't aware that she exists, or for that matter, that Alette existed. But Toni and Alette know each other. It's interesting. Toni has a lovely singing voice, and Alette is a talented painter." He held up the painting that the male nurse had brought him. "I think their talents may be the key to getting through to them."

Ashley received a letter from her father once a week. After she read them, she would sit in her room quietly, not wanting to talk to anyone.

"They're her only link to home," Dr. Keller said to Otto Lewison. "I think it increases her desire to get out of here and start leading a normal life. Every little bit helps. . . ."

Ashley was becoming used to her surroundings. The patients seemed to walk about, although there were attendants at every door and in the corridors. The gates to the grounds were always locked. There was a recreation room where they could gather and watch television, a gymnasium where inmates could work out and a common dining room. There were many kinds of people there: Japanese, Chinese, French, Americans. . . . Every effort had been made to make the hospital as ordinary-looking as possible, but when Ashley went to her room, the doors were always locked behind her.

"This isn't a hospital," Toni complained to Alette. "It's a bloody prison."

"But Dr. Keller thinks he can cure Ashley. Then we can get out of here."

"Don't be stupid, Alette. Don't you see? The only way he can cure Ashley is to get rid of us, make us disappear. In other words, to cure her, we have to die. Well, I'm not going to let that happen."

"What are you going to do?"

"I'm going to find a way for us to escape."

Chapter Twenty-four

THE following morning a male nurse was escorting Ashley back to her room. He said, "You seem different today."

"Do I, Bill?"

"Yeah. Almost like another person."

Toni said softly, "That's because of you."

"What do you mean?"

"You make me feel different." She touched his arm and looked into his eyes. "You make me feel wonderful."

"Come on."

"I mean it. You're very sexy. Do you know that?"

"No."

"Well, you are. Are you married, Bill?"

"I was, once."

"Your wife was mad to ever let you go. How long have you worked here, Bill?"

"Five years."

"That's a long time. Do you ever feel you want to get out of here?"

"Sometimes, sure."

Toni lowered her voice. "You know there's nothing really wrong with me. I admit I had a little problem when I came in, but I'm cured now. I'd like to get out of here, too. I'll bet you could help me. The two of us could leave here together. We'd have a wonderful time."

He studied her a moment. "I don't know what to say."

"Yes, you do. Look how simple it would be. All you have to do is let me out of here one night when everyone's asleep, and we'll be on our way." She looked over at him and said softly, "I'll make it worth your while."

He nodded. "Let me think about it."

"You do that," Toni said confidently.

When Toni returned to the room, she said to Alette, "We're getting out of this place."

The following morning, Ashley was escorted into Dr. Keller's office.

"Good morning, Ashley."

"Good morning, Gilbert."

"We're going to try some Sodium Amytal this morning. Have you ever had it?"

"No."

"Well, you'll find it's very relaxing."

Ashley nodded. "All right. I'm ready."

Five minutes later, Dr. Keller was talking to Toni. "Good morning, Toni."

"Hi, Dockie."

"Are you happy here, Toni?"

"It's funny you should ask that. To tell you the truth, I'm really beginning to like this place. I feel at home here."

"Then why do you want to escape?"

Toni's voice hardened. "What?"

"Bill tells me that you asked him to help you escape from here."

"That son of a bitch!" There was fury in her voice. She flew out of the chair, ran over to the desk, picked up a paperweight and flung it at Dr. Keller's head.

He ducked.

"I'll kill you, and I'll kill him!"

Dr. Keller grabbed her. "Toni—"

He watched the expression on Ashley's face change. Toni had gone. He found that his heart was pounding.

"Ashley!"

When Ashley awakened, she opened her eyes, looked around, puzzled, and said, "Is everything all right?"

"Toni attacked me. She was angry because I found out she was trying to escape."

"I—I'm sorry. I had a feeling that something bad was happening."

"It's all right. I want to bring you and Toni and Alette together.''

"No!''

"Why not?''

"I'm afraid. I—I don't want to meet them. Don't you understand? They're not *real.* They're my imagination.''

"Sooner or later, you're going to have to meet them, Ashley.
You have to get to know one another. It's the only way you're
going to be cured.''

Ashley stood up. "I want to go back to my room.''

When she was returned to her room, Ashley watched the attendant
leave. She was filled with a deep sense of despair. She thought,
*I'm never going to get out of here. They're lying to me. They can't
cure me.* She could not face the reality that other personalities were
living inside of her. . . . Because of them, people had been murdered, families destroyed. *Why me, God?* She began to weep. *What
did I ever do to you?* She sat down on the bed and thought, *I can't
go on like this. There's only one way to end it. I have to do it
now.*

She got up and walked around the small room, looking for
something sharp. There was nothing. The rooms had been carefully
designed so that there was nothing in them that would allow the
patients to harm themselves.

As her eyes darted around the room, she saw the paints and
canvas and paintbrushes and walked over to them. The handles
of the paintbrushes were wooden. Ashley snapped one in half,
exposing sharp, jagged edges. Slowly, she took the sharp edge
and placed it on her wrist. In one fast, deep movement, she cut
into her veins and her blood began to pour out. Ashley placed
the jagged edge on her other wrist and repeated the movement.
She stood there, watching the blood stain the carpet. She began
to feel cold. She dropped to the floor and curled up into a fetal
position.

And then the room went dark.

When Dr. Gilbert Keller heard the news, he was shocked. He went
to visit Ashley in the infirmary. Her wrists were heavily bandaged.
Watching her lying there, Dr. Keller thought, *I can't ever let this
happen again.*

"We almost lost you," he said. "It would have made me look bad."

Ashley managed a wry smile. "I'm sorry. But everything seems so—so hopeless."

"That's where you're wrong," Dr. Keller assured her. "Do you want to be helped, Ashley?"

"Yes."

"Then you have to believe in me. You have to work with me. I can't do it alone. What do you say?"

There was a long silence. "What do you want me to do?"

"First, I want a promise from you that you'll never try to harm yourself again."

"All right. I promise."

"I'm going to get the same promise now from Toni and Alette. I'm going to put you to sleep now."

A few minutes later, Dr. Keller was speaking to Toni.

"That selfish bitch tried to kill us all. She thinks only about herself. Do you see what I mean?"

"Toni—"

"Well, I'm not having it. I—"

"Will you be quiet and listen to me?"

"I'm listening."

"I want you to promise that you'll never harm Ashley."

"Why should I promise?"

"I'll tell you why. Because you're part of her. You were born out of her pain. I don't know yet what you've had to go through, Toni, but I know that it must have been terrible. But you have to realize that she went through the same thing, and Alette was born for the same reason as you. The three of you have a lot in common. You should help each other, not hate each other. Will you give me your word?"

Nothing.

"Toni?"

"I suppose so," she said grudgingly.

"Thank you. Do you want to talk about England now?"

"No."

"Alette. Are you there?"

"Yes." *Where do you think I am, stupid?*

"I want you to make me the same promise that Toni did. Promise never to harm Ashley."

That's the only one you care about, isn't it? Ashley, Ashley, Ashley. What about us?
"Alette?"
"Yes. I promise."

The months were going by, and there were no signs of progress. Dr. Keller sat at his desk, reviewing notes, recalling sessions, trying to find a clue to what was wrong. He was taking care of half a dozen other patients, but he found that it was Ashley he was most concerned about. There was such an incredible chasm between her innocent vulnerability and the dark forces that were able to take over her life. Every time he talked to Ashley, he had an overpowering urge to try to protect her. *She's like a daughter to me,* he thought. *Who am I kidding? I'm falling in love with her.*

Dr. Keller went to see Otto Lewison. "I have a problem, Otto."
"I thought that was reserved for our patients."
"This involves one of our patients. Ashley Patterson."
"Oh?"
"I find that I'm—I'm very attracted to her."
"Reverse transference?"
"Yes."
"That could be very dangerous for both of you, Gilbert."
"I know."
"Well, as long as you're aware of it . . . Be careful."
"I intend to."

NOVEMBER
I gave Ashley a diary this morning.

"I want you and Toni and Alette to use this, Ashley. You can keep it in your room. Anytime that any of you has any thoughts or ideas that you prefer to write down instead of talking to me, just put them down."
"All right, Gilbert."
A month later, Dr. Keller wrote in his diary:

DECEMBER
The treatment is at a standstill. Toni and Alette refuse to discuss the past. It is becoming more difficult to persuade Ashley to undergo hypnosis.

MARCH
The diary is still blank. I'm not sure whether the most resistance is coming from Ashley or Toni. When I do hypnotize Ashley, Toni and Alette come out very briefly. They are adamant about not discussing the past.

JUNE
I meet with Ashley regularly, but I feel there's no progress. The diary is still untouched. I have given Alette an easel and a set of paints. I am hoping that if she begins to paint, there may be a breakthrough.

JULY
Something happened, but I'm not sure if it's a sign of progress. Alette painted a beautiful picture of the hospital grounds. When I complimented her on it, she seemed pleased. That evening the painting was torn to shreds.

Dr. Keller and Otto Lewison were having coffee.

"I think I'm going to try a little group therapy," Dr. Keller said. "Nothing else seems to be working."

"How many patients did you have in mind?"

"Not more than half a dozen. I want her to start interacting with other people. Right now she's living in a world of her own. I want her to break out of that."

"Good idea. It's worth a try."

Dr. Keller led Ashley into a small meeting room. There were six people in the room.

"I want you to meet some friends," Dr. Keller said.

He took Ashley around the room introducing them, but Ashley was too self-conscious to listen to their names. One name blurred into the next. There was Fat Woman, Bony Man, Bald Woman, Lame Man, Chinese Woman and Gentle Man. They all seemed very pleasant.

"Sit down," Bald Woman said. "Would you like some coffee?"

Ashley took a seat. "Thank you."

"We've heard about you," Gentle Man said. "You've been through a lot."

Ashley nodded.

Bony Man said, "I guess we've all been through a lot, but we're being helped. This place is wonderful."

"They have the best doctors in the world," Chinese Woman said.

They all seem so normal, Ashley thought.

Dr. Keller sat to one side, monitoring the conversations. Forty-five minutes later he rose. "I think it's time to go, Ashley."

Ashley stood up. "It was nice meeting all of you."

Lame Man walked up to her and whispered, "Don't drink the water here. It's poisoned. They want to kill us and still collect the money from the state."

Ashley gulped. "Thanks. I'll—I'll remember."

As Ashley and Dr. Keller walked down the corridor, she said, "What are their problems?"

"Paranoia, schizophrenia, MPD, compulsive disorders. But, Ashley, their improvement since they came here has been remarkable. Would you like to chat with them regularly?"

"No."

Dr. Keller walked into Otto Lewison's office.

"I'm not getting anywhere," he confessed. "The group therapy didn't work, and the hypnotism sessions aren't working at all. I want to try something different."

"What?"

"I need your permission to take Ashley to dinner off the grounds."

"I don't think that's a good idea, Gilbert. It could be dangerous. She's already—"

"I know. But right now I'm the enemy. I want to become a friend."

"Her alter, Toni, tried to kill you once. What if she tries again?"

"I'll handle it."

Dr. Lewison thought about it. "All right. Do you want someone to go with you?"

"No. I'll be fine, Otto."

"When do you want to start this?"

"Tonight."

* * *

"You want to take me out to dinner?"

"Yes. I think it would be good for you to get away from this place for a while, Ashley. What do you say?"

"Yes."

Ashley was surprised at how excited she was at the thought of going out to dinner with Gilbert Keller. *It will be fun to get out of here for an evening,* Ashley thought. But she knew that it was more than that. The thought of being with Gilbert Keller on a date was exhilarating.

They were having dinner at a Japanese restaurant called Otani Gardens, five miles from the hospital. Dr. Keller knew that he was taking a risk. At any moment, Toni or Alette could take over. He had been warned. *It's more important that Ashley learns to trust me so that I can help her.*

"It's funny, Gilbert," Ashley said, looking around the crowded restaurant.

"What is?"

"These people don't look any different from the people at the hospital."

"They aren't really different, Ashley. I'm sure they all have problems. The only difference is the people at the hospital aren't able to cope with them as well, so we help them."

"I didn't know I had any problems until— Well, you know."

"Do you know why, Ashley? Because you buried them. You couldn't face what happened to you, so you built the fences in your mind and shut the bad things away. To one degree or another, a lot of people do that." He deliberately changed the subject. "How's your steak?"

"Delicious, thank you."

From then on, Ashley and Dr. Keller had meals away from the hospital once a week. They had lunch at an excellent little Italian restaurant called Banducci's and dinners at The Palm, Eveleene's and The Gumbo Pot. Neither Toni nor Alette made an appearance.

One night, Dr. Keller took Ashley dancing. It was at a small nightclub with a wonderful band.

"Are you enjoying yourself?" he asked.

"Very much. Thank you." She looked at him and said, "You're not like other doctors."

"They don't dance?"

"You know what I mean."

He was holding her close, and both of them felt the urgency of the moment.

"That could be very dangerous for both of you, Gilbert. . . ."

Chapter Twenty-five

"**I** know what the bloody hell you're trying to do, Dockie.
You're trying to make Ashley think you're her friend."

"I am her friend, Toni, and yours."

"No, you're not. You think she's great, and I'm nothing."

"You're wrong. I respect you and Alette as much as I respect
Ashley. You're all equally important to me."

"Is that true?"

"Yes. Toni, when I told you that you had a beautiful singing
voice, I meant it. Do you play an instrument?"

"Piano."

"If I could arrange for you to use the piano in the recreation
hall so you can play and sing, would you be interested?"

"I might be." She sounded excited.

Dr. Keller smiled. "Then I'll be happy to do it. It will be there
for you to use."

"Thanks."

Dr. Keller arranged for Toni to have private access to the recreation room for one hour every afternoon. In the beginning, the
doors were closed, but as other inmates heard the piano music and
the singing from inside, they opened the door to listen. Soon, Toni
was entertaining dozens of patients.

Dr. Keller was looking over his notes with Dr. Lewison.

Dr. Lewison said, "What about the other one—Alette?"

"I've set it up for her to paint in the garden every afternoon.
She'll be watched, of course. I think it's going to be good therapy."

*   *   *

But Alette refused. In a session with her, Dr. Keller said, "You don't use the paints I gave you, Alette. It's a shame to let them go to waste. You're so talented."

How would you know?

"Don't you enjoy painting?"

"Yes."

"Then why don't you do it?"

"Because I'm no good." *Stop pestering me.*

"Who told you that?"

"My—my mother."

"We haven't talked about your mother. Do you want to tell me about her?"

"There's nothing to tell."

"She died in an accident, didn't she?"

There was a long pause. "Yes. She died in an accident."

The following day, Alette started to paint. She enjoyed being in the garden with her canvas and brushes. When she painted, she was able to forget everything else. Some of the patients would gather around her and watch. They talked in multicolored voices.

"Your paintings should be in a gallery." Black.

"You're really good." Yellow.

"Where did you learn to do that?" Black.

"Can you paint a picture of me sometime?" Orange.

"I wish *I* knew how to do that." Black.

She was always sorry when her time was up and she had to go back into the big building.

"I want you to meet someone, Ashley. This is Lisa Garrett." She was a woman in her fifties, small and wraithlike. "Lisa is going home today."

The woman beamed. "Isn't that wonderful? And I owe it all to Dr. Keller."

Gilbert Keller looked at Ashley and said, "Lisa suffered from MPD and had thirty alters."

"That's right, dear. And they're all gone."

Dr. Keller said pointedly, "She's the third MPD patient leaving us this year."

And Ashley felt a surge of hope.

*   *   *

Alette said, "Dr. Keller is sympathetic. He really seems to like us."

"You're bloody stupid," Toni scoffed. "Don't you see what's happening? I told you once. He's pretending to like us so we'll do what he wants us to do. And do you know what that is? He wants to bring us all together, luv, and then convince Ashley that she doesn't need us. And do you know what happens then? You and I die. Is that what you want? I don't."

"Well, no," Alette said hesitantly.

"Then listen to me. We go along with the doctor. We make him believe that we're really trying to help him. We string him along. We're in no hurry. And I promise you that one day I'll get us out of here."

"Whatever you say, Toni."

"Good. So we'll let old Dockie think he's doing just great."

A letter arrived from David. In the envelope was a photograph of a small boy. The letter read:

Dear Ashley,

I hope that you're coming along well and that the therapy is progressing. Everything's fine here. I'm working hard and enjoying it. Enclosed is a photograph of our two-year-old, Jeffrey. At the rate he's growing, in a few minutes, he'll be getting married. There's no real news to report. I just wanted you to know that I was thinking about you.

Sandra joins me in sending our warm regards,

David

Ashley studied the photograph. *He's a beautiful little boy,* she thought. *I hope he has a happy life.*

She went to lunch, and when she returned, the photograph was on the floor of her room, torn to bits.

June 15, 1:30 P.M.

Patient: Ashley Patterson. Therapy session using Sodium Amytal. Alter, Alette Peters.

"Tell me about Rome, Alette."

"It's the most beautiful city in the world. It's filled with great museums. I used to visit all of them." *What would you know about museums?*

"And you wanted to be a painter?"

"Yes." *What did you think I wanted to be, a firefighter?*
"Did you study painting?"
"No, I didn't." *Can't you go bother someone else?*
"Why not? Because of what your mother told you?"
"Oh, no. I just decided that I wasn't good enough." *Toni, get him away from me!*
"Did you have any traumas during that period? Did any terrible things happen to you that you can recall?"
"No. I was very happy." *Toni!*

August 15, 9:00 A.M.
Patient: Ashley Patterson. Hypnotherapy session with alter, Toni Prescott.
"Do you want to talk about London, Toni?"
"Yes. I had a lovely time there. London is so civilized. There's so much to do there."
"Did you have any problems?"
"Problems? No. I was very happy in London."
"Nothing bad happened there at all that you remember?"
"Of course not." *What are you going to make of that, you willy?*

Each session brought back memories to Ashley. When she went to bed at night, she dreamed that she was at Global Computer Graphics. Shane Miller was there, and he was complimenting her on some work she had done. *"We couldn't get along without you, Ashley. We're going to keep you here forever."* Then the scene shifted to a prison cell, and Shane Miller was saying, *"Well, I hate to do this now, but under the circumstances, the company is terminating you. Naturally, we can't afford to be connected with anything like this. You understand, don't you? There's nothing personal in this."*
In the morning, when Ashley awakened, her pillow was wet with tears.

Alette was saddened by the therapy sessions. They reminded her of how much she missed Rome and how happy she had been with Richard Melton. *We could have had such a happy life together, but now it is too late. Too late.*

*   *   *

Toni hated the therapy sessions because they brought back too many bad memories for her, too. Everything she had done had been to protect Ashley and Alette. But did anybody appreciate her? No. She was locked away as though she were some kind of criminal. *But I'll get out of here,* Toni promised herself. *I'll get out of here.*

The pages of the calendar were wiped away by time, and another year came and went. Dr. Keller was getting more and more frustrated.

"I've read your latest report," Dr. Lewison told Gilbert Keller. "Do you think there's a genuine lacuna, or are they playing games?"

"They're playing games, Otto. It's as though they know what I'm trying to do, and they won't let me. I think Ashley genuinely wants to help, but they won't allow her to. Usually under hypnosis you can get through to them, but Toni is very strong. She takes complete control, and she's dangerous."

"Dangerous?"

"Yes. Imagine how much hatred she must have in her to murder and castrate five men."

The rest of the year went no better.

Dr. Keller was having success with his other patients, but Ashley, the one he was most concerned about, was making no progress. Dr. Keller had a feeling that Toni enjoyed playing games with him. She was determined that he was not going to succeed. And then, unexpectedly, there was a breakthrough.

It started with another letter from Dr. Patterson.

June 5
   Dear Ashley,
   I'm on my way to New York to take care of some business, and I would like very much to stop by and see you. I will call Dr. Lewison, and if there's no objection, you can expect me around the 25th.
   Much love,
   Father

Three weeks later, Dr. Patterson arrived with an attractive, dark-haired woman in her early forties and her three-year-old daughter, Katrina.

They were ushered into Dr. Lewison's office. He rose as they entered. "Dr. Patterson, I'm delighted to meet you."

"Thank you. This is Miss Victoria Aniston and her daughter, Katrina."

"How do you do, Miss Aniston? Katrina."

"I brought them along to meet Ashley."

"Wonderful. She's with Dr. Keller right now, but they should be finished soon."

Dr. Patterson said, "How is Ashley doing?"

Otto Lewison hesitated. "I wonder if I could speak to you alone for a few minutes?"

"Certainly."

Dr. Patterson turned to Victoria and Katrina. "It looks like there's a beautiful garden out there. Why don't you wait for me, and I'll join you with Ashley."

Victoria Aniston smiled. "Fine." She looked over at Otto Lewison. "It was nice to meet you, Doctor."

"Thank you, Miss Aniston."

Dr. Patterson watched the two of them leave. He turned to Otto Lewison. "Is there a problem?"

"I'll be frank with you, Dr. Patterson. We're not making as much progress as I had hoped we would. Ashley says she wants to be helped, but she's not cooperating with us. In fact, she's fighting the treatment."

Dr. Patterson was studying him, puzzled. "Why?"

"It's not that unusual. At some stage, patients with MPD are afraid of meeting their alters. It terrifies them. The very thought that other characters can be living in their mind and body and take over at will— Well, you can imagine how devastating that can be."

Dr. Patterson nodded. "Of course."

"There's something that puzzles us about Ashley's problem. Almost always, these problems start with a history of molestation when the patient is very young. We have no record of anything like that in Ashley's case, so we have no idea how or why this trauma began."

Dr. Patterson sat there silently for a moment. When he spoke, he said heavily, "I can help you." He took a deep breath. "I blame myself."

Otto Lewison was watching intently.

"It happened when Ashley was six. I had to go to England. My wife couldn't go. I took Ashley with me. My wife had an elderly cousin over there named John. I didn't realize it at the time, but John had . . . emotional problems. I had to leave to give a lecture one day, and John offered to baby-sit. When I got back that evening, he was gone. Ashley was in a state of complete hysteria. It took a long, long time to calm her down. After that, she wouldn't let anyone come near her, she became timid and withdrawn and a week later, John was arrested as a serial child molester." Dr. Patterson's face was filled with pain. "I never forgave myself. I never left Ashley alone with anyone after that."

There was a long silence. Otto Lewison said, "I'm terribly sorry. But I think you've given us the answer to what we've been looking for, Dr. Patterson. Now Dr. Keller will have something specific to work on."

"It's been too painful for me even to discuss before."

"I understand." Otto Lewison looked at his watch. "Ashley's going to be a little while. Why don't you join Miss Aniston in the garden, and I'll send Ashley out when she comes."

Dr. Patterson rose. "Thank you. I will."

Otto Lewison watched him leave. He could not wait to tell Dr. Keller what he had learned.

Victoria Aniston and Katrina were waiting for him. "Did you see Ashley?" Victoria asked.

"They'll send her out in a few minutes," Dr. Patterson said. He looked around the spacious grounds. "This is lovely, isn't it?"

Katrina ran up to him, "I want to go up to the sky again."

He smiled. "All right." He picked her up, threw her into the air and caught her as she came down.

"Higher!"

"Hang on. Here we go." He threw her up again and caught her, and she was screaming with delight.

"Again!"

Dr. Patterson's back was to the main building, so he did not see Ashley and Dr. Keller come out.

"Higher!" Katrina screamed.

Ashley stopped in the doorway, frozen. She watched her father playing with the little girl, and time seemed to fragment. Everything after that happened in slow motion.

There were flashes of a little girl being thrown into the air. . . . "Higher, Papa!"
"Hang on. Here we go."
And then the girl being tossed onto a bed . . .
A voice saying, "You'll like this. . . ."
An image of the man getting into bed beside her. The little girl was screaming, "Stop it. No. Please, no."
The man was in the shadow. He was holding her down, and he was stroking her body. "Doesn't that feel good?"

And suddenly the shadow lifted, and Ashley could see the man's face. It was her father.

Looking at him now, in the garden, playing with the little girl, Ashley opened her mouth and began to scream, and could not stop.

Dr. Patterson, Victoria Aniston and Katrina turned around, startled.

Dr. Keller said quickly, "I'm terribly sorry. This is a bad day. Could you come back another time?" And he carried Ashley inside.

They had her in one of the emergency rooms.

"Her pulse is abnormally high," Dr. Keller said. "She's in a fugue state." He moved close to her and said, "Ashley, you have nothing to be frightened about. You're safe here. No one's going to hurt you. Just listen to my voice and relax . . . relax . . . relax. . . ."

It took half an hour. "Ashley, tell me what happened. What upset you?"

"Father and the little girl . . ."

"What about them?"

It was Toni who answered. "She can't face it. She's afraid he's going to do to the little girl what he did to her."

Dr. Keller stared at her a moment. "What—what did he do to her?"

It was in London. She was in bed. He sat down next to her and said, "I'm going to make you very happy, baby," and began tickling her, and she was laughing. And then . . . he took her pajamas off, and he started playing with her. "Don't my hands feel good?" Ashley started screaming, "Stop it. Don't do that." But he wouldn't stop. He held her down and went on and on. . . .

Dr. Keller asked, "Was that the first time it happened, Toni?"

"Yes."

"How old was Ashley?"

"She was six."

"And that's when you were born?"

"Yes. Ashley was too terrified to face it."

"What happened after that?"

"Father came to her every night and got into bed with her." The words were pouring out now. "She couldn't stop him. When they got home, Ashley told Mother what happened, and Mother called her a lying little bitch.

"Ashley was afraid to go to sleep at night because she knew Papa was going to come to her room. He used to make her touch him and then play with himself. And he said to her, 'Don't tell anyone about this or I won't love you anymore.' She couldn't tell anyone. Mama and Papa were yelling at each other all the time, and Ashley thought it was her fault. She knew she had done something wrong, but she didn't know what. Mama hated her."

"How long did this go on?" Dr. Keller asked.

"When I was eight . . ." Toni stopped.

"Go on, Toni."

Ashley's face changed, and it was Alette sitting in the chair. She said, "We moved to Roma, where he did research at Policlinico Umberto Primo."

"And that's where you were born?"

"Yes. Ashley couldn't stand what happened one night, so I came to protect her."

"What happened, Alette?"

"Papa came into her room while she was asleep, and he was naked. And he crawled into her bed, and this time he forced himself inside her. She tried to stop him, but she couldn't. She begged him never to do it again, but he came to her every night. And he always said, 'This is how a man shows a woman he loves her, and you're my woman, and I love you. You must never tell anyone about this.' And she could never tell anyone."

Ashley was sobbing, tears running down her cheeks.

It was all Gilbert Keller could do not to take her in his arms and hold her and tell her that he loved her and everything was going to be all right. But, of course, it was impossible. *I'm her doctor.*

When Dr. Keller returned to Dr. Lewison's office, Dr. Patterson, Victoria Aniston and Katrina had left.

"Well, this is what we've been waiting for," Dr. Keller told Otto Lewison. "We finally got a breakthrough. I know when Toni and Alette were born and why. We should see a big change from now on."

Dr. Keller was right. Things began to move.

Chapter Twenty-six

THE hypnotherapy session had begun. Once Ashley was under, Dr. Keller said, "Ashley, tell me about Jim Cleary."

"I loved Jim. We were going to run away together and get married."

"Yes . . . ?"

"At the graduation party, Jim asked me if I would go to his house with him, and I . . . I said no. When he brought me home, my father was waiting up for us. He was furious. He told Jim to get out and stay out."

"What happened then?"

"I decided to go to Jim. I packed a suitcase and I started toward his house." She hesitated. "Halfway to his house, I changed my mind and I went back home. I—"

Ashley's expression started to change. She began to relax in her chair, and it was Toni sitting there.

"Like hell she did. She went to his house, Dockie."

When she reached Jim Cleary's house, it was dark. "My folks will be away for the weekend." *Ashley rang the doorbell. A few minutes later, Jim Cleary opened the door. He was in his pajamas.*

"Ashley." His face lit up in a grin. "You decided to come." He pulled her inside.

"I came because I—"

"I don't care why you came. You're here." He put his arms around her and kissed her. "How about a drink?"

"No. Maybe some water." She was suddenly appre-hensive.

"Sure. Come on." He took her hand and led her into the kitchen. He

*poured a glass of water for her and watched her drink it. "You look ner-
vous."*

"I—I am."

*"There's nothing to be nervous about. There's no chance that my folks
will come back. Let's go upstairs."*

"Jim, I don't think we should."

*He came up behind her, his arms reaching for her breasts. She turned.
"Jim . . ."*

*His lips were on hers, and he was forcing her against the kitchen
counter.*

*"I'm going to make you happy, honey." It was her father saying, "I'm
going to make you happy, honey."*

*She froze. She felt him pulling her clothes off and entering her as she
stood there naked, silently screaming.*

And the feral rage took over.

*She saw the large butcher knife sticking out of a wooden block. She
picked it up and began stabbing him in the chest, screaming, "Stop it,
Father. . . . Stop it . . . Stop it . . . Stop it. . . ."*

*She looked down, and Jim was lying on the floor, blood spurting out of
him.*

*"You animal," she screamed. "You won't do this to anyone again." She
reached down and plunged the knife into his testicles.*

At six o'clock in the morning, Ashley went to the railroad station to wait for Jim. There was no sign of him.

She was beginning to panic. What could have happened? Ashley
heard the train whistle in the distance. She looked at her watch:
7:00. The train was pulling into the station. Ashley rose to her feet
and looked around frantically. *Something terrible has happened to
him.* A few minutes later, she stood there watching the train pull
out of the station, taking her dreams with it.

She waited another half hour and then slowly headed home.
That noon, Ashley and her father were on a plane to London. . . .

The session was ending.

Dr. Keller counted, ". . . four . . . five. You're awake now."

Ashley opened her eyes. "What happened?"

"Toni told me how she killed Jim Cleary. He was attacking
you."

Ashley's face went white. "I want to go to my room."

*   *   *

Dr. Keller reported to Otto Lewison. "We're really beginning to make some advances, Otto. Up to now, it's been a logjam, with each one of them afraid to make the first move. But they're getting more relaxed. We're going in the right direction, but Ashley is still afraid to face reality."

Dr. Lewison said, "She has no idea how these murders took place?"

"Absolutely none. She's completely blanked it out. Toni took over."

It was two days later.

"Are you comfortable, Ashley?"

"Yes." Her voice sounded far away.

"I want us to talk about Dennis Tibble. Was he a friend of yours?"

"Dennis and I worked for the same company. We weren't really friends."

"The police report says that your fingerprints were found at his apartment."

"That's right. I went there because he wanted me to give him some advice."

"And what happened?"

"We talked for a few minutes, and he gave me a glass of wine with a drug in it."

"What's the next thing you remember?"

"I—I woke up in Chicago."

Ashley's expression began to change.

In an instant, it was Toni talking to him. "Do you want to know what really happened . . . ?"

"Tell me, Toni."

Dennis Tibble picked up the bottle of wine and said, "Let's get comfortable." He started leading her toward the bedroom.

"Dennis, I don't want to—"

And they were in the bedroom, and he was taking off her clothes.

"I know what you want, baby. You want me to screw you. That's why you came up here."

She was fighting to get free. "Stop it, Dennis!"

"Not until I give you what you came here for. You're going to love it, baby."

He pushed her onto the bed, holding her tightly, his hands moving down

to her groin. It was her father's voice. "You're going to love it, baby."
And he was forcing himself into her, again and again, and she was silently
screaming, "No, Father. Stop!" And then the unspeakable fury took over.
She saw the wine bottle. She reached for it, smashed it against the edge of
the table and jammed the ragged edge of the bottle into his back. He
screamed and tried to get up, but she held him tightly while she kept
ramming the broken bottle into him. She watched him roll onto the floor.
  "Stop it," he whimpered.
  "Do you promise to never do that again? Well, we'll make sure." She
picked up the broken glass and reached for his groin.

Dr. Keller let a moment of silence pass. "What did you do after
that, Toni?"

"I decided I'd better get out of there before the police came. I
have to admit I was pretty excited. I wanted to get away from
Ashley's boring life for a while, and I had a friend in Chicago, so
I decided to go there. It turned out he wasn't home, so I did a
little shopping, hit some of the bars and had a good time."

"And what happened next?"

"I checked into a hotel and fell asleep." She shrugged. "From
then on it was Ashley's party."

She awakened slowly, knowing something was wrong, terribly wrong. She
felt as though she had been drugged. Ashley looked around the room and
began to panic. She was lying in bed, naked, in some cheap hotel room.
She had no idea where she was or how she had gotten there. She managed
to sit up, and her head started to pound.

She got out of bed, walked into the tiny bathroom and stepped into the
shower. She let the stream of hot water pound against her body, trying to
wash away whatever terrible, dirty things had happened to her. What if
he had gotten her pregnant? The thought of having his child was sickening.
Ashley got out of the shower, dried herself and walked over to the closet.
Her clothes were missing. The only things inside the closet were a black
leather miniskirt, a cheap-looking tube top and a pair of spiked high-heeled
shoes. She was repelled by the thought of putting the clothes on, but she
had no choice. She dressed quickly and glanced in the mirror. She looked
like a prostitute.
  "Father, I—"
  "What's wrong?"
  "I'm in Chicago and—"
  "What are you doing in Chicago?"
  "I can't go into it now. I need an airline ticket to San Jose. I don't have
any money with me. Can you help me?"

"Of course. Hold on. . . . There's an American Airlines plane leaving O'Hare at ten-forty A.M., *Flight 407. There will be a ticket waiting for you at the check-in counter."*

"Alette, can you hear me? Alette."

"I'm here, Dr. Keller."

"I want us to talk about Richard Melton. He was a friend of yours, wasn't he?"

"Yes. He was very . . . *simpático*. I was in love with him."

"Was he in love with you?"

"I think so, yes. He was an artist. We would go to museums together and look at all of the wonderful paintings. When I was with Richard I felt . . . alive. I think if someone had not killed him, then one day we would have been married."

"Tell me about the last time you were together."

"When we were walking out of a museum, Richard said, 'My roommate is at a party tonight. Why don't we stop at my place? I have some paintings I'd like to show you.' "

" 'Not yet, Richard.' "

" 'Whatever you say. I'll see you next weekend?' "

" 'Yes.' "

"I drove away," Alette said. "And that was the last time I—"

Dr. Keller watched her face begin to take on Toni's animation.

"That's what she wants to think," Toni said. "That's not what happened."

"What did happen?" Dr. Keller asked.

She went to his apartment on Fell Street. It was small, but Richard's paintings made it look beautiful.

"It makes the room come alive, Richard."

"Thank you, Alette." He took her in his arms. "I want to make love to you. You're beautiful."

"You're beautiful," her father said. And she froze. Because she knew the terrible thing that was going to happen. She was lying on the bed, naked, feeling the familiar pain of him entering her, tearing her apart.

And she was screaming, "No! Stop it, Father! Stop it!" And then the manic-depressive frenzy took over. She had no recollection of where she got the knife, but she was stabbing his body over and over, yelling at him, "I told you to stop it! Stop it!"

Ashley was writhing in her chair, screaming.

"It's all right, Ashley," Dr. Keller said. "You're safe. You're going to wake up now, at the count of five."

Ashley awoke, trembling. "Is everything all right?"

"Toni told me about Richard Melton. He made love to you. You thought it was your father, so you—"

She put her hands over her ears. "I don't want to hear any more!"

Dr. Keller went to see Otto Lewison.

"I think we're finally making the breakthrough. It's very traumatic for Ashley, but we're nearing the end. We still have two murders to retrieve."

"And then?"

"I'm going to bring Ashley, Toni and Alette together."

Chapter Twenty-seven

"Toni ? Toni, can you hear me?" Dr. Keller watched Ashley's expression change.

"I hear you, Dockie."

"Let's talk about Jean Claude Parent."

"I should have known he was too good to be true."

"What do you mean?"

"In the beginning, he seemed like a real gentleman. He took me out every day, and we really had a good time. I thought he was different, but he was like all the others. All he wanted was sex."

"I see."

"He gave me a beautiful ring, and I guess he thought that he owned me. I went with him to his house."

The house was a beautiful two-story, redbrick house filled with antiques.

"It's lovely."

"There's something special I want to show you upstairs in the bedroom." And he was taking her upstairs, and she was powerless to stop him. They were in the bedroom, and he took her in his arms and whispered, "Get undressed."

"I don't want to—"

"Yes, you do. We both want it." He undressed her quickly, then laid her down on the bed and got on top of her. She was moaning, "Don't. Please don't, Father!"

But he paid no attention. He kept plunging into her until suddenly he said, "Ah," and then stopped. "You're wonderful," he said.

And the malevolent explosion shook her. She grabbed the sharp letter

*opener from the desk and plunged it into his chest, up and down and up
and down.*
"You won't do that to anyone again." She reached for his groin.
*Afterward, she took a leisurely shower, dressed and went back to the
hotel.*

"Ashley . . ." Ashley's face began to change. "Wake up now."
Ashley slowly came awake. She looked at Dr. Keller and said,
"Toni again?"
"Yes. She met Jean Claude on the Internet. Ashley, when you
were in Quebec, were there periods when you seemed to lose time?
When suddenly it was hours later or a day later, and you didn't
know where the time had gone?"
She nodded slowly. "Yes. It—it happened a lot."
"That's when Toni took over."
"And that's when . . . when she—?"
"Yes."

The next few months were uneventful. In the afternoons, Dr. Keller would listen to Toni play the piano and sing, and he would
watch Alette painting in the garden. There was one more murder
to discuss, but he wanted Ashley to be relaxed before he started
talking about it.
It had been five years now since she had come to the hospital.
She's almost cured, Dr. Keller thought.
On a Monday morning, he sent for Ashley and watched her walk
into the office. She was pale, as though she knew what she was
facing.
"Good morning, Ashley."
"Good morning, Gilbert."
"How are you feeling?"
"Nervous. This is the last one, isn't it?"
"Yes. Let's talk about Deputy Sam Blake. What was he doing
in your apartment?"
"I asked him to come. Someone had written on my bathroom
mirror, 'You Will Die.' I didn't know what to do. I thought some-
one was trying to kill me. I called the police, and Deputy Blake
came over. He was very sympathetic."
"Did you ask him to stay with you?"
"Yes. I was afraid to be alone. He said that he would spend
the night, and then in the morning, he would arrange for twenty-

four-hour protection for me. I offered to sleep on the couch and
let him sleep in the bedroom, but he said he would sleep on the
couch. I remember he checked the windows to make sure they
were locked, and then he double-bolted the door. His gun was on
the table next to the couch. I said good night and went into the
bedroom and closed the door."

"And then what happened?"

"I—The next thing I remember is being awakened by someone
screaming in the alley. Then the sheriff came in to tell me that
Deputy Blake had been found dead." She stopped, her face pale.

"All right. I'm going to put you to sleep now. Just relax. . . .
Close your eyes and relax. . . ." It took ten minutes. Dr. Keller
said, "Toni . . ."

"I'm here. You want to know what really happened, don't you?
Ashley was a fool to invite Sam to stay at the apartment. I could
have told her what he would do."

*He heard a cry from the bedroom, quickly rose from the couch and scooped
up his gun. He hurried over to the bedroom door and listened a moment.
Silence. He had imagined it. As he started to turn away, he heard it again.
He pushed the door open, gun in hand. Ashley was in bed, naked, asleep.
There was no one else in the room. She was making little moaning sounds.
He moved to her bedside. She looked beautiful lying there, curled up in a
fetal position. She moaned again, trapped in some terrible dream. He
meant only to comfort her, to take her in his arms and hold her. He lay
down at her side and gently pulled her toward him, and he felt the heat
of her body and began to be aroused.*

*She was awakened by his voice saying, "It's all right now. You're safe."
And his lips were on hers, and he was moving her legs apart and was
inside her.*

And she was screaming, "No, Father!"

*And he moved faster and faster in a primal urgency, and then the savage
revenge took over. She grabbed the knife from the dresser drawer at her
bedside and began to slash into his body.*

"What happened after you killed him?"

"She wrapped his body in the sheets and dragged him to the
elevator and then through the garage to the alley in back."

". . . and then," Dr. Keller told Ashley, "Toni wrapped his body
in the sheets and dragged him into the elevator and through the
garage to the alley in back."

Ashley sat there, her face dead white. "She's a mon— *I'm* a monster."

Gilbert Keller said, "No. Ashley, you must remember that Toni was born out of your pain, to protect you. The same is true of Alette. It's time to bring this to a closure. I want you to meet them. It's the next step to your getting well."

Ashley's eyes were tightly shut. "All right. When do we . . . do this?"

"Tomorrow morning."

Ashley was in a deep hypnotic state. Dr. Keller started with Toni.

"Toni, I want you and Alette to talk to Ashley."

"What makes you think she can handle us?"

"I think she can."

"All right, Dockie. Whatever you say."

"Alette, are you ready to meet Ashley?"

"If Toni says it's all right."

"Sure, Alette. It's about time."

Dr. Keller took a deep breath and said, "Ashley, I want you to say hello to Toni."

There was a long silence. Then, a timid, "Hello, Toni . . ."

"Hello."

"Ashley, say hello to Alette."

"Hello, Alette . . ."

"Hello, Ashley . . ."

Dr. Keller breathed a deep sigh of relief. "I want you all to get to know one another. You've suffered through the same terrible traumas. They've separated you from one another. But there's no reason for that separation anymore. You're going to become one whole, healthy person. It's a long journey, but you've begun it. I promise you, the most difficult part is over."

From that point on, Ashley's treatment moved swiftly. Ashley and her two alters talked to one another every day.

"I had to protect you," Toni explained. "I suppose every time I killed one of those men, I was killing Father for what he had done to you."

"I tried to protect you, too," Alette said.

"I—I appreciate that. I'm grateful to both of you."

Ashley turned to Dr. Keller and said wryly, "It's really all me, isn't it? I'm talking to myself."

"You're talking to two other parts of yourself," he corrected her gently. "It's time for all of you to unify and become one again."

Ashley looked at him and smiled. "I'm ready."

That afternoon, Dr. Keller went to see Otto Lewison.

Dr. Lewison said, "I hear good reports, Gilbert."

Dr. Keller nodded. "Ashley's made remarkable progress. In another few months, I think she can be released and go on with her treatment as an outpatient."

"That's wonderful news. Congratulations."

I'll miss her, Dr. Keller thought. *I'll miss her terribly.*

"Dr. Salem is on line two for you, Mr. Singer."

"Right." David reached for the phone, puzzled. Why would Dr. Salem be calling? It had been years since the two men had talked. "Royce?"

"Good morning, David. I have some interesting information for you. It's about Ashley Patterson."

David felt a sudden sense of alarm. "What about her?"

"Do you remember how hard we tried to find the trauma that had caused her condition, and we failed?"

David remembered it well. It had been a major weakness in their case. "Yes."

"Well, I just learned the answer. My friend, Dr. Lewison, who's head of the Connecticut Psychiatric Hospital, just called. The missing piece of the puzzle is Dr. Steven Patterson. He's the one who molested Ashley when she was a child."

David asked incredulously, *"What?"*

"Dr. Lewison just learned about it."

David sat listening as Dr. Salem went on, but his mind was elsewhere. He was recalling Dr. Patterson's words. *"You're the only one I trust, David. My daughter means everything in the world to me. You're going to save her life. . . . I want you to defend Ashley, and I won't have anyone else involved in this case. . . ."*

And David suddenly realized why Dr. Patterson had been so insistent on his representing Ashley alone. The doctor was sure that if David had ever discovered what he had done, he would have protected him. Dr. Patterson had had to decide between his daughter and his reputation, and he had chosen his reputation. *The son of a bitch!*

"Thanks, Royce."

* * *

That afternoon, as Ashley passed the recreation room, she saw a copy of the *Westport News* that someone had left there. On the front page of the newspaper was a photograph of her father with Victoria Aniston and Katrina. The beginning of the story read, "Dr. Steven Patterson is to be married to socialite Victoria Aniston, who has a three-year-old daughter from a previous marriage. Dr. Patterson is joining the staff of St. John's Hospital in Manhattan, and he and his future wife have bought a house on Long Island. . . ."

Ashley stopped and her face contorted into a mask of rage. "I'll kill the son of a bitch," Toni screamed. "I'll kill him!"

She was completely out of control. They had to put her in a padded room where she could not hurt herself, restrained by handcuffs and leg-irons. When the attendants came to feed her, she tried to grab them, and they had to be careful not to get too close to her. Toni had taken total possession of Ashley.

When she saw Dr. Keller, she screamed, "Let me out of here, you bastard. Now!"

"We're going to let you out of here," Dr. Keller said soothingly, "but first you have to calm down."

"I'm calm," Toni yelled. "Let me go!"

Dr. Keller sat on the floor beside her and said, "Toni, when you saw that picture of your father, you said you were going to hurt him, and—"

"You're a liar! I said I was going to *kill* him!"

"There's been enough killing. You don't want to stab anyone else."

"I'm not going to stab him. Have you heard of hydrochloric acid? It will eat through anything, including skin. Wait until I—"

"I don't want you to think like that."

"You're right. Arson! Arson is better. He won't have to wait until hell to burn to death. I can do it so they'll never catch me if—"

"Toni, forget about this."

"All right. I can think of some other ways that are even better."

He studied her a moment, frustrated. "Why are you so angry?"

"Don't you know? I thought you were supposed to be such a great doctor. He's marrying a woman with a three-year-old daughter. What's going to happen to that little girl, Mr. Famous Doctor?

I'll tell you what. The same thing that happened to us. Well, I'm going to stop it!"

"I'd hoped we'd gotten rid of all that hate."

"Hate? You want to hear about hate?"

It was raining, a steady downpour of raindrops hitting the roof of the speeding car. She looked at her mother sitting at the wheel, squinting at the road ahead, and she smiled, in a happy mood. She began to sing:

> *"All around the mulberry bush,*
> *The monkey chased—"*

Her mother turned to her and screamed, "Shut up. I told you I detest that song. You make me sick, you miserable little—"

After that, everything seemed to happen in slow motion. The curve ahead, the car skidding off the road, the tree. The crash flung her out of the car. She was shaken, but unhurt. She got to her feet. She could hear her mother, trapped in the car, screaming, "Get me out of here. Help me! Help me!"

And she stood there watching until the car finally exploded.

"Hate? Do you want to hear more?"

Walter Manning said, "This has to be a unanimous decision. My daughter's a professional artist, not a dilettante. She did this as a favor. We can't turn her down. . . . This has to be unanimous. We're either giving him my daughter's painting or we don't give him anything at all."

She was parked at the curb, with the motor running. She watched Walter Manning cross the street, headed for the garage where he kept his car. She put the car in gear and slammed her foot down on the accelerator. At the last moment, he heard the sound of the car coming toward him, and he turned. She watched the expression on his face as the car smashed into him and then hurled his broken body aside. She kept driving. There were no witnesses. God was on her side.

"*That's* hate, Dockie! That's real hate!"

Gilbert Keller listened to her recital, appalled, shaken by the cold-blooded viciousness of it. He canceled the rest of his appointments for the day. He needed to be alone.

The following morning when Dr. Keller walked into the padded cell, Alette had taken over.

"Why are you doing this to me, Dr. Keller?" Alette asked. "Let me out of here."

"I will," Dr. Keller assured her. "Tell me about Toni. What has she told you?"

"She said we have to escape from here and kill Father."

Toni took over. "Morning, Dockie. We're fine now. Why don't you let us go?"

Dr. Keller looked into her eyes. There was cold-blooded murder there.

Dr. Otto Lewison sighed. "I'm terribly sorry about what's happened, Gilbert. Everything was going so well."

"Right now, I can't even reach Ashley."

"I suppose this means having to start the treatment all over."

Dr. Keller was thoughtful. "Not really, Otto. We've arrived at the point where the three alters have gotten to know one another. That was a big breakthrough. The next step was to get them to integrate. I have to find a way to do that."

"That damned article—"

"It's fortunate for us that Toni saw that article."

Otto Lewison looked at him in surprise. "Fortunate?"

"Yes. Because there's that residual hate in Toni. Now that we know it's there, we can work on it. I want to try an experiment. If it works, we'll be in good shape. If it doesn't"—he paused and added quietly—"then I think Ashley may have to be confined here for the rest of her life."

"What do you want to do?"

"I think it's a bad idea for Ashley's father to see her again, but I want to hire a national clipping service, and I want them to send me every article that appears about Dr. Patterson."

Otto Lewison blinked. "What's the point?"

"I'm going to show them all to Toni. Eventually, her hate has to burn itself out. That way I can monitor it and try to control it."

"It may take a long time, Gilbert."

"At least a year, maybe longer. But it's the only chance Ashley has."

Five days later Ashley had taken over.

When Dr. Keller walked into the padded cell, Ashley said, "Good morning, Gilbert. I'm sorry that all this happened."

"I'm glad it did, Ashley. We're going to get all of our feelings out in the open." He nodded to the guard to remove the leg-irons and handcuffs.

Ashley stood up and rubbed her wrists. "That wasn't very comfortable," she said. They walked out into the corridor. "Toni's very angry."

"Yes, but she's going to get over it. Here's my plan. . . ."

There were three or four articles about Dr. Steven Patterson every month. One read: "Dr. Steven Patterson is to wed Victoria Aniston in an elaborate wedding ceremony on Long Island this Friday. Dr. Patterson's colleagues will fly in to attend . . ."

Toni was hysterical when Dr. Keller showed the story to her.

"That marriage isn't going to last long."

"Why do you say that, Toni?"

"Because he's going to be dead!"

"Dr. Steven Patterson has resigned from St. John's Hospital and will head the cardiac staff at Manhattan Methodist Hospital. . . ."

"So he can rape all the little girls there," Toni screamed.

"Dr. Steven Patterson received the Lasker Award for his work in medicine and is being honored at the White House. . . ."

"They should hang the bastard!" Toni yelled.

Gilbert Keller saw to it that Toni received all the articles written about her father. And as time went by, with each new item, Toni's rage seemed to be diminishing. It was as though her emotions had been worn out. She went from hatred to anger and, finally, to a resigned acceptance.

There was a mention in the real estate section. "Dr. Steven Patterson and his new bride have moved into a home in Manhattan, but they plan to purchase a second home in the Hamptons and will be spending their summers there with their daughter, Katrina."

Toni started sobbing. "How could he do that to us?"

"Do you feel that that little girl has taken your place, Toni?"

"I don't know. I'm—I'm confused."

Another year went by. Ashley had therapy sessions three times a week. Alette painted almost every day, but Toni refused to sing or play the piano.

At Christmas, Dr. Keller showed Toni a new clipping. There

was a picture of her father and Victoria and Katrina. The caption read: THE PATTERSONS CELEBRATE CHRISTMAS IN THE HAMPTONS.

Toni said wistfully, "We used to spend Christmases together. He always gave me wonderful gifts." She looked at Dr. Keller. "He wasn't all bad. Aside from the—you know—he was a good father. I think he really loved me."

It was the first sign of a new breakthrough.

One day, as Dr. Keller passed the recreation room, he heard Toni singing and playing the piano. Surprised, he stepped into the room and watched her. She was completely absorbed in the music.

The next day, Dr. Keller had a session with Toni.

"Your father's getting older, Toni. How do you think you'll feel when he dies?"

"I—I don't want him to die. I know I said a lot of stupid things, but I said them because I was angry with him."

"You're not angry anymore?"

She thought about it. "I'm not angry, I'm hurt. I think you were right. I did feel that the little girl was taking my place." She looked up at Dr. Keller and said, "I was confused. But my father has a right to get on with his life, and Ashley has a right to get on with hers."

Dr. Keller smiled. *We're back on track.*

The three of them talked to one another freely now.

Dr. Keller said, "Ashley, you needed Toni and Alette because you couldn't stand the pain. How do you feel about your father now?"

There was a brief silence. She said slowly, "I can never forget what he did to me, but I can forgive him. I want to put the past behind me and start my future."

"To do that, we must make you all one again. How do you feel about that, Alette?"

Alette said, "If I'm Ashley, can I still go on painting?"

"Of course you can."

"Well, then, all right."

"Toni?"

"Will I still be able to sing and play the piano?"

"Yes," he said.

"Then, why not?"

"Ashley?"

"I'm ready for all of us to be one. I—I want to thank them for helping me when I needed them."

"My pleasure, luv."

"Minièra anche," Alette said.

It was time for the final step: integration.

"All right. I'm going to hypnotize you now, Ashley. I want you to say good-bye to Toni and Alette."

Ashley took a deep breath. "Good-bye, Toni. Good-bye, Alette."

"Good-bye, Ashley."

"Take care of yourself, Ashley."

Ten minutes later, Ashley was in a deep hypnotic state. "Ashley, there's nothing more to be afraid of. All your problems are behind you. You don't need anyone to protect you anymore. You're able to handle your life without help, without shutting out any bad experiences. You're able to face whatever happens. Do you agree with me?"

"Yes, I do. I'm ready to face the future."

"Good. Toni?"

There was no answer.

"Toni?"

There was no answer.

"Alette?"

Silence.

"Alette?"

Silence.

"They're gone, Ashley. You're whole now and you're cured."

He watched Ashley's face light up.

"You'll awaken at the count of three. One...two... three..."

Ashley opened her eyes and a beatific smile lit her face. "It— it happened, didn't it?"

He nodded. "Yes."

She was ecstatic. "I'm free. Oh, thank you, Gilbert! I feel—I feel as though a terrible dark curtain has been taken away."

Dr. Keller took her hand. "I can't tell you how pleased I am. We'll be doing some more tests over the next few months, but if they turn out as I think they will, well, we'll be sending you home. I'll arrange for some outpatient treatment for you wherever you are."

Ashley nodded, too overcome with emotion to speak.

Chapter Twenty-eight

OVER the next few months, Otto Lewison had three psychiatrists examine Ashley. They used hypnotherapy and Sodium Amytal.

"Hello, Ashley. I'm Dr. Montfort, and I need to ask you some questions. How do you feel about yourself?"

"I feel wonderful, Doctor. It's as though I've just gotten over a long illness."

"Do you think you're a bad person?"

"No. I know some bad things have happened, but I don't believe I'm responsible for them."

"Do you hate anyone?"

"No."

"What about your father? Do you hate him?"

"I did. I don't hate him anymore. I don't think he could help what he did. I just hope he's all right now."

"Would you like to see him again?"

"I think it would be better if I didn't. He has his life. I want to start a new life for myself."

"Ashley?"

"Yes."

"I'm Dr. Vaughn. I'd like to have a little chat with you."

"All right."

"Do you remember Toni and Alette?"

"Of course. But they're gone."

"How do you feel about them?"

"In the beginning, I was terrified, but now I know I needed them. I'm grateful to them."

"Do you sleep well at night?"

"Now I do, yes."

"Tell me your dreams."

"I used to have terrible dreams; something was always chasing me. I thought I was going to be murdered."

"Do you still have those dreams?"

"Not anymore. My dreams are very peaceful. I see bright colors and smiling people. Last night, I dreamed I was at a ski resort, flying down the slopes. It was wonderful. I don't mind cold weather at all anymore."

"How do you feel about your father?"

"I want him to be happy, and I want to be happy."

"Ashley?"

"Yes."

"I'm Dr. Hoelterhoff."

"How do you do, Doctor?"

"They didn't tell me how beautiful you were. Do you think you're beautiful?"

"I think I'm attractive. . . ."

"I hear that you have a lovely voice. Do you think you do?"

"It's not a trained voice, but, yes"—she laughed—"I do manage to sing on key."

"And they tell me you paint. Are you good?"

"For an amateur, I think I'm quite good. Yes."

He was studying her thoughtfully. "Do you have any problems that you would like to discuss with me?"

"I can't think of any. I'm treated very well here."

"How do you feel about leaving here and getting out into the world?"

"I've thought a lot about it. It's scary, but at the same time it's exciting."

"Do you think you would be afraid out there?"

"No. I want to build a new life. I'm good with computers. I can't go back to the company I worked for, but I'm sure I can get a job at another company."

Dr. Hoelterhoff nodded. "Thank you, Ashley. It was a pleasure talking to you."

* * *

Dr. Montfort, Dr. Vaughn, Dr. Hoelterhoff and Dr. Keller were gathered in Otto Lewison's office. He was studying their reports. When he finished, he looked up at Dr. Keller and smiled.

"Congratulations," he said. "These reports are all positive. You've done a wonderful job."

"She's a wonderful woman. Very special, Otto. I'm glad she's going to have her life back again."

"Has she agreed to outpatient treatment when she leaves here?"

"Absolutely."

Otto Lewison nodded. "Very well. I'll have the release papers drawn up." He turned to the other doctors. "Thank you, gentlemen. I appreciate your help."

Chapter Twenty-nine

Two days later, she was called into Dr. Lewison's office. Dr. Keller was there. Ashley was to be discharged and would return to her home in Cupertino, where regular therapy and evaluation sessions had been arranged with a court-approved psychiatrist.

Dr. Lewison said, "Well, today's the day. Are you excited?"

Ashley said, "I'm excited, I'm frightened, I'm—I don't know. I feel like a bird that's just been set free. I feel like I'm flying." Her face was glowing.

"I'm glad you're leaving, but I'm—I'm going to miss you," Dr. Keller said.

Ashley took his hand and said warmly, "I'm going to miss you, too. I don't know how I . . . how I can ever thank you." Her eyes filled with tears. "You've given me my life back."

She turned to Dr. Lewison. "When I'm back in California, I'll get a job at one of the computer plants there. I'll let you know how it works out and how I get on with the outpatient therapy. I want to make sure that what happened before never happens to me again."

"I don't think you have anything to worry about," Dr. Lewison assured her.

When she left, Dr. Lewison turned to Gilbert Keller. "This makes up for a lot of the ones that didn't succeed, doesn't it, Gilbert?"

It was a sunny June day, and as she walked down Madison Avenue in New York City, her radiant smile made people turn back to look at her. She had never been so happy. She thought of the wonderful life ahead of her, and all that she was going to do. There could have been a terrible ending for her, she thought, but this was the happy ending she had prayed for.

She walked into Pennsylvania Station. It was the busiest train station in America, a charmless maze of airless rooms and passages. The station was crowded with people. *And each person has an interesting story to tell,* she thought. *They're all going to different places, living their own lives, and now, I'm going to live my own life.*

She purchased a ticket from one of the machines. Her train was just pulling in. *Serendipity,* she thought.

She boarded the train and took a seat. She was filled with excitement at what was about to happen. The train gave a jerk and then started picking up speed. *I'm on my way at last.* And as the train headed toward the Hamptons, she began to sing softly:

> *"All around the mulberry bush,*
> *The monkey chased the weasel.*
> *The monkey thought 'twas all in fun,*
> *Pop! goes the weasel. . . ."*

Afterword

D URING the past twenty years, there have been dozens of criminal trials involving defendants claiming to have multiple personalities. The charges covered a wide range of activities, including murder, kidnapping, rape and arson.

Multiple personality disorder (MPD), also known as dissociative identity disorder (DID), is a controversial topic among psychiatrists. Some psychiatrists believe that it does not exist. On the other hand, for years many doctors, hospitals and social services organizations have been treating patients who suffer from MPD. Some studies estimate that between 5 and 15 percent of psychiatric patients are afflicted with it.

Current statistics from the Department of Justice indicate that approximately one third of juvenile victims of sexual abuse are children under six years of age, and that one out of three girls is sexually abused before the age of eighteen.

Most reported cases of incest involve a father and daughter.

A research project in three countries suggests that MPD affects 1 percent of the general population.

Dissociative disorders are often misdiagnosed, and studies have shown that, on average, people with MPD have spent seven years seeking treatment, prior to an accurate diagnosis.

Two thirds of the cases of multiple personality disorder are treatable. Following is a list of some of the organizations devoted to helping and treating patients. In addition, I have included a list of books and articles that may be of interest.

United States Organizations
B.E.A.M. (Being Energetic About Multiplicity)
P.O. Box 20428
Louisville, KY 40250-0428
(502) 493-8975 (fax)

The Center for Post-Traumatic & Dissociative Disorders
Program
The Psychiatric Institute of Washington
4228 Wisconsin Avenue, N.W.
Washington, D.C. 20016
(800) 369-2273

The Forest View Trauma Program
1055 Medical Drive, S.E.
Grand Rapids, MI 49546-3671
(800) 949-8437

International Society for Traumatic Stress Studies (ISTSS)
60 Revere Drive, Suite 500
Northbrook, IL 60062
(847) 480-9028
(847) 480-9282 (fax)

Justus Unlimited
P.O. Box 1221
Parker, CO 80134
(303) 643-8698

Masters and Johnson's Trauma and Dissociative Disorders
Programs
Two Rivers Psychiatric Hospital
5121 Raytown Road
Kansas City, MO 64133
(800) 225-8577

Mothers Against Sexual Abuse (MASA)
503½ South Myrtle Avenue, No. 9
Monrovia, CA 91016
(626) 305-1986
(626) 503-5190 (fax)

The Sanctuary Unit
Friends Hospital
4641 Roosevelt Boulevard
Philadelphia, PA 19124
(215) 831-4600

The Sidran Foundation
2328 West Joppa Road, Suite 15
Lutherville, MD 21093
(410) 825-8888

The Timberlawn Trauma Program
4600 Samuell Boulevard
Dallas, TX 75228
(800) 426-4944

Foreign Organizations
ARGENTINA
Grupo de Estudio de
Trastornos de disociación y trauma de Argentina
Dr. Gracaiela Rodriguez
Federico Lacroze 1820 7mo. A
(1426) Buenos Aires
Argentina
Tel/Fax 541-775-2792

AUSTRALIA
Australian Association for Trauma and Dissociation (AATD)
P.O. Box 85
Brunswick
Melbourne, Victoria 3056
Australia
(03) 9663 6225

Beyond Survival: A Magazine on Abuse, Trauma and Dissociation
P.O. Box 85
Annandale, NSW 2038
Australia
(02) 9566 2045

CANADA
Canadian Mental Health Association
Metro Toronto Branch
970 Lawrence Avenue West, Suite 205
Toronto, Ontario
Canada M6A 3B6
(416) 789-7957
(416) 789-9079 (fax)

Canadian Society for the Study of Dissociation
c/o John O'Neil, MD, FRCPC
4064 Wilson Avenue
Montreal, Quebec
Canada H4A 2T9
(514) 485-9529

*MPD Reaching Out: A Newsletter About Multiple Personality
Disorder*
Royal Ottawa Hospital
Public Relations Department
1145 Carling Avenue
Ottawa, Ontario
Canada K1Z 7K4
(613) 722-6521

ISRAEL
Maytal-Israel Institute for Treatment & Research on Stress
Eli Somer, Ph.D., Clinical Director
3 Manyan Street
Haifa, Israel 34484
+972-4-8381999
+972-4-8386369 (fax)

NETHERLANDS
Nederlands-Vlaamse Vereniging voor de bestudering van Dissociatieve Stoornissen (NVVDS)
(Netherlands-Flemish Society for the Study of Dissociative Disorders)
c/o Stichting RBC, location P.C. Bloemendaal
Kliniek voor Intensieve Behandeling Atlantis
Fenny ten Boschstraat 23
2555 PT Den Haag
The Netherlands
+31 (070) 391-6117
+31 (070) 391-6115 (fax)

Praktijk voor psychotherapie
en hypnose
Els Grimminck, M.D.
Wielewaal 17
1902 KE Castricum
The Netherlands
(+31-0) 251650264
(+31-0) 251653306 (fax)

UNITED KINGDOM
British Dissociative Disorders Professional Study Group
c/o Jeanie McIntee, MSo
Chester Therapy Centre
Weldon House
20 Walpole Street
Chester
England CH1 4HG
1244-390121

Books

Calof, David L., with Mary Leloo. *Multiple Personality and Dissociation: Understanding Incest, Abuse, and MPD.* Park Ridge, IL: Parkside Publishing, 1993.

Putnam, Frank. *Diagnosis and Treatment of Multiple Personality Disorder.* New York: Guilford Press, 1989.

―――. *Dissociation in Children and Adolescents: A Developmental Perspective.* New York: Guilford Press, 1997.

Roseman, Mark, Gini Scott, and William Craig. *You the Jury.* Santa Ana, CA: Seven Locks Press, 1997.

Saks, Elyn R., with Stephen H. Behnke. *Jekyll on Trial.* New York: New York University Press, 1997.

Schreiber, Flora Rheta. *Sybil.* New York: Warner Books, 1995.

Thigpen, Corbett H., and Hervey M. Cleckley. *Three Faces of Eve.* Rev. ed. Augusta, GA: Three Faces of Eve, 1992.

Articles

Abrams, S. "The Multiple Personality: A Legal Defense." *American Journal of Clinical Hypnosis* 25 (1983): 225–31.

Allison, R. B. "Multiple Personality and Criminal Behavior." *American Journal of Forensic Psychiatry* 2 (1981–82): 32–38.

On the Internet

The Sidran Foundation Online
http://www.sidran.org

Pat McClendon's Home Page
http://www.users.mis.net/Zpatmc/

International Society for the Study of Dissociation
E-mail: *into@issd.org*